MW01656945

Say You Love Me

Rachel Murphy

Copyright © 2023 by Rachel Murphy

All rights reserved.

ISBN-13: 9798395422194

This book is a work of fiction. Names, characters, organization, places and events are either products of the author's imagination or used fictitiously.

For lovers of love.

Chapter One

Brooke Lewis stared at the cellphone being handed to her and rolled her hazel eyes as she read the word prompt on the screen. "If I could travel to any time in the past, it would be to before I had this conversation with you," she said in agitation.

Her best friend, Nina, laughed before she pulled the phone back and dramatically spread her legs apart on the couch. "I thought you'd be more supportive since I'm trying to help you get laid."

Brooke leaned forward to grab her wine glass off the wooden coffee table and took a long sip. After all, it was the Pinot Noir that dropped her reservations about online dating, along with a year's worth of pressure from Nina. Maybe it could be the wine to help her finally complete her profile and get Nina off her back.

"I don't want to get laid," Brooke said simply as she placed the glass back down on the table. "I mean, yes, that's great but I'm forty now and not looking for just fun."

What *was* Brooke looking for? She had no idea other than someone she could trust. Someone she could laugh with. Someone who would care about her just as much as she cared about them. She was definitely going to need more wine to accept the fact that this ideal woman wasn't going to be easy to find through a click. Or a swipe. It was a swipe nowadays, right?

"The quickest way to my heart," Nina read aloud before pausing and looking deep in thought. Brooke raised her eyebrow in anticipation of what ridiculous answer Nina was going to come up with now. "Hell, if I knew maybe we would have wound up together."

Brooke laughed and ran her fingers through her wavy brown hair trying to release the tension brewing beneath her scalp so she could relax. "You wish."

Brooke and Nina had been best friends for more than half their lives at this point. Brooke still fondly remembered the day they met on the Georgetown campus when Nina was speed walking like a true native New Yorker and accidently, or so she says, pummeled her way into Brooke. What oddly started as a cantankerous introduction, quickly turned into an unbreakable friendship the moment they sat down next to each other in their Freshman Sociology class and bonded over their shared passion for a better world.

Nina was a constant rock in Brooke's life ever since. They were roommates when Brooke moved from Washington DC to New York. Brooke was Nina's maid of honor at her wedding and then Nina was hers. But most importantly, Nina had been there for the last two years after Brooke's divorce. When Brooke found out her ex-wife, Jaclyn, was cheating on her, she felt like her entire world was going to fall apart, and it likely would have if it wasn't for her best friend. Nina cried with her, lamented with her, but most importantly encouraged her to move on and help her realize nothing was wrong with *her* – it was all Jaclyn's shortcomings and issues. It was easier said than done but all these months later, Brooke was starting to believe it and was finally ready to meet someone new. She would try at least.

"Okay, okay, this is it," Nina said as she cleared her throat and pulled her leg in under her on the couch. "My secret skill is what I can do with my tongue."

"Nina!" Brooke exclaimed. "I'm going to take away your profile creation rights if you don't stop it." She should have known Nina would act like this. Despite being a lawyer, Nina had no filter after work hours. As if all the things she wanted to say had to be repressed until she was in a safe space. It probably didn't help that Nina had been begging to get Brooke on dating apps like this for almost a year now and it was evident she had given it a lot of thought while she wore her best friend down.

"Fine! How about my dream dinner guest is Michelle Obama?" Nina questioned, almost proud of herself for having a genuine answer. "Anyone who doesn't love her is not someone you should be dating."

"Fair," Brooke said with a relaxed breath. Maybe this whole dating thing wouldn't be so hard if she could just focus on the simple parts. The things she liked and didn't. If someone disagreed, they wouldn't willingly talk to her. Right?

Nina got up to tie her black hair into a ponytail before she grabbed a slice of leftover pizza from the kitchen. What was supposed to be a relaxing Friday night with pizza and wine had turned into a much more stressful evening. At least for Brooke. Nina was having the time of her life. "You still promise you'll try to have a date a week?" she asked between bites. "It's the only way to get back out there."

That seemed daunting but nevertheless, Brooke promised. For the next forty-five minutes, Brooke let Nina complete her profile, select her pictures, and even swipe on several women. It was terrifying. Not because Nina was currently in control, but because when she left to go home to her husband and two kids, Brooke would be alone with her phone and the worry of whether or not she'd meet anyone decent. And when she did, how would it go? Would it be a disaster? Would she have fun? Would she be nervous and throw in the towel immediately?

There was only one way to find out.

Taylor Thompson slid onto a barstool at the wine bar down the block from her apartment. When she picked this bar for her second date with Georgia, she didn't do it with any intentions of inviting her back over for a nightcap or anything more. She was just really looking forward to getting home as early as possible. She should have known this was not a good sign about her interest in Georgia.

The only reason why she agreed to go out with Georgia again was because she felt a little rusty in the dating game. Ever since she and Stella broke up six months ago, she was only going on dates here and there but none of them were proving to be worthy of investing time into. Sure, some of them resulted in some fun outings and enjoyable hookups, but none of them had substance. Till this day, she had yet to meet a woman that she felt challenged her and inspired her; made her want to aspire for greatness just by being in their presence. The more she thought about it, none of her previous long-term girlfriends provided that either. She could only see that now that she was removed from the situation to not be blinded by emotions. Or lust.

Maybe this was what it meant to grow up. When Taylor was in her early twenties, she could be a bit shallow and initially only care about looks. She wouldn't lie and say that wasn't the same case now, but she knew looks faded. She knew they didn't define a person's caliber. Now, she wanted to find someone who could open up new worlds for her, enlighten her mind, make her want to be a better person in every possible way. Maybe that type of woman didn't even exist. Maybe she had been watching too many straight-to-streaming cheesy movies lately as a way to fill a void in her life.

"Hi, Taylor," Georgia said as she placed her hand on Taylor's shoulder blade and leaned in to kiss her on the cheek.

"Hey," Taylor said with a smile. She watched as Georgia pulled her denim jacket off to hang it on the hook under the bar and tried to prepare herself to be present in the moment. Georgia was twenty-seven and had just moved to New York from Texas and Taylor could relate to her. She knew what it was like to be a transplant from a slower town and feel like the entire city was passing her by.

"This is such a cute bar," she said with a genuine smile.

"Yeah, I like it here," Taylor admitted while she handed Georgia the menu to look over. Georgia pondered aloud about whether she liked white or red wine more and for some reason, that annoyed Taylor. Shouldn't someone know whether they liked red or white wine? Of course, there was a time and a place for certain pairing preferences, but Taylor knew that her go-to was always a nice red wine, preferably a Malbec or Pinot Noir. Georgia on the other hand seemed to be completely lost. It was almost as reflective of the two different places the women on the date seemed to be in. Maybe Taylor should have declined this date after all.

As they sipped their wine, after Georgia finally settled on a Chardonnay, Taylor felt herself start to get distracted by a couple sitting at the end of the bar. Two men were laughing and smiling as they looked into each other's eyes, completely ignoring the rest of the bar and only having eyes on each other. When one leaned in to press a light kiss on the other's lips before he got up to go to the bathroom, Taylor had an epiphany. *That's* what she wanted. Not a man, but someone who made her feel like the only person in the world. Someone who's absence would make her feel incomplete, not that she *needed* someone else to complete her. She didn't believe that true love was about a missing piece being found – she was already a whole human and she wanted a whole human. She was just looking for something real. A soulmate if you believed in that sort of thing. Did Taylor even believe in that? She wasn't sure until now when she realized it might actually exist.

Taylor drank another glass of wine as she grappled with these thoughts and tried to stay engaged in conversation with her date. That was proving harder than she would have imagined before she walked in the door. When Georgia placed her hand on Taylor's thigh, she didn't feel anything besides a sense of loneliness and disappointment that crept throughout her body and mind. Moving forward, Taylor knew she needed to only seek out dates with someone who seemed like they could fit the bill of everything she wanted. As tall of a bill as that might be. Until then, maybe Georgia could provide her company. After all, who knew when she would ever meet a woman like that. She could be entering a very long dry spell.

"Do you want to get out of here?" she found herself asking without thinking about the repercussions. "I live down the block."

A megawatt smile crept across Georgia's face as she said yes. As soon as Georgia went to the bathroom, Taylor decided to help out the Taylor of tomorrow, and force her to be true to her word today. She opened her phone and deleted the dating apps off her home screen. She knew she'd need to rely on them soon enough to vet new women to see if any could be of the caliber she was looking for, but for now, she wanted to sever ties. She needed a fresh start with a new perspective and not have profiles mislead her. Maybe she could meet someone in person and feel the spark from the start. Maybe she could tap into her friends' network and see if someone knew a perfect and available woman she could be set up with. Either way, Georgia had to be the last rendezvous without feelings.

Would she regret all of this? Maybe, but there was only one way to find out.

Chapter Two

"I absolutely loved Jackson Hole. You should definitely visit and go hiking at Grand Teton National Park and go to the National Elk Refuge – you will not believe how breathtaking it is and how graceful the elks are just being in their natural habitat in the wild."

Brooke started to drift away as Laura continued to ramble about all the things to do in Jackson Hole. No offense to the great people of Wyoming, but this was not a topic that Brooke cared to discuss on a first date. Fifteen minutes into the conversation and Brooke already regretted asking about Laura's last vacation immensely. She regretted even asking her out on a date to begin with.

The saddest part was that this wasn't even the worst date Brooke had recently. Two weeks ago, she went out with a woman who ended the date by telling her it wouldn't work out because she was still in love with her ex-girlfriend, not that Brooke saw it going anywhere either. That date alone was enough to almost make her throw in the towel but Nina harshly reminded her that she needed to keep dating. That was her first real date in almost a year and the odds were likely it wouldn't be a success.

Brooke suppressed a sigh that wanted to escape her lips as she thought about how dismal this first month of dating had been. She never should have allowed Nina to woo her with wine and pizza as a ploy to put herself on the line. Laura was date three and it was a disaster. Just more collateral damage from Jaclyn, surely. Maybe Brooke wasn't meant to find love again and she'd just have to deal with a lifetime of loneliness as a divorcée.

"You know there's a reason why they say three strikes you're out," a sultry voice said to bring Brooke back into the present from her internal abysmal thoughts. She looked up to see the young bartender leaning on the bar in front of her. The chair next to Brooke was vacant and Brooke hadn't even processed that Laura got up. She did vaguely hear herself say 'okay' which was probably in response to Laura saying she was going to the restroom. Given the fact that her bag was still on her chair, she clearly didn't leave the bar. Not that Brooke would have been offended or cared if she did leave.

"Are we talking about baseball?" Brooke questioned with a raised brow.

"Yes and no," the woman said with a smile. Brooke couldn't help but watch her lips as they moved when she spoke. The way they parted with each word and seemed to be inviting Brooke closer. "Three strikes and it's time to sit down and wait for the next chance. Kind of like you."

"What about me?" Brooke asked with a touch of hostility in her voice, no longer lingering on the supple, glossy lips a foot away from her. Who did this woman think she was to be talking to her like this, seeming to pass judgement on her?

"Tonight is the third time I've seen you here with a different woman, and each time it didn't seem to be going well."

While this was completely true, Brooke didn't appreciate having a complete stranger point out that her dating experience lately was a complete joke. Only she was allowed to do that. Brooke didn't really know why she chose this bar again for her two last dates other than it was convenient. It was a relatively quiet bar, by New York standards, where she could enjoy a good cocktail and conversation with someone new that she was supposed to be getting to know. When the first date was a bust, she just recycled the location for the next, and the current. She didn't think anyone would notice. Except for the apparently attentive and painfully attractive bartender.

Brooke forced a laugh as she leaned back in her chair, trying to mask her embarrassment. "Oh really? What gives you that impression?" How did this bartender know that Brooke didn't go home alone? It's not like she actually knew for a fact that Brooke wound up on her couch watching comfort episodes of *30 Rock* and *Parks and Recreation* to make her feel better about herself.

The judgmental stranger leaned on her elbows to grow closer to the woman on the other side of the wooden divide. "I know what it's like to not be satisfied and long for more," she said in a way that made Brooke feel exposed. Did her dates notice that too? Except right now, she also felt kind of turned on which she definitely didn't feel before. "You've looked at your phone at least five times already tonight. You've barely smiled, which I did see previously, but since you're here with this extremely talkative woman, I guess the two blondes didn't make the cut either."

Damn. She was paying attention.

"Are you stalking me or something?" Brooke questioned with a smile in an attempt to hide her vulnerabilities, and that fact that she felt mortified that there were witnesses to her failed dates.

"I've just been observing," the bartender said with a wink before she stepped back as Laura approached and returned to her seat beside Brooke.

Who even winks at strangers? Brooke thought to herself as her eyes followed the woman walking away towards the other end of the bar.

"They have a delicious smelling lavender soap in the bathroom, you should try it out," Laura said completely oblivious to the conversation that just happened and the looks the bartender was still sending her date.

Brooke knew the soap smelt good. She also relished in the scent when she hid in there the week prior for a few minutes longer than necessary. "I love lavender everything," Brooke said in an attempt to keep the conversation going.

"Another amazing place you need to go are the lavender fields in Provence. Completely stunning." As Laura started another long-winded explanation about a destination Brooke should visit, she let her ramble on without telling her that she had already been to Provence twice. She found herself nodding and sipping her cocktail as she looked at the bartender stealing glances at her.

Brooke would be lying if she said she hadn't noticed her the past two times she was there. Brooke had eyes and was attracted to women, after all. She wasn't their server during the previous visits since Brooke and her dates sat at a table with a waitress, but the beautiful woman was hard to miss. Even across a room, she was captivating with gorgeous green eyes and light brown hair that cascaded down her slightly tanned shoulders over her black V-neck t-shirt uniform that perfectly showcased her breasts, probably on display for a good tip. She was everything Brooke was physically attracted to in a woman, except she was far too young. The bold playfulness in her conversation attempt was a sign of just how different they were in age and personality.

Brooke pushed herself through the rest of her drink and the conversation to focus on her date, but when Laura asked about another round, Brooke lied and said she had to get up early. She motioned to the bartender for the check and when it was placed down in front of her, Brooke decided to pay the bill rather than split it in half. She felt like the least she could do for being so distant would be to buy Laura a drink. She seemed like a nice person, just not right for her.

When Brooke opened the black check holder after it was returned, her eyes were immediately drawn to a napkin tucked inside with a note written on it. She quickly signed the bill and discretely pulled the napkin away without Laura noticing. As she put her credit card back in her wallet, she dropped the napkin into her purse to read it in full in private.

"If you want to go on a real first date that will have you smile, laugh, and so much more, text me.
– Taylor"

Under the message was her phone number.

Brooke looked back up at Taylor and felt herself grow warm. It had been over a decade since anyone openly flirted with her like that and boldly tried to ask her out. Despite how foreign it felt in this moment, she liked it. She wanted it. She knew she had looked at the alluring bartender more than each of the women that had been seated beside her or across from her the past three weeks. That should have been a sign that the dates weren't going well. Even Taylor knew that.

As Laura and Brooke walked away from their seats, Brooke turned around one last time to see Taylor smiling sweetly at her. The napkin felt like it was burning a hole in Brooke's purse the entire commute home but she knew she wouldn't follow through with it. She *couldn't*. Taylor was far too young for her and very obviously just a flirt. Weren't all bartenders a bit flirtatious for a good tip? For her date next week, she'd just have to find a new bar to go. After all, this one wasn't bringing her any luck anyway.

"How are the dates going?" Nina casually questioned during Sunday brunch days later. Once a month, the best friends vowed to have dinner or brunch together and not let their careers and personal lives get in the way. "Who's the lucky lady of the week?"

Brooke looked down at her French toast and sighed, wishing she could hide herself behind a wall of whipped cream and strawberries rather than admit the bleak reality. "They're all failing miserably and nobody has been lucky." Brooke hadn't even bothered trying to coordinate a next date with anyone she had been messaging on the app.

"Give it time. You're just getting your feet wet again," Nina offered in support. "Hopefully amongst other things."

Brooke laughed at her friend's ability to turn a simple conversation into something dirty. There definitely hadn't been any of that on her dates. There hadn't been any of that in almost six months after her last attempt of moving on resulted in an extremely short-lived friends with benefits situation with someone she knew there would be no future with. And the sex wasn't even worth it either.

Brooke reflected back on her last three dates and exhaled sharply as she reminded herself of the lack of spark. There was no interest. No chemistry. Their conversations that moved them from dating app to real life were utterly disappointing and almost seemed transactional in an attempt to move things to the next stage. The only time she felt something brewing inside of her was with the flirtatious bartender.

The note-covered napkin had been sitting on her desk at home since Thursday night. She hadn't thrown it out as much as she thought about it because part of her was intrigued. Maybe Taylor could be a fun date. Maybe it could be just another disaster. Was it worth avoiding entirely?

"A young, hot bartender gave me her number though," Brooke shared with her best friend, hoping that she could add some fresh perspective to the situation and tell her what she should do. "Do you think I should follow through?"

Nina dramatically dropped her fork against the side of her plate as if Brooke just confessed a dark secret she had been hiding from her for two decades. "Um, yes! What are you even waiting for?"

Brooke wasn't sure. All she knew was that she was scared. *Terrified.* Everyone she had gone on dates with had been around the same age as her. She had read their profiles and was able to ascertain that they had at least some things in common or foundational grounds for basing initial conversations around. A date with Taylor would be starting from complete scratch. No profile to pull topics from. No pictures to bring up as ice breakers. It would be a completely fresh start. "She's young," Brooke started to open up as she thought about how much it wouldn't work before it even started. "Do you know how shitty it's going to feel seeing her react to the fact that I'm forty and divorced?"

Nina rolled her eyes and returned to her avocado toast. "She clearly liked what she saw enough to ask you out and plenty of people are divorced. I don't know why you still think that's such a scarlet letter anymore."

The truth was, Brooke was still ashamed of it. She knew over fifty percent of marriages ended in divorce, but she naïvely never thought she would contribute to that statistic. She thought she and Jaclyn would be together until one of them died. How could she foresee it all come crumbling down two years ago? She'd been left in shambles questioning just how loyal her wife was for the eight years they were together prior to that and now she was expected to trust strangers to not hurt her? "It just feels like an easier conversation to have with someone my own age."

"You act like you're sixty for fuck's sake," Nina scoffed. Brooke always loved how blunt her best friend was, even though in this moment, she didn't feel the same affection for it. "Do I need to have Jayson give you an eye exam? You are hot as hell, who cares if you're forty and divorced? Only you."

Brooke smirked at Nina, biting back with her own rebuttal. "My contacts are the perfect prescription. I can see crystal clear that you're being an asshole."

Nina pretended to be offended as she clutched her hand against her chest. "You're so sweet, I have no idea why those dates were a bust."

"You really think I should go out with the bartender?" Brooke asked to bring the conversation back to the topic at hand.

"Yes," Nina said simply. "What do you have to lose? Absolutely nothing. And you said she's hot, so why not treat yourself?"

A smile spread across Brooke's face. She couldn't control it even if she tried. It was an involuntary reaction to what her body already knew it wanted. "She's gorgeous. I can't remember the last time I was physically drawn to someone like that."

"See!" Nina exclaimed. "You'd just be denying yourself of what your body wants to not text her and see what happens."

Brooke pondered over what her friend was telling her and knew that it was true, despite how much it scared her. She shifted the conversation back to Nina and her three-year old daughter, Allison, who had quickly started to pick up all the curse words that Jayson said while playing video games on weekends. As funny as it was to Brooke as an outsider, it also made her sad that she didn't have a child to pick up traits after her. Maybe it was a good thing she and Jaclyn broke up; their child might have picked up watching trashy reality TV that Brooke couldn't stand. Or picked up being a cheater. Brooke didn't know which one was worse.

As soon as Brooke got home from brunch, she returned her father's two phone calls and listened as he recapped the latest news about her mother. For the past several weeks, Mary had been bouncing from doctor to doctor trying to understand her options for her recent lung cancer diagnosis. She even came up to New York to meet with specialists after Brooke relentlessly insisted, but Mary was nothing but stubborn and wanted to remain with her doctor and chemotherapy and radiation treatment plan in DC. The plan that was truly wiping her out now and bringing her husband to tears as he talked to his daughter.

The diagnosis was pretty grim given she was already in stage three, in part to her decades' long cigarette habit. Brooke could still clearly remember her mom picking her up from elementary school and her needing to wait in the car so her mom could finish another cigarette before getting inside. It was almost comical how many packs she found out Mary went through when Brooke told her she was a lesbian and crushed her mother's dreams of Brooke marrying Prince William. True story.

Brooke heard the lighter flick when she called her mother crying hysterical that Jaclyn cheated on her and they were getting divorced. Cigarettes and her mother went together like peanut butter and jelly. Wine and cheese. Gin and tonic. All of the above Mary also overindulged in, just not at the same time. As a daughter, Brooke always pleaded with her mom to stop smoking. She couldn't understand why Mary couldn't quit the habit knowing the consequences. Now the damage was done and Brooke and her father had to deal with the unavoidable reality.

During these troubling times, Brooke could really use a distraction. Her life couldn't become only dealing with her mother's illness and work; she'd drive herself insane. It was this thought that led her feet over to her desk to pick up Taylor's napkin. Dating had been a challenge so far rather than a pleasant distraction. Maybe this could be the change she needed.

> **Brooke [4:39pm]**
> Hey it's Brooke – the woman from the bar with the bad dates. Still think you can show me a better first date?

She couldn't believe that was how she was describing herself to a complete stranger she wanted to go out with. She was so much more than that, including someone full of nerves as she waited for a reply. Ten minutes later she couldn't control the smile on her face.

> **Taylor [4:51pm]**
> I know I can. How about you meet me at the same bar Saturday at 9? I get off at 10 and I've heard 4th first dates there are the best

> **Brooke [4:53pm]**
> I'll see you then

What she'd have in common with a younger woman, she had no idea. Yet the prospect of finding out exhilarated her in ways she didn't anticipate. Saturday couldn't come soon enough.

Chapter Three

Taylor sat cross-legged on her bed in her studio apartment laughing at her best friend, Liam, struggle to close his suitcase. "I don't understand why this goddamn thing won't close," he complained as he finally tried to sit on the bag in an attempt to zip it shut.

"Because you insisted you had to go to Bloomingdales, and Saks, and Macy's." Taylor got up from the bed and offered a hand to help her friend. After she sat on top of the blue suitcase, Liam was finally able to zip it completely. "Did you even tell James how much shopping you did this week?"

The look that Liam shot up to his best friend could have burned a hole through her skin. "No, and we will not be telling him about any of that."

Taylor laughed as she threw herself back on her bed. "Already keeping secrets from your fiancé? Not a good sign."

"It's not a secret. It's just personal information," he replied with a cheeky grin.

Taylor missed this banter. Ever since Liam moved to London over a year-and-a-half ago to be with his now fiancé, Taylor felt a bit lonely in New York. Even though she had plenty of other friends, none compared to Liam. They had been best friends since elementary school back in Phoenix. They moved to New York together. They got tattoos for the first, and last, time together. They both almost had a crush on the same girl before Liam realized he was most definitely gay and not bisexual. It was a bond that Taylor would always cherish, but him leaving now after only having forty-eight hours together made her incredibly sad.

"I really hope the next time I see you isn't the wedding," Taylor said as she watched Liam search in her refrigerator for something to eat.

"We just got engaged last month," Liam said behind the opened door. "God, you really have no food in here. Such a bachelorette lifestyle."

Taylor rolled her eyes. "I didn't have time to go shopping when I was watching you, well, go shopping."

While Liam continued to search through bare cabinets, a text from an unrecognized number appeared on Taylor's phone. "Holy shit," she internally exclaimed to herself, or so she thought.

"Holy shit, what?" Liam inquired, confirming that Taylor hadn't kept those words inside of her head as intended.

Taylor quickly locked her phone, knowing that Liam was all too keen on sending inappropriate messages to people for a good laugh. Taylor could already tell that would not be the way to make a good first impression on Brooke. "Remember how I told you I gave my number to that woman at the bar?"

"The hot older woman who's date you sabotaged?" Liam asked with a raised brow.

When you put it that way... Taylor didn't think she was sabotaging anything, mainly because she could tell that it wasn't going well. In that moment, all she could think about was that this beautiful, sophisticated looking woman deserved to be happy. Taylor was naïve and foolish to think she could provide that happiness for her, but it was what gave her that boost of adrenaline to give Brooke her number. She had never done something so bold and slightly outrageous before but she thought the new her that was trying to find a real partner could also try a new approach in the process. Even if it seemed a bit wild and presumptuous.

"Yeah," she finally said softly.

"What about her?"

"She just texted me."

Liam sprung across the small apartment to jump on the bed. "What did she say?"

Taylor smiled as she thought about the look and tint of rose on Brooke's face when she saw the napkin in the check holder. A similar blush started to creep throughout Taylor's body now as she thought about the possibility of actually going on a date together. The bold move that she didn't expect to lead to anything now had a glimmer of opportunity peeking through. "She, uh, asked if I think I could still be a better first date."

Liam playfully slapped Taylor on the thigh. "You can. And a better second. Third. Twentieth."

"One date at a time!" Taylor exclaimed, trying to find a way to not get ahead of herself. This was just a first date. It could be a disaster. She could have absolutely nothing in common with Brooke and find her to be someone that's only enjoyable to look at. Which was exactly the type of woman she was trying to avoid dating. If she wanted that, she could reinstall the dating apps and be vain and picky.

She could hate Brooke's personality. There had to be a reason why she was on three consecutive failed dates. *Maybe she's the problem.* Although, from what Taylor overheard at the bar, Brooke sounded smart and witty. She definitely seemed like the type of woman that had a serious job and enjoyed obscure artsy films and music. On the flip side, maybe Brooke could hate Taylor's playful personality or think she's not attractive enough to date or not as successful. She could think Taylor was just a basic girl who liked pop music and Pumpkin Spice Lattes. *Damn, maybe I'm going to be the problem.*

"Earth to Taylor," Liam said as he snapped his fingers to get Taylor's attention. "You just went into total la-la land on me."

"Sorry," she apologized as she ran her fingers through her hair, trying to get a grip on herself. She never worried this much when someone from an app sent her a text, so why was she suddenly so nervous now? "I was just thinking about how I can't believe she texted me."

"She might be desperate," Liam said before catching himself. "Not that you're not worth dating but like hello, being single does suck. You should know."

Taylor dramatically flung herself back on her bed. She really *did* know. When she and Stella broke up last year, she was reminded how much it sucked to be single mostly because it was ahead of the holidays – the one time of the year you wished you had someone to celebrate with and curl up next to during cold nights. Instead, Taylor had to deal with her family's inquisition into what happened and what Taylor must have done to ruin things, which really made for a festive Thanksgiving and Christmas, since no one knew how to drop the topic.

Taylor spent most of the winter wondering if she truly really loved Stella or just liked the idea of her. Stella came into her life at the perfect time after Liam moved to London and managed to fill a void that Taylor wondered if she confused with love. They only dated for ten months, which wasn't that long in the grand scheme of things, and deep down she knew they were a terrible match for each other. Yet, Taylor was still distraught to see Stella move on quickly with her aspiring Influencer girlfriend that she constantly posted on Instagram.

Taylor thought about whether or not she should delete that app too before she realized the past was the past for a reason. Now she had the future to look forward to and she didn't want to screw it up. She had enough failed relationships to know she wanted one that would truly work. She didn't want to date someone for two years like she did with Diana and feel the deep disappointment of two people just growing apart. She wanted someone who was going to be there for the long haul. She wanted true love.

"What do I say to her?" Taylor asked Liam while looking at her ceiling seeking answers.

Liam laid down on the bed and turned on his side to face her. This felt like all the nights in high school when they'd curl up in the same position talking about their crushes. Not much seemed to change except for their age, and improved sense of style and taste in crushes. "Tell her yes and you're going to make her scream your name." Taylor shoved her best friend for his predictable comment. His humor certainly hadn't changed since they were teenagers. "Don't pretend it's not true!"

Taylor grabbed her phone and re-read the text again. Without overthinking it, she confirmed she could show Brooke a good first date and told her to meet her at the bar on Saturday. If she tried to plan a more intricate date, she knew she'd botch it out of nerves of wanting to impress Brooke. Instead, she decided to just be cute. She could do cute. Offering Brooke a better first date at the bar was a playful way for them to have their own beginning. Then she'd take her to the quaint Spanish restaurant she liked down the block after and they could talk and get to know each other.

When Taylor finally stopped picturing the date behind her eyes, she realized that Liam was still talking and discussing all the possible sexual scenarios she and Brooke could wind up in. "I'm starting to worry that you and James don't have sex with the way you talk and fantasize."

Liam leaned over and placed a kiss on Taylor's cheek. "It's just you, babe. You get me going." He glanced at the time on his watch and pulled himself up from the bed. "And I have to get going if I'm ever making it back to London."

"You could stay," Taylor suggested. "Move back here with James."

"To go on double dates with you and Brooke?" Liam inquired with a wink.

Wouldn't that be nice. "If it's not her, I'm going to need to be dating someone else by the time you get married. I will not attend your wedding alone."

"You have a year to figure your shit out," Liam declared as he grabbed his suitcase handle and struggled to lift it up. There was no way that bag wasn't going to be overweight, but Taylor knew Liam would somehow talk himself out of paying any fees. It was a gift.

As she walked her best friend outside to the street, they hugged tightly and said their goodbyes. Taylor waved as the Uber started to pull away and felt a pang of sadness radiate in her chest. Having a taste of her old life back was so comforting, only to be a stark reminder of what it felt like to be without it once Liam was gone. It kind of felt like dating. And that scared Taylor just as much.

Chapter Four

"So, your idea of a good first date is to bring me back to the same place I just had three bad first dates at?" Brooke questioned playfully when she sat down at Taylor's bar and met the bartender's smiling face. She was trying to muster up all of her strength to remain confident and not give off the impression that she was extremely nervous. Or that she spent the last four hours getting ready and deciding what to wear that could be perceived as hip and sexy without looking like she was trying too hard. Which ironically proved harder than she thought since she overthought everything. Including her underwear selection that she had no intention of Taylor seeing tonight. If ever.

Now that she was looking at Taylor without any sense of reservation like she had the week before, her nerves went into overdrive. Taylor was even more beautiful than she remembered and those green eyes peering back at her were pulling her in to a mental state of complete panic. *This could be dangerous.*

"I want you to have a positive connotation with this place now," Taylor said with a sweet smile. At first, Brooke thought it was unoriginal for Taylor to suggest they meet here, but then she started to find it cute and playful. Could she handle cute and playful when she wanted something serious and substantial? She was about to find out. "What can I make you?"

Brooke thought about what she was in the mood to drink and decided she wanted to see what Taylor would come up with. Maybe this would be her first way to figure out something else about Taylor besides her flawless exterior. "Surprise me."

Taylor's eyes scanned Brooke as she gave her a once over before she stepped away to start mixing ingredients. Brooke watched as she gracefully reached up to grab two bottles and started eyeballing her pour into the silver shaker. Brooke always thought that bartenders at upscale bars moved with such grace that it was practically an artform as they measured and maneuvered. It was a stark difference from the hustle and frantic pace of a crowded, more casual bar. Taylor certainly looked like an artist as she shook the shaker and Brooke couldn't help but watch as Taylor kept stealing glances her way.

Taylor carefully placed a drink in front of Brooke and leaned her hands on the bar as she grinned at her date. Her toned arms were on display in that pose and Brooke wondered what she did when she worked out. She probably looked really good while doing it, too. "This is an Aviation. It's strong, classic, and tastes delicious. Seems fitting for you."

This could be extremely dangerous. "Thanks," Brooke said as she raised the glass to sip her violet-colored cocktail in silence. Taylor made a good drink, not that she had any doubts. And she was still just as flirtatious as the week prior. Another point scored in the cute and playful category.

As Taylor stepped away to tend to other patrons, Brooke watched in awe as the bartender mixed martinis, poured glasses of wine, and engaged in small talk. Brooke then watched all the people at the bar like a spectator. She tried to figure out who was there with friends versus who was there on a date. The presumed dates all seemed to be going better than any of the ones Brooke had been on at this bar. Except maybe tonight's. She and Taylor had barely spoken and yet she felt more optimistic about the night than she had during her full dates the previous three weeks but she knew better than to get ahead of herself. The night was still young.

At the end of Taylor's shift, she led them three doors over from the bar to a small tapas restaurant where she had reserved a table. As they walked towards the back of the intimate restaurant, Brooke took a deep breath while Taylor's back was to her to prepare herself for the real date now. The talking. The getting to know each other. Brooke always believed in trusting her instincts on first dates. She'd either be interested or not. This was now either going to be a deal breaker or a game changer.

"I'm starving, I hope you don't mind if I order some food," Taylor announced as she sat down and quickly started to scan the menu.

"Go for it. I'll just have something light. I usually don't eat this late." In reality, Brooke didn't like eating on a first date at all. She was always too self-conscious of something miniscule and irrelevant happening like a piece of arugula getting stuck in her teeth or oil dripping on her shirt. If that was enough for someone to find her unattractive or deem it a bad date and not want a second, then they weren't worthy of Brooke's time to begin with. Yet it still terrified her regardless.

"Live a little," Taylor said playfully.

Brooke laughed and put the laminated menu down. "Funny, coming from a twenty-five-year-old who hasn't discovered indigestion yet." Not only did Brooke not like eating on first dates, she also wasn't used to *starting* a date at nine o'clock at night. She hadn't done that since her twenties.

Taylor laughed boisterously before she became sullen. "Wait. You're serious. You think I'm twenty-five?"

"Twenty-six?" Brooke questioned with a touch of uncertainty in her voice.

Taylor smiled and leaned back against the wooden chair. "I'm turning thirty in September, but thanks for the compliment. Or insult, I'm not sure."

"You just have a youthful energy," Brooke said as she looked back at the menu, trying to hide her relief that Taylor wasn't as young as she assumed but still embarrassed that they were ten years apart. An entire decade existed between them. They probably didn't even like the same music, movies, celebrities. Brooke could feel herself spiraling as she thought about all the reasons why this was not going to work out.

Taylor leaned forward and perched her elbows on the table, very similar to how she did at the bar the first time they spoke. It was as if she was trying to close the space between them and establish a sense of dominance. Brooke found it oddly sexy. "Thirty-seven?" Brooke raised her eyes and shook her head. "Thirty-nine."

"Warmer."

"No way are you over forty," Taylor said loudly, sending a wave of insecurity through Brooke's body. What would happen when she confirmed the unthinkable?

"Turned forty in February," Brooke admitted sheepishly, trying to gauge the reaction on Taylor's face, but one never came. Just that same sweet smile that brought out an adorable dimple on her left cheek.

"Does that bother you?" Taylor asked softly.

"What?"

"Being forty?"

It bothered Brooke more than she wanted to admit. She had always been cognizant of age and despite how much she wanted to view it as just a number, she knew it wasn't. It was also a symbol of days gone by and the unknown limited number that were still remaining. She wanted to always enjoy every day to its fullest knowing how short life was, but at certain moments she found herself too afraid to venture too far out of her comfort zone out of fear. Being here in this small restaurant with Taylor was definitely teetering into that zone. "Do *you* want to be forty?"

Taylor bit her bottom lip and smirked. "If I looked like you, then yes, I wouldn't mind."

Brooke laughed at the compliment. "You might want to get your eyes checked. I've heard vision starts to deteriorate at twenty-nine."

Taylor was unfazed by the rebuttal as she continued to lean in to the table towards Brooke. "Have you seen Cate Blanchett? She's over fifty and gorgeous."

"I have and I'm far from that even at forty," Brooke said as her eyes moved over to the waiter arriving at their table asking for their order. Brooke went against her first date rules and ordered a goat cheese bruschetta and a glass of red wine while Taylor ordered two appetizers and a glass of prosecco.

"Just to be clear," Taylor started when the waiter walked away and Brooke's full attention was back on her. "I think you're far more beautiful than Cate Blanchett."

Brooke laughed again and shook her head in complete disbelief. "Okay, now I'm convinced you're insane and I should leave before I find out you're also a murderer. My safety is in question."

Brooke didn't feel unsafe at all, but that type of compliment felt almost impossible to be true and something had to be wrong with the woman sitting across from her. She was either extremely bold and flirtatious or crazy. Neither was a compatible match.

"I'm serious! I mean how else would I notice you at a crowded bar while I'm busy working if you weren't so breathtaking?" Taylor leaned back and crossed her arms probing Brooke to have a response to that.

She didn't. She could only blush in return. If she was being honest, that was the same exact reason why Taylor stood out to her as well. She wasn't just someone working at the bar; she was someone she couldn't keep her eyes off.

"Do you pick up a lot of people bartending?" Brooke asked as she took a sip of water, needing to deviate the attention off of herself and start to learn more about Taylor. Her friends had gone home with a few bartenders over the years and she just assumed that Taylor was one who could have easily gotten dates and hookups just by meeting different people each night. Brooke must be the flavor of the week.

"I've been asked out quite a few times and always decline," Taylor said as she picked up the glass of prosecco that was placed in front of her. "You're the first I've given my number to."

Brooke lifted her glass of wine and tapped the glass against Taylor's raised in the air, focusing on the toast more than the warmth that started to rise in her chest. "I'm honored."

"You should be," Taylor said simply. "I don't just give my number out to anyone."

As a silence came over them, Taylor seemed to be studying Brooke's face. At first it made Brooke a little uncomfortable, but she quickly found herself just as intrigued at the features of the woman across from her. The way Taylor's cheekbones looked like they were airbrushed. Those lips that were perfectly plump and screamed caution for how dangerous they could be to land on. The way her blue manicured fingers lingered on her collarbone for a moment. Who knew a clavicle could be sexy?

"Three failed dates, huh?" Taylor finally asked when she broke their lingering stare. "Maybe I should be the one concerned about the type of people you pick up."

Brooke never thought about how her own actions might have been perceived when she was so focused on Taylor. Three dates at the same bar really wasn't a good look. It almost seemed promiscuous and lazy. "It's really not like that," she started before she took a sip of her wine to give her the slightest confidence boost to rip the Band-Aid off and spill the truth. "I was trying to have a date a week to get back out there. You were witness to my first three failures."

Taylor's lips rose in a smile. "Hopefully not to the fourth."

"Hopefully," Brooke agreed. She already knew she didn't want this to be a failure, despite the high likelihood that it would.

"Why did you need to get back out there though?"

If being forty didn't falter Taylor's interest, would this? "I got divorced two years ago," she said nervously. "Dating hasn't really been a priority for me until now."

Just like her age, Taylor didn't react. *Maybe I'm the only one who cares? Or maybe she just has one hell of a poker face.* "Divorce happens even to the best of couples."

Relief washed over Brooke before it almost seemed comical. "Jaclyn and best don't belong in the same sentence."

A reaction finally appeared on Taylor's face as her eyes went wide before she closed them and sighed softly. "Thank God, you're actually into women. I started to panic that you were trying to figure yourself out now. Not that there is anything wrong with figuring out your sexuality at any age but now I'm rambling and I'll shut up."

Brooke laughed and felt herself finally start to relax. She never would have thought that Taylor could have assumed she might have been straight, questioning, or just as nervous as she was. It was a relief to know that she wasn't the only one with some sort of first date jitters. "I'm a lesbian. What about you?"

"Oh, I'm straight and just like to pick up women in bars for fun," Taylor said with a devilish smile. "I really don't like labels so I prefer Queer but I am a lady-only-loving-lady for sure."

"Glad we got that sorted out," Brooke declared with a smile. "Would definitely be four bad dates in a row if you were straight."

"I promised you a good date and I don't break promises," Taylor said proudly, "but back to the original topic. What happened with your ex?"

Talking about Jaclyn wasn't exactly high on first date material Brooke wanted to cover, so she went with the SparkNotes version to speed it up. Not talking about it at all could give the impression it was a sore spot, which it was, but not one that had to be avoided like landmines because she had lingering feelings for the woman who broke her heart. The pain remained, but the love was gone. "We were together for eight years until she cheated on me. We broke up. The end."

Taylor picked up her glass and raised it in a toast. "To her being an idiot and giving me a chance to be here with you right now."

Brooke smiled as she listened to the voice in her head start to tell her that this was too good to be true. Taylor couldn't be such a catch. She couldn't be a gorgeous, nice, funny, single, *and* sapphic woman she just happened to stumble upon at a bar. There had to be, well, a catch, besides being ten years younger. "I'll toast to that," she said before she took a sip and returned her glass to the table. "What about you? Ex-wives? Children? Pet custody?"

"None of the above," Taylor started with a smile. "Been there done that with the rough breakups though. Guess I've been kind of unlucky in that department."

If there was an obvious reason why, Brooke never found out on the remainder of the date. They talked about everything from Brooke's job as a publicist to their favorite music, which they did mostly agree on, and Taylor's obsession with pickles. It was lighthearted, fun and most importantly, Brooke didn't want it to end. This was nothing like any of the dates she had been on since Jaclyn. She actually wanted this date to continue and have Taylor's voice fill her ears as she learned about this mysterious woman from Phoenix who came into her life unexpectedly.

"I guess we should head out," Brooke said two hours after they walked in the door when she noticed their waiter standing over Taylor's shoulder impatiently waiting for them to clear out. They were the last patrons in the restaurant and all other chairs were already flipped over on the empty tables. Taylor had paid the bill at least thirty minutes ago, but there was no real urgency to leave. Walking out now almost felt like they were deprived of more time together, but the night had to end at some point.

"Maybe we can have a real dinner next week?" Taylor asked as they stood on the street corner and Brooke pulled out her phone to order an Uber. "One where you eat more than just a tiny appetizer."

"That sounds nice," Brooke said with a soft smile, internally celebrating the knowledge that Taylor wanted a second date, just like herself. "Are you going to be okay getting home?"

"I'll manage," Taylor said simply as she looked at Brooke order a car.

When the sedan pulled up to the curb, Taylor stepped towards Brooke and placed an unexpected, but much appreciated, soft kiss on Brooke's cheek. "Goodnight, Brooke."

"Goodnight," Brooke repeated before she got in the car and watched

Taylor wave goodbye to her. In the loneliness of the backseat of a Toyota Prius, Brooke realized she didn't look at her phone once during the date. Taylor was right. It was the best first date she had since she was married. And she could still feel the skin on her cheek burning hours later.

Chapter Five

Brooke came home from work on Tuesday night feeling exhausted. She was in back-to-back meetings for most of the day and her so-called free time was spent focusing on preparing a presentation for the following week and picking at the soggy salad she didn't have time to fully eat. This was one of those mundane days that made her want to get inside and open a bottle of wine after she took off her bra. Was there really anything more freeing than that?

She picked up her package of overpriced candles from the doorman before she checked her mailbox for the first time in a week. As she rode up the elevator to the seventeenth floor, she started to sort through the mail in her hands. Behind the political flyers and credit card offers she was supposed to be opt-ed out of was a thick envelope with her name in black calligraphy.

The elevator door opened up and she stepped into the hallway clutching the mail to her chest as she walked towards her apartment door. She stepped inside and dropped the box on the hallway bench before she turned the envelope over and saw the names she was dreading. She tore open the envelope to reveal a wedding invitation. Jaclyn was marrying the man she left Brooke for. The man she already had her dream child with. The man that brought down Brooke's entire world.

Brooke sank into the couch in a daze. *At least she's marrying the bastard she cheated on me with.* As a long exhale left her lips, she looked at the invitation. *Brooke Lewis and Guest.* That somehow hurt even more. Like Jaclyn inviting her to begin with was a joke at her expense to remind her that she was single. Not that Brooke would ever attend the wedding so all of Jaclyn's friends and family could look at her with pity or judgement.

"Brooklyn Botanical Gardens," Brooke said aloud as she tossed the invitation on the table. She had wanted to get married there but Jaclyn said it would be too much for her allergies. She didn't want to mess up her makeup with watery eyes, which in hindsight, should have been a sign to Brooke that Jaclyn had no intention of crying at their wedding.

Brooke and Jaclyn were together for eight years and married for almost four when everything came crashing down. Early in their relationship, they had talked about having kids in the future and Jaclyn said that she didn't want them. Brooke came to terms with that and focused on the fact that she was in love with Jaclyn and was so busy with work that she'd enjoy their lavish vacations and freedom over having a baby. She truly enjoyed being a DINK family: Double Income No Kids. She thought they were still on the same page with that but it seemed that Jaclyn had started to come up with her own ideas of what she wanted for her future.

Jaclyn met Charlie at work and they started a torrid affair behind Brooke's back for almost a year. It probably would have gone on for longer if Jaclyn hadn't been forced to reveal the truth since Brooke obviously couldn't get her pregnant. Brooke was inconsolable during their breakup. Jaclyn didn't put up a fight – she accepted her punishment of Brooke wanting a divorce immediately and moved in with Charlie. Meanwhile, Brooke was heartbroken and divorced at thirty-eight with her prime child-bearing years behind her now. Jaclyn being three years younger gave her a wonderful advantage and she and Charlie had their unplanned but wanted baby together and now they were getting married. Two years after they broke up, Brooke was still single and barely dipping her toe into the dating pool again out of fear of getting hurt. How could she even have everything she always wanted now?

Taylor drifted into her mind for a moment and despite how much she wanted to disregard the thought, she couldn't. Taylor was younger. Maybe there was hope for her having a family after all. Brooke started to laugh to herself realizing she was fantasizing something beyond far-fetched. Despite their undeniable chemistry, she shouldn't get ahead of herself. They had one simple date. They were far from ever getting married and having kids together, but she decided to throw in the towel and surrender to her own desires. She had a goal of a date a week – neither she nor Nina ever specified if it had to be a different person each week. Brooke hadn't even opened the dating app over the past week so reaching out to Taylor was simply her keeping up with her own rules.

Brooke [7:42pm]
There's a new Cuban restaurant I've been wanting to check out. Want to go this weekend?

Taylor [8:10pm]
You had me at mojitos... I'm working Saturday night but free Friday

Brooke made a reservation and sent Taylor confirmation of the time and place to meet her. It was the first second date she had in a decade and the nerves were already starting to kick in where it remained for the rest of the week.

"What's your work schedule like? Do you work almost every night?" Brooke asked as they started to dig in to their empanada starter on Friday night. As promised, Brooke would eat more than just an appetizer on this date, even if she gave Taylor the larger portion of the empanada she just cut in half.

"I don't just bartend," Taylor nonchalantly said between bites.

Brooke furrowed her brow as she questioned the response. "You have another job? I didn't know that."

"You didn't ask," Taylor pointed out. "Is that why your previous dates didn't work out? You didn't ask the right questions?"

Brooke felt herself replay their entire conversation the week prior. They didn't have a moment of silence. They talked *a lot*. Brooke confirmed that Taylor had been working at the bar for a while and that she also bartended for a year after she graduated college. Brooke didn't ask a follow up question nor did she ever think to ask if Taylor had another job. Why would she?

"You're right. I'm sorry," Brooke said, not wanting Taylor to think she was self-absorbed. How could she be so foolish to not ask more about her job? Taylor easily asked her at least five questions about her career.

"I'm just teasing you," Taylor said as she quickly placed her hand on Brooke's forearm on the table. "I kind of liked that you agreed to see me again thinking I was a bartender. Like that doesn't bother you."

"Why would it bother me?"

Taylor shrugged and when she brushed a strand of hair behind her ear, Brooke couldn't help but want to be the one to move it. To be so close to her skin. To caress her face. "You're super sophisticated. You could think it's beneath you or something. Or maybe jealous that people give me extra tips because they think I'm cute." Taylor winked and Brooke felt herself grow warm. Did she care? Sure, it had crossed her mind but she was trying not to get her hopes up that this could lead to anything at all.

"Well, you *are* cute," Brooke said with a smile, sending an adorable blush across Taylor's cheeks. "So, what's your day job?"

When Brooke raised her glass for a sip, Taylor replied with, "I'm a stripper."

Brooke's mojito almost shot across the table directly at Taylor. Her wide eyes retracted to normal size before she wiped the side of her mouth in embarrassment. "Oh," she said softly. Bartender she could deal with. Stripper would be impossible. Knowing that the person she was dating was getting naked for other people. *You're getting ahead of yourself. You're not dating. But you'd be no better than a patron at the strip club salivating for the chance to see her naked.*

Taylor started laughing to break Brooke out of the downward spiral of thoughts she was having. "I'm totally kidding. You're really easy to get going." A wave of relief washed over Brooke to know that Taylor was not a stripper. Although, now all she could think about was what Taylor would look like if she was and it was a very enticing image. "I work in marketing analytics. A real nine-to-five office job where I keep my clothes on. I'm just bartending for a while to pay off business school loans and have a nice cushion for rent, savings, and vacation. I don't like the idea of carrying debt."

Any judgments Brooke had about Taylor's career ambitions were immediately squished and replaced with a sense of guilt for momentarily panicking. Taylor may have been younger, but she had her act together enough to be focused and driven. "That's impressive," Brooke said as she collected her thoughts. "I've been there but remember work and money aren't everything. You need to enjoy your life too."

Taylor batted her eyelashes at Brooke as her lips raised in a smile. "I'm enjoying it plenty right now."

Taylor wasn't the only one.

After dinner, and possibly one mojito too many, Taylor suggested that they go out to a gay bar. It was her spur of the moment idea of getting to spend more time with Brooke in a relaxed environment where maybe they could dance and have fun as they got to know each other more. It didn't hurt that one of her friends was doing a DJ set tonight for ladies' night and it was the perfect reason for them to go to a very crowded Stonewall Inn.

It was a bold choice, but Taylor hoped it would pay dividends as she laced her fingers with Brooke's to lead her upstairs to the bar's second floor through a crowd of people. She walked straight towards the DJ booth where Marianna saw her and threw her hands in the air before stepping out to wrap her arms around Taylor. Even while hugging Marianna, Taylor kept her left hand in Brooke's, not wanting to break contact. She could get used to this.

"Mari, this is Brooke," she said with a proud smile. "I dragged her here against her will."

Marianna smiled widely at Brooke. Almost too widely for Taylor's taste. She knew *exactly* what that look meant. "Let me get you ladies a round of drinks to make up for it."

Taylor leaned over to Brooke to ask her what she wanted to drink before she finally separated their hands to meet her friend at the bar. After ordering them both a gin and tonic, Taylor glanced over her shoulder to see Brooke looking towards the group of girls dancing on the stage celebrating a bachelorette party. "Brooke is gorgeous," Marianna announced as she followed Taylor's eyes. "Are you dating or do I have a shot?"

"We're dating," Taylor declared feeling instantly territorial, even though there truly wasn't a label to what they were doing. *This was a second date, right?*

"Damn," Marianna said before she turned back towards the bartender to thank him for the drinks. Taylor stepped back towards Brooke to hand her the cocktail which she raised in a toast to Marianna across the room.

"When was the last time you were here?" Taylor asked as she leaned in to talk into Brooke's ear over the blaring music. Being this close to her was everything she wanted, but nothing she was prepared for. Whenever Taylor started dating someone new, she was always nervous about those initial moments of getting too close, wondering if the other woman felt the same. Right now, Taylor struggled to think about how Brooke was feeling because she was too distracted by the other woman. Being across from her at dinner tonight was a bit of torture as she wanted nothing more than to close the gap as much as possible. Never had she wanted to be so close to someone.

Brooke looked up towards the ceiling almost lost in thought as Taylor watched her perfectly structured face move. Aside from wanting to be with her, Taylor couldn't help but admire Brooke as a woman. She was truly stunning. "Maybe three years ago."

"Three?" Taylor questioned sharply, quickly losing her train of thought over the exposed skin on Brooke's neck. "Where the hell do you go out then?"

Brooke smiled and took a sip of her drink. "I haven't really been going out that much."

As a smile started to drift off of Brooke's face, a terrifying thought entered Taylor's mind. Had Brooke actually *been* with anyone since her divorce? The dates she had been on recently clearly didn't work out, but what if she hadn't had any successful ones before then? What if she was still figuring out how to be with someone else again in every possible way? What if Taylor was going to be some sort of rebound? "So, uh, does that mean you haven't been with anyone since your ex?" Taylor nervously asked.

Brooke raised a brow as she leaned in to respond. "That's what you gathered from me not coming to Stonewall for three years?"

Shit. Too far. "I'm sorry that's really none of my business," Taylor started to backtrack as she panicked about how she could salvage this conversation. "I just meant like you haven't really gone out with anyone since then. Aside from your bar dates."

"I haven't had a real relationship since her, no," Brooke said as she looked into Taylor's eyes. "But if you're trying to find out if I've had sex since then, the answer is yes."

Taylor didn't know whether she was relieved or jealous. Neither made much sense in the moment. What did Brooke's sex life since her divorce have to do with anything? Either she was ready to move on or she wasn't. Taylor already knew that she wished it could be with her, as long as she wasn't just a rebound.

"I don't think I want to ask a follow-up question," Taylor said with a smile as she took a long sip of her drink. "I've put my foot in my mouth enough for one night."

Brooke smiled and silently nursed her drink. How could someone drinking a mediocre cocktail from a paper straw be so attractive? This wasn't something that Taylor would have ever paid attention to before but now she was transfixed. It was the only thing she could do to distract her mind from wondering what kind of women Brooke was with before. What they looked like. What did they for a living. What Brooke liked in every possible way. Including in bed.

"Do you want to dance?" Taylor finally asked minutes later to stop her mind from going down a rabbit hole that would be difficult to get out of. She was nervous Brooke would say no, but all she wanted to do was get closer to her date and maybe for a moment, get to feel her body against hers.

Brooke surprisingly nodded and followed Taylor's lead as they dropped their empty glasses on the edge of the bar. When they moved closer to the crowd of people swaying to the sounds of Bad Bunny, Taylor turned around to look at Brooke. Blue and white lights were illuminating her pale skin from up above. She looked like a cinematic vision out of a movie; almost too good to be true to be standing here in her presence. Taylor didn't know how she got so lucky to be here tonight dancing with the most beautiful woman in the room but she surely wouldn't take it for granted as she inched herself closer and held her breath in anticipation of being able to wrap her arms around Brooke.

The younger woman smiled at Brooke as they started to dance and sway with a noticeable gap between them. It gave Taylor the perfect opportunity to let her gaze linger over Brooke's body. She was in such good shape, and the curve of her hips was enough to make Taylor's mouth water at the idea of getting to hold them. Her eyes traveled upwards and like a pubescent teenager, she swallowed hard at the sight of Brooke's chest. Her breasts were moving with each movement of Brooke's dancing shoulders and Taylor needed to get closer to them; closer to Brooke.

Taylor delicately wrapped her arm around Brooke's waist as she closed the gap between them. Her leg parted Brooke's thighs as she swayed to the music, nervous that every moment they danced was bringing her closer to an increasing desire she didn't know if she could keep at bay, despite how much she knew she should. That thought became even more difficult to process when she swore she could feel heat radiating off of Brooke's body through her jeans.

Sure, Taylor had high hopes of maybe getting closer to Brooke here at the bar but now that it was happening, she wanted to find the nearest exit. She was so enchanted by touching this exotic woman that it seemed to have thrown her for a complete loop. She couldn't control her thoughts and the reaction her body was having. Taylor's eyes moved off of Brooke's neck where they had been staring for the past few moments in a daze thinking about how it would feel to kiss the exposed skin. She returned her focus to Brooke's eyes that were twinkling right back at her.

"What are you looking at?" Brooke asked after a moment as she leaned in towards Taylor, pressing their chests fully flush against one another's.

Taylor wished she could find something eloquent to say. To say something profound about how much she enjoyed tonight and how much more she wanted to enjoy. Although, most of the words she'd say probably would have been more expletive rather than eloquent. It didn't help that her mind was completely frazzled by the scent of Brooke's floral perfume entering her nostrils as it had all night. She was truly intoxicating. "You're so beautiful," Taylor finally whispered back into Brooke's ear as their bodies swayed in sync to the music.

A cheek pressed against Taylor's jaw and every pore on her skin raised in chills. "You're sweet," Brooke said softly.

Sweet wasn't what Taylor wanted to be described as. Of course, that was nice, and Taylor *was* sweet. But right now, with their bodies moving on the dancefloor, Taylor wanted to be sexy. She wanted Brooke to want her just as much as she wanted her.

Brooke pulled back to look into Taylor's eyes before she dropped her gaze to Taylor's lips. Taylor felt herself grow still as the thought entered her mind that Brooke might actually kiss her. Maybe encouraging that third mojito at the restaurant was a good idea if it meant that Brooke was letting her guard down. Before Taylor could close the gap between them, Brooke leaned in and gently pressed her lips against Taylor's. It was so faint that Taylor almost didn't realize it was happening until she felt that their lips were indeed moving against one another's and her entire body was ablaze.

Taylor's hands landed on Brooke's hips and pulled her closer as their lips danced in sync with the movement of their bodies. These had to be the softest and most intoxicating lips Taylor had ever encountered in her lifetime. As Brooke's hands lowered to the dip of Taylor's lower back, she couldn't help but hope that she felt the same. That she was also feeling explosions behind her eyelids as her pillowy lips molded with Taylor's.

"Not where I imagined us having our first kiss," Brooke said with a smug smile as she pulled away far too soon. The daze was broken. They weren't swirling in space. They were in the middle of a packed Stonewall Inn on a Friday night and not a single person around them seemed to notice what just transpired between them.

"You've imagined it?" Taylor asked as she ran her hand up Brooke's back to hold her closer.

Brooke brought her bottom lip between her teeth. "Maybe."

"I've thought about it too," Taylor admitted as she dragged her hand across Brooke's shoulder. "It was going to go something like this," she stated as she gently cupped Brooke's face in her hand and leaned in, pressing her lips against Brooke's gently before she moved her hand to the nape of Brooke's neck to bring her closer.

Unlike their kiss a moment earlier, this one continued for longer and was much more intense. When Brooke opened her mouth and grazed her tongue against Taylor's, the younger woman felt her knees almost betray her and give out underneath her. Despite how loud the bar was, the only sound Taylor could hear was the faintest moan that left Brooke's mouth. *Good God, this is the most erotic kiss of my life,* Taylor thought to herself as her own tongue entered Brooke's mouth where it wanted to stay forever.

As the song abruptly changed to Beyoncé and the crowd erupted in excitement, Brooke pulled back with hooded eyes. *Did she feel that too?*

"I liked your kiss better," Brooke said with a smile as she took a step backwards, leaving more than just space for air between them.

Taylor found herself unable to move or respond. All she wanted to do was lean in and kiss Brooke until neither of them could breathe but she was suddenly reminded of the crowded bar and the people moving around them. As she glanced to her left, she could see Marianna grinning at her. Their make out session was no longer something that existed just for them.

"I'm going to head out," Brooke declared, immediately sending Taylor into a panic. Was she leaving because of their kiss? Was it too much? Or worse, did she not actually like it?

"What? Why?" She scrambled to find the words to say.

Brooke brought her hand to Taylor's cheek and the action alone sent a wave of relief down the younger woman's spine. "It's late. And as nice as this has been, it's not my scene."

Taylor nodded and considered asking if she wanted to go somewhere else but remembered the first reason for why Brooke wanted to leave. "Let me walk you out," she said as she laced their fingers together again and moved through the sea of people towards the stairs. Once they got outside, Brooke quietly looked for a taxi on the street before glancing down at her phone, weighing the options between taxi and Uber.

"Are you leaving because we kissed?" Taylor found the courage to ask. "Did I do something wrong?"

Brooke turned back to look at her, her face softening under the streetlight. "I did. I shouldn't have kissed you like that, I'm sorry."

Sorry? There was absolutely nothing to be sorry about in Taylor's eyes. One thing was certain: the only regret she had over the kiss was that it ended. "There is no reason to apologize to me. I'm glad you kissed me."

Brooke shook her head and glanced back towards the street. It was obvious that she was embarrassed, for reasons that Taylor couldn't quite understand. "It wasn't the right time or place."

"I completely disagree," Taylor countered back quickly, trying to reel Brooke back in from the deep-end she was veering off to. "Was it unexpected? Yes. Would I have it any other way? No." Brooke remained expressionless and still very clearly regretted her actions and that made Taylor fill with disappointment. "Are you leaving because I'm a bad kisser or something?"

"I'm leaving because it was too good," Brooke said with a smile that Taylor was relieved to see appear. "And it's late. I'm not thirty anymore." The playful tone of Brooke's voice quieted all the anxiety that bubbled up in Taylor's mind. She might have regretted how and where they kissed, but she didn't deny how good it was.

When a cab pulled up to the curb and Brooke opened the door, Taylor's worry was quickly replaced with a longing for the night to not end. Before dinner, she never thought about the possibility of kissing Brooke today, let alone making out in the middle of a dancefloor at a bar. Now that she had a taste of Brooke, figuratively and literally, she didn't know how to quiet her cravings for more.

"Goodnight," Brooke said as she leaned in and gently pressed her lips against Taylor's one last time. "I had a great night."

"Me too," Taylor said as she watched Brooke get in the car and close the door. As the cab drove off, Taylor couldn't help but wonder where exactly Brooke was off to. What her apartment looked like. How she decorated. What she wore to bed. She stopped there as she became fixated on the idea of Brooke in bed.

If this was any other night, Taylor would have gone back into the bar and hung out with Marianna. Tonight, she just wanted to go home and revel in the fact that she and Brooke kissed. Plus, maybe she didn't want Marianna to know they didn't go home together. Just maybe.

Chapter Six

Taylor was in the middle of a child's pose at her Monday morning yoga class trying to find a sense of inner calm amidst her stretch, but she couldn't seem to find it. No matter how many poses they did, how many inhales and exhales she took, how many attempts at mindfulness she made, her brain was elsewhere.

She hadn't stopped thinking about her kiss with Brooke since Friday night. If she was being honest with herself, she hadn't stopped thinking about Brooke in general since they met at the bar. She wasn't used to this type of nagging feeling that quickly appeared and thwarted everything. She had gone out with Stella four times before they even kissed. Her girlfriend before that she did sleep with on the first date. Neither of those had worked out and clearly there wasn't a playbook for what was the right way to date someone, but Taylor really wished there was. She could use a guide to help her understand the proper way to court a woman like Brooke because she was truly lost.

She and Brooke texted a bit over the weekend but Taylor was growing antsy at trying to wait to ask to see her again. She didn't want to come across as needy, which would be how she would perceive someone who asked her out again so soon, but this was different. She didn't want to play games and wait pretending she didn't really care or she was busy with someone else. She left the yoga studio with the decision that during lunch later that day, she would ask Brooke out again. To hell with waiting. Life was too short.

Taylor [1:17pm]
Since you like to eat early and hate loud music in crowded bars... how about an early bird Central Park brunch picnic Saturday at 1:00? I start at the bar at 6

Brooke [3:02pm]
Thoughtful. But for the record I don't hate loud music. I just prefer something a bit quieter when I'm trying to talk to someone

Taylor [3:09pm]
Stonewall isn't for talking. It's for dancing, drinking, and kissing

Taylor really hoped that wasn't taking it too far. They hadn't talked about their kiss yet, despite how much Taylor wanted to bring it up. She didn't know what would be too flirtatious or cross a line that could scare Brooke off when she only wanted her so much closer.

Brooke [3:15pm]
I did enjoy all three of those

Taylor smiled widely, feeling relieved that she wasn't the only one who enjoyed it.

Taylor [3:16pm]
Me too

Taylor [3:16pm]

Sooooo Saturday?

Brooke [3:17pm]
Yes

On Friday afternoon, Taylor knew she was going to lose her battle with Mother Nature. Saturday's forecast was calling for rain all day long; a literal dampen on her plans for a picture-perfect picnic in Central Park. As she hopped from store-to-store to pick up everything she wanted for their time together, she finally caved and told Brooke to come over to her apartment for an indoor makeshift picnic. She didn't want to cancel their plans and miss the chance to see Brooke again, despite how different an indoor picnic would feel.

Taylor frantically cleaned her apartment all of Saturday morning. She always kept her studio in presentable condition, but she was feeling extra pressure now that Brooke would be in her apartment. It was moments like this that she was relieved she didn't have a larger place to clean nooks and crannies. After she set up a picnic blanket on the floor and put a bottle of champagne in the fridge, she jumped in the shower and tried to wash away her nerves.

When Brooke arrived at her door an hour later, Taylor took a deep breath that didn't help alleviate any of the fleeting feelings she had when she opened the door and saw Brooke standing across from her. She looked absolutely flawless in a loose white button-down shirt, a pair of light blue jeans and white sneakers – a casual look she didn't think the woman would have eased into so quickly judging by how pristine she had been dressed every time she saw her previously. There were no blazers, blouses, plunging V-neck t-shirts that wouldn't deteriorate after one wash, tight pants or cute shoes that would impress anyone. "I dressed for a picnic," Brooke declared as she obviously sensed Taylor looking at her outfit.

"You look perfect," Taylor said as her eyes moved upwards and back to Brooke's face – well, mostly her lips. How were they supposed to greet one another now? Were they still solely in cheek-kiss territory? Were kisses on the lips reserved only for dimly lit crowded bars? "Hi," Taylor finally said as she leaned in and placed a safe, soft kiss on Brooke's cheek.

"Cute place," Brooke said as she entered into the apartment still holding a small bouquet of flowers and a bottle of prosecco.

"It's smaller than I'd like but I'm too old for a roommate."

Brooke laughed, as if it was supposed to be comical that Taylor considered herself old. "Yes, you're *so* old."

Taylor smiled to herself as she grabbed a vase from above the refrigerator before taking the gifts from Brooke's hands. "We can talk about 401(k) plans and Roth IRAs if that's more your speed."

Brooke slid beside Taylor to lean against the kitchen counter. "Way to get me hot and bothered."

Taylor knew it was a joke but something stirred inside of her. It was a mix of desire and trepidation. She very obviously already knew she wanted Brooke, but could she live up to Brooke's expectations? If she even had any.

"Well, good thing I have chilled champagne to cool you off," Taylor deflected as she stepped back towards the fridge and removed the bottle. She started to scold herself for already losing control mere minutes after Brooke walked through the door. This was ridiculous – Taylor had dated plenty of people and had survived plenty of initial first dates, kisses, sex, and yet none of them prepared her for this. None of them prepared her for a real woman. Maybe there was a reason why they say be careful what you wish for. She wished for a woman like Brooke and now she had no idea what to do with her to not screw it all up.

"I know this doesn't compare to Central Park but I found a two-hour long bird chirping meditation that can make it seem like we're there," Taylor nervously said as she found the playlist on her phone and connected it to her Bluetooth speaker. Brooke silently looked on and laughed when Taylor pressed play and birds filled the apartment. For some reason, Taylor loved making Brooke laugh. The sound alone brought her joy because even her laugh was adorable.

"But I think the food is more important, go sit down and get comfortable," Taylor ushered for Brooke to leave her small kitchen to give her a moment to pull the already prepared charcuterie board out of the fridge. And help her get a grip on herself.

"Can I help?" Brooke asked.

"You can take this to the blanket," Taylor said as she handed the chilled bottle and glasses to Brooke, desperate for her to leave her proximity so she could breathe.

Brooke sat on the floor and crossed her legs as she watched Taylor across the apartment. Taylor suddenly wished her apartment had walls. She would have preferred a moment of privacy to look at her reflection, see if her lips were still glossy, spray another puff of perfume before sitting mere inches apart on the floor. Instead, she hoped for the best as she grabbed their meal and walked over to her date.

As they sat in the middle of Taylor's apartment sharing a wide assortment on a perfectly displayed charcuterie board, Taylor found herself simply admiring Brooke. Never had she met a woman who she could talk to endlessly and learn about facets of her life that only peaked more of her interest. She wanted to know everything about Brooke and each time she had a chance to ask a follow-up question, she took advantage of it. She also had no qualms sharing pieces of her own personal life. From her family dynamic to her failed relationships. She'd willingly tell Brooke anything and everything.

When they finished eating and Taylor started to clean up, she put on non-bird related music and watched as Brooke looked at some of the artwork on her wall. "My mom painted those," she said as she watched Brooke's eyes remained focused on the scattered frames.

"They're beautiful," Brooke said before she finally stepped away and returned to the couch. "She's an artist?"

"In her spare time," Taylor noted with a smile. She was always so impressed and proud of her mother's accomplishments. "She's a realtor and does a lot of volunteering. I don't know how she has time for anything to be honest."

"She sounds like a great woman," Brooke said softly.

"What about your parents?" Taylor asked. Surprisingly, they hadn't come up previously and Taylor learned the hard way to not prematurely ask personal questions about someone's parents. She once asked a girl about her parents on their first date and she broke down in tears at the table because she had been recently disowned. Taylor could still see the distraught look on her face all these years later.

Brooke looked back towards the wall of paintings. "My dad works part-time for an environmental agency and my mom is a retired teacher."

"And they still live in DC?" Taylor asked as she sat down besides Brooke on the couch.

"Yeah, I don't think they'll ever leave," Brooke said with a smile. "My dad enjoys protesting things too much."

Taylor laughed and took the final sip of her champagne. "He'd fit in here. There's basically a protest every day somewhere."

"True," Brooke agreed. "But I think he gets joy out of potentially running into politicians in restaurants. You should hear some of the speeches he has mentally planned for the day he sees Ted Cruz."

Taylor laughed and leaned back on the couch. "I hope he gets the chance to deliver it one day. Every time my sister talks about taking the kids to Disney World, my mom complains about Ron DeSantis."

"He's vile," Brooke declared as she turned towards Taylor. "You have nieces and nephews?"

"Yep," Taylor beamed as she grabbed her phone and started to pull up pictures on her sister's Instagram. "This is Ella and this is Eli."

"They're adorable!" Brooke gushed as she held Taylor's phone in her hand and looked at the recent photo of the two children smiling as they clutched their Easter baskets filled with candy. "You look like your sister."

Taylor unconsciously rolled her eyes. She knew it was true; she had been hearing it her entire life, yet it still annoyed her that she and Harper looked so similar. Especially when Harper was always what Taylor needed to live up to. "I like to think she looks like me," Taylor said softly before she looked down at her phone again. "Hey, do you have Instagram?"

"I do," Brooke sounded.

Taylor handed her phone back to Brooke. "Can I add you?"

Brooke smiled and typed her handle into Taylor's phone. "I suppose you can."

It was a small win in getting to know more about Brooke and she'd take it. "I think that calls for a refill," she said as she got up and picked up their empty glasses. She walked to the kitchen and popped open the bottle of prosecco Brooke brought. She looked over at Brooke and decided that there was no time like the present to address the elephant in the room. Or maybe it was the alcohol putting it there to begin with.

Taylor placed their glasses down on the table before she leaned over towards Brooke, who judging by how she smiled, wasn't bothered by Taylor sitting significantly closer to her than she was previously. "I have to tell you something," Taylor started, knowing she was being a bit dramatic but didn't know how else to eloquently deliver what she was about to say. "I've been thinking about our kiss all week."

The slightest hint of pink rose over Brooke's fair cheeks. "What about it?"

About how I want to reenact it right now. "About how good it felt," Taylor said as she inched closer to bring their faces closer together. "But mostly that little moan you let out when our tongues touched." She hovered over Brooke's ear as she whispered, "I'd give anything to hear you moan again."

She pressed her lips to the side of Brooke's jaw and started to pepper kisses until she reached her chin and she lifted her mouth to look into Brooke's eyes that were lust ridden and surely matched her own.

Taylor was relieved that Brooke was the one to lean in and bring their lips together yet again. Just like the week prior, Brooke's kiss was nothing short of intoxicating. All the blood in Taylor's body rushed to her brain in an overload of emotion and sensations before it shot elsewhere in a pang of desire and lust.

Taylor shifted her weight and repositioned herself to sit on Brooke's lap. She needed to feel more of Brooke. The warmth of her body underneath her. The pounding of her heart against her own chest. The scent of her perfume filling her nostrils, permanently etching the fragrance into her memory.

Brooke wrapped her arms around Taylor to hold her closer, instantly informing Taylor that she never wanted someone's hands to go under her shirt more than she did right now. She could feel the heat radiating from Brooke's palms on her back all the way down to her core and she found herself getting more and more distracted the second they danced across her ribs.

She trailed her hand from Brooke's neck down to her chest, nervously gauging how far she could go before Brooke stopped her, or she bailed from own fear of not being able to stop. She slowly undid one button at a time before she slipped her hand under the fabric to touch Brooke's skin directly. The faintest moan left Brooke's mouth the second Taylor's hand grazed the side of her breast and Taylor felt her entire stomach drop in desire.

Taylor was fully aware that she was practically grinding her body on top of Brooke but she couldn't even control herself in this moment. She was desperate for more contact in ways she didn't even know was possible. This was by far the most arousing make out session she had ever had in her entire life and nothing was happening except kissing.

She shifted her hand from Brooke's back desperate for more contact and now she was the one moaning as she felt Brooke's breast in her hand with only the thin material of a bra keeping them apart. "You're killing me," Brooke said as she arched her hips up and they battled for control over who could kiss who harder, faster, more desperately.

Brooke gave Taylor what she was yearning for when her hand finally moved up under Taylor's shirt and caressed her breasts. Taylor's body immediately reacted with stiff peaks pressing into Brooke's fingertips that she was gently squeezing to send Taylor squirming on top of her.

"God," Taylor moaned as she threw her head back, giving Brooke an opportunity to lean forward and kiss her neck. She gently nibbled her way across the skin while Taylor boldly went a step further and maneuvered her hand to try to open Brooke's bra behind her back with only one hand because there was no way she was going to stop touching Brooke's breast with the other.

"Fuck," Taylor said in frustration, not because she was unable to unclasp it, because she most certainly had in one swift move. She was cursing because her phone alarm was blaring across the apartment, ruining the moment. She dragged herself off of Brooke's lap to turn off her phone that she left on the kitchen counter when she got them a refill. She quickly walked back to Brooke who hadn't moved an inch and got back into her lap to kiss her deeply. "I have to get ready for work," she said amidst kisses.

Brooke nodded her head and continued to kiss Taylor with just as much passion as before. If only her hands returned to the same position as before, then Taylor would have surely decided today was a good day to just not show up to work. She would even be content to get fired if it meant that she could go back to what they started and get that bra fully off Brooke's body, along with the rest of her clothes. "I get off at midnight if you want to come back later," Taylor said without thinking.

When Brooke slowed her kiss before stopping entirely, Taylor wondered if she went too far. It was one thing to make out, even if there was some fondling involved, but it was another to imply taking things further and potentially having sex. This was only their third date after all.

"Let's have a raincheck," Brooke said as she pulled back and ran her fingers through her long dark hair. She reached behind her back to close her bra and Taylor did everything in her power to not pout at the realization that this was over. It was over before it even began.

There was no denying that Taylor was disappointed. Both that she had to go to work and that Brooke was declining to pick up where they left off later. She should have known better. Brooke wasn't someone that seemed to like casual hookups. Not that Taylor did either, but she'd been there and done that enough to know that wasn't something she wanted with Brooke. She wanted it to mean something. And this couch exploration meant a lot, but wouldn't mean as much as taking things further.

"Okay," she sounded as she reluctantly got off of Brooke's lap and painfully watched her get up and button her shirt before she grabbed her purse. "Thanks for coming over."

Brooke quietly slipped back into her sneakers and looked up with a smile. "Thanks for the picnic."

"I'd say I wish it didn't rain but I kind of enjoyed our time inside," Taylor shared, hoping that Brooke would know she truly meant it. And not just the making out; she enjoyed her company in general.

"Me too," Brooke said softly before leaning over and placing a very quick kiss on Taylor's lips. "Have a good day at work."

As Brooke grabbed her umbrella and walked out the door, Taylor felt like a fool. She pushed them too far and it resulted in Brooke practically running out of the apartment. She leaned her forehead against the closed door and sighed. She was definitely not going to be able to pay attention to anything at work today.

Chapter Seven

Brooke sat on her couch watching the third episode in a row of a show she didn't even have any interest in. Was she supposed to care about the personal lives of real estate agents that got into petty arguments every episode and made more money in commission than some people made in an entire year? She was desperately trying to distract her mind and the ache that had been burning through her body the entire afternoon but this show wasn't doing the trick. Would anything?

Even after she took a cold shower when she got home from Taylor's apartment, she was still ignited with desire. She chalked it up to the fact that she hadn't had sex in roughly six months, and that wasn't very satisfying. When she initially developed a short-lived on-again-off-again friends with benefits situation with a woman she was acquainted with, it became another sad attempt to not feel so lonely post-divorce. Every time they got together, Brooke hoped it would be better, but it lacked everything, including passion. It was simply a means to an end and she decided to end it once and for all.

To have sex with Taylor, someone she was actually interested in, would be a complete game changer. She hadn't done that since Jaclyn which felt like an eternity ago. Now she wanted to prolong the experience and try to get to know each other more before crossing any physical lines, knowing it would change everything. Yet, she was the one who kissed Taylor first at Stonewall. She was the one who closed the gap this afternoon and ached in disappointment when they were forced to part. Her body was betraying her mind. All of her inhibitions were suddenly dropped and all she could be reminded of was desire; the one thing she hadn't felt in so long and didn't know how to repress now that it was unleashed.

Brooke picked up her phone looking for something else to distract her racing thoughts. The dating app she had been neglecting peered back at her, reminding her of what she was doing. *Dating*. She opened the app and saw Morgan who she had briefly messaged with a few weeks ago asked if she wanted to meet for coffee. Bianca told her she was beautiful and asked how her week was going. As she glanced at the phone and looked at Bianca's profile, she knew this was pointless. She couldn't possibly talk to another person while she was doing whatever it was she was doing with Taylor, let alone go on a date. She didn't want to put all her hope into this, but she knew herself. She wasn't the type of person to juggle others. She wanted to focus on actively dating only one person at a time and right now that was Taylor.

In this moment, she realized she was ready to jump in head first with Taylor which is why she involuntarily moved her finger to her account settings and deactivated her account. If she needed to come back here in days, weeks, months, she'd reinstate it to make Nina proud. For now, she was off the apps and into the real world.

She looked at the time in the corner of her screen and saw it was ten-twenty. *What the hell am I doing?* She got up and quickly applied some basic makeup before throwing on a pair of jeans and a sweater and grabbing her purse. It had been too long since she had meaningful sex, and if Taylor was ready to cross that bridge with her tonight, who was she to say no? After all, she just committed herself to Taylor without giving it a second thought.

When Brooke walked into Taylor's bar, she took a deep breath as she stepped towards the crowded countertop. Taylor didn't notice her at first until she moved her eyes down the bar just as Brooke sat in a vacant seat. A wide smile appeared on the bartender's face as she stepped towards the latest patron. "I'm surprised to see you."

"Why?" Brooke asked, suddenly nervous that maybe Taylor didn't actually want her to come back. Had it really been that long since she dated that she didn't even know how to read the signs?

"Because it's past your bedtime," Taylor said with a playful smirk.

"I have no problem staying up late for the right reasons," Brooke flirted.

Taylor rolled her bottom lip between her teeth. "And what are those?"

"Maybe you'll find out later."

Taylor began to blush before walking away to start making a drink. Brooke watched her at the other end of the bar and swallowed hard at the thought of what could happen later; what she *knew* was going to happen because she wanted it and Taylor was looking back at her silently saying the same thing.

"This is the Bee's Knees," Taylor said when she returned to place a drink in front of Brooke. "Which you are to me."

Brooke chuckled as she held Taylor's serious gaze, finding the joke the perfect reprieve from the heart palpitations she was starting to have. "That might be the corniest pickup line I've ever heard."

"Do I really need a pickup line with someone I've already picked up?" Taylor asked with a raised brow.

Challenge accepted. "I didn't realize I was picked up."

Taylor licked her lips as she leaned closer on the bar before her name was yelled out behind her. "Taylor! I need another round of four negronis for table eight." The bartender stepped away and winked at her date. Brooke sipped her drink and tried to convince herself that she wasn't picked up, despite knowing she was and wouldn't have it any other way.

"What the hell was I thinking calling her the Bee's Knees?" Taylor mumbled to herself. That was definitely one of the corniest lines that could have ever left her mouth and she did it without even thinking about how it would sound. Brooke seemed to have that effect on her. Taylor wanted to be perfect for her but she found herself just being genuinely herself. She was a bit corny and dorky at times. She always said what she felt. She did her best to not be fake about anything and the one thing that'd been increasingly clear over the last three weeks was that she had a massive crush on the woman at the end of the bar.

She could still feel Brooke's lips on hers from hours prior and judging by the fact she came back, she hoped there'd be more of that. The end of her shift couldn't come fast enough and as soon as the clock struck midnight, she practically ran towards the back of the bar to get her bag so she could continue the rest of her night with the woman patiently waiting for her by the front door.

"I think it's only fitting that since I saw your place earlier you come to mine now," Brooke said as they stepped outside into the cool Spring air. Brooke exuded such confidence in her suggestion that Taylor started to wonder if she might be the only one that was nervous. Which gave her even more anxiety over whether she could manage to not screw it all up in the next few hours, because this night was definitely going to go on for hours if she had her way.

"I'd like that," Taylor said as she focused on the fact that there was nothing more that she wanted right now than to go back to Brooke's apartment.

After the short drive to Chelsea, they silently rode the elevator up and walked into Brooke's impeccable apartment. Where Taylor's apartment was cute and cozy, Brooke's was modern and elegant. One panel of the floor-to-ceiling windows had more light shining through at nighttime than the three windows in Taylor's apartment combined during the day. The marble island in her kitchen was practically the same size as Taylor's bathroom. There was a black leather Eames lounge chair and ottoman in the corner of the living room. The chair her father always wanted but was never willing to spend the money on because of its high price tag.

This apartment was everything Taylor wished she could have, and the moment she started to question how much it all cost, other thoughts started to enter her mind. Was Brooke out of her league? Did Brooke think Taylor was just a young, cute, woman to pass the time? Was this where Brooke lived with her ex-wife? Was this a divorce settlement? A place that was haunted by ghosts Taylor wanted nothing to do with?

As Taylor turned around and saw Brooke stepping towards her, all her questions went out the floor-to-ceiling windows. Now all she could focus on was how breathtaking Brooke was in the low light of her apartment. How she was walking towards Taylor like a supermodel on a runway knowing everyone's eyes were on her. "Do you want a glass of wine or anything?" Brooke asked.

Don't tell her you want her. Taylor's mind was already racing on what *not* to say. The Bee's Knees comment was embarrassing enough for one night, maybe a lifetime. Instead, she stepped towards Brooke and gently placed her hand on the back of her neck before bringing their lips together. There was no turning back now. There was only one thing Taylor wanted and judging by the way Brooke kissed her back, she wanted it too.

Taylor pushed Brooke backwards, really hoping that the other open doorway in the apartment led to Brooke's bedroom. Judging by what she had already seen, Taylor wouldn't have been surprised if there was a full home office or a guest room tucked behind the corner. Brooke's backwards steps seemed to guide them in the right direction until her legs hit the edge of her bed and she pulled Taylor down with her.

"God," Taylor moaned into Brooke's mouth as she felt herself mold onto Brooke's body. Lying on top of her was so much better than sitting on her lap earlier, especially now that they were in her bed.

"I'm just Brooke," she teased as her lips raised into a smirk.

Taylor smiled and pulled back to look at Brooke beneath her. She may have fantasized about this moment a few times but right now reality was better than any vision she conjured in her head. Sprawled out against a charcoal gray duvet, Brooke was radiant and for at least tonight, she was Taylor's. "Well, I do think you're a goddess."

Brooke licked her lips and stared up at Taylor with such tender eyes that it would have been heartwarming if Taylor wasn't so turned on. The events from this afternoon left her in shambles. She had been aroused for hours and needed to pick up where they left off so she could find a release. Taylor went to lift her own shirt over her head before Brooke grabbed her hand to stop her. "I really want to do that myself," she said as she ran her hand down Taylor's side. "And go nice and slow."

Taylor gulped as Brooke's hands slowly lifted the cotton fabric over her head before she tossed it to the floor. Brooke gently trailed her fingers down the center of Taylor's chest, feeling the goosebumps on Taylor's skin beneath her fingertips. Taylor's chest rose and fell in anticipation of where Brooke's hand was going to go next and the realization that Brooke was going to kill her by taking her time.

Needing more contact, Taylor leaned in to kiss Brooke's swollen lips and immediately felt her heart sink into her stomach. Brooke slowly moved her lips with such an erotic ease that it made Taylor feel like she had a secret expertise in making out. No one she ever kissed before was this good. No one moved their tongue this delicately and deliberately with such a sensual power from each turn and swipe. Taylor groaned as she thought about how that tongue would feel elsewhere on her body.

Taylor had been with a fair share of women over the years, but never had she yearned for anyone the way she did for the woman she was latched onto. Sure, they had only hung out together three times, four of you counted their first formal interaction that day at the bar. But Taylor knew how much she wanted the other woman. Her soaked underwear reminded her of that every time she thought of Brooke. This wasn't going to be just a hookup for Taylor, this was going to be life-changing and her body knew it.

"I've been thinking about you all night," Brooke said as she moved her lips to Taylor's ear and gently tugged on her earlobe. The way she flicked the skin with her tongue sent Taylor into a tizzy. She pushed Brooke back onto the bed and hovered over her with her hands on both sides of Brooke's head as she pressed into the mattress.

"I've been thinking about you since the first day I saw you at the bar," Taylor confessed. It might have been a bit much, but it was true, and she needed Brooke to know this before they crossed any further lines. "You owe me a lot of underwear."

Brooke smiled and leaned up to meet Taylor's hungry kiss. Taylor bit Brooke's lip more roughly than she anticipated but Brooke didn't seem to mind as she dug her short nails into Taylor's back before flipping their positions entirely and pinned Taylor down on the bed.

Taylor stared up at her and felt her mouth go dry, unlike another part of her body. She was about to undress Brooke in real life, not just in her mind. She moaned to herself that Brooke was about to be more exposed than she ever had been before yet it wasn't enough. Taylor needed to see all of her – *feel* all of her.

Taylor slowly lifted Brooke's sweater over her head and reveled in the sight before her. She suspected that underneath the posh clothing was a toned body and mouthwatering breasts she got a partial glimpse of earlier, but Taylor wasn't expecting to be biting her own lip at the sight of them in a black lace bra. When she got trapped in a mental loop wondering if there were matching panties underneath her jeans, Brooke took advantage of the hesitation and returned her lips to Taylor's.

Brooke hovered over her as she dipped her head to pepper kisses from Taylor's neck down to her bra. She pulled the hot pink fabric back to expose Taylor's nipple before flicking her tongue over it in a painfully slow circle. Taylor pressed her hips into the bed seeking support for the sensations running through her body, especially when Brooke began to suck on her nipple as she pulled her forward to undo the bra entirely. When she removed it from Taylor's body, she tossed it across the room and shifted her attention to Taylor's other breast.

Taylor pressed her leg between Brooke's thighs and moved her thigh slowly knowing how much she loved that sensation. Brooke seemed to feel the same as she slowed her tongue against Taylor's nipple while she moaned. Taylor could feel heat radiating through her jeans – a stark reminder that they both were still wearing too much clothing.

"These have to go," Taylor said breathlessly as she sat up and started to undo Brooke's jeans. Brooke stood up from the bed and slowly pulled her jeans to the floor as Taylor watched with an open jaw. She felt her stomach drop out entirely at confirmation that there were matching black lace panties underneath. Brooke was a goddess after all.

"You are so incredibly sexy," she found the strength to say.

Brooke remained silent as she got back on the bed and looked into Taylor's eyes, almost seeking confirmation that this was really happening. That they were getting completely naked and about to have sex that surely was going to be mind-blowing if the buildup already felt like this.

Brooke slowly undid the button of Taylor's jeans and moved the zipper down at a snail's pace while not breaking eye contact with Taylor. Taylor was convinced it was some sort of powerplay to see if Taylor would beg her to undress her and Taylor had no shame begging if it came down to it. That's how badly she wanted the woman slowly torturing her. Brooke finally got the denim down Taylor's legs and added it to the growing pile of discarded clothes on the floor before a greater sense of need started to intensify between the two of them.

Well, at least for Taylor, who practically ripped Brooke's bra off in desperation before she groaned at the sight of Brooke's exposed breasts. *Finally*. She reached out to hold them in her hands like they were delicate glass that she needed to treat carefully. Taylor dragged her tongue across each breast with determination. She wanted Brooke to feel just as good as she made her feel doing the same thing. As Brooke moaned and rocked her hips into Taylor, the younger woman felt her core twitch with need. While there was nothing more she wanted than to relish in enjoying this first time of truly seeing all of Brooke, her desire to feel her took over.

Her hand traveled from Brooke's breast down her stomach and under the lace band of her underwear. Taylor's fingers slipped lower to be met with folds wet with arousal.

"Fuck," Brooke grunted softly as her eyes rolled back before she closed them tightly. Never had a curse word sounded so sexy to Taylor before. All she wanted was to give Brooke the best orgasm of her life before Brooke grabbed her hand and pulled it out of underwear. "Me first," she said as she slowly licked herself off of Taylor's fingers.

Taylor shuddered at the sensation of her fingers in Brooke's mouth and how sensual that move was. She also had a pang of jealously that she wasn't able to do that herself. She imagined that Brooke tasted delicious and she couldn't wait to find out.

Brooke slowly moved down Taylor's body and when her fingertips grazed the fabric of Taylor's underwear, Taylor felt her soul leave her body. She forced her mouth closed to prevent a gasp at the contact, thinking she needed to at least have some composure right now. Brooke had barely touched her and she was already coming apart at the seams.

"You're so wet," Brooke stated the obvious as she quickly moved her fingers lower to draw circles on Taylor's thighs. Taylor would have been embarrassed if she wasn't so turned on. She knew she was drenched. She never wanted someone more than she wanted Brooke right now. Not the first girl she had sex with. Not any of her ex-girlfriends. It was Brooke. And the desire was pooling between her legs.

"Touch me," Taylor pleaded as she twisted her legs in agony. "Please."

A devilish smirk sprawled across Brooke's face. It was very clear that she had every intention of drawing this out. Taylor would have hated her if she wasn't enjoying every second of it. "Touch you where?"

"Oh God, Brooke, please," Taylor gasped again. She would never last any more foreplay if she couldn't have this first release. At least she hoped it would be the first, hopefully of many.

Brooke raised Taylor's right leg to kiss her way from Taylor's ankle to her knee before she placed Taylor's calf on her shoulder to rest. After she placed one more kiss on the skin, she turned towards the woman breathing erratically on the bed. "How about here?"

Taylor shook her head and watched as a hand moved to her stomach. "Here?"

"Brooke," she sounded again, almost in pain this time which only seemed to please Brooke more.

With a lick of her lips, she moved her hand from Taylor's stomach straight down to place her palm flat against soaked underwear. "Maybe it's here," she said softly. Taylor grunted in frustration as she bucked her hips up, desperate for more contact. "Or maybe you want to be touched here?" Brooke asked as she dropped Brooke's calf from her shoulder to pick up her left leg that had been ignored.

Taylor was about to complain that Brooke was pure evil before fingertips quickly slipped into the waistband of her underwear to fully pull them off of her body. Taylor wanted to sigh in relief but she was too distracted by Brooke trailing kisses up Taylor's leg and when she reached Taylor's inner thigh, she didn't stop to ask where Taylor wanted her. She knew and she just went for it.

"Holy shit," Taylor exclaimed the second Brooke's tongue finally faintly touched her clit. If Brooke was the best kisser she had ever met, she sure as hell was going to be the best at giving her an orgasm and Taylor couldn't wait.

Every swirl of her tongue into the circular patterns she was making were driving Taylor wild. She was ready to explode when Brooke abruptly pulled back and removed her perfect mouth from Taylor's body. Taylor lifted her head up to make eye contact and tell Brooke not to stop but she became frozen and transfixed. Brooke was staring back at her and she was absolutely stunning. And seeing her between Taylor's legs was hotter than Taylor could have ever imagined.

Brooke smiled softly as she looked into Taylor's eyes while she slowly inserted a finger inside of Taylor, quickly followed by another, moving in a perfect slow rhythm. "Oh my fucking God," Taylor moaned as she gripped the sheets and angled her hips up to meet Brooke's movement.

Brooke hummed in satisfaction before she lowered herself to bring her tongue back to Taylor's clit where she moved swiftly in sync with her fingers curling in and out of Taylor.

"Brooke," Taylor moaned as she raised her hips. "I'm going to come."

Brooke increased her speed just enough to send a spasm through Taylor's entire body as she yelled out in pleasure and rode out an orgasm that she would surely never forget. Her body fell limp on the bed as her labored breaths filled the room. Brooke slowly removed her fingers and placed a chaste kiss on Taylor's thigh before she slid up the bed beside Taylor.

"I can't feel my body," Taylor said breathlessly as she turned her head to look at Brooke on the pillow beside her. Her hair was completely disheveled from Taylor's hands wrapped up in it and she couldn't have looked more beautiful. "That was incredible."

Brooke smiled softly. "I aim to please."

Please was an understatement but Taylor wasn't willing to overshare just how earthshattering that was, mainly because she still had to reciprocate and the last thing she wanted was for Brooke to not be as satisfied as she was. She had a lot to live up to now.

Taylor leaned in and kissed Brooke, tasting herself on her lips, as her hand gently caressed Brooke's breasts and pinched her nipples between her fingers. "I'm dying to taste you," Taylor whispered into Brooke's ear as she bit her earlobe before pulling away and crawling down Brooke's body.

She decided not to tease Brooke and draw this out any further. She nestled herself between Brooke's legs, throwing her legs over her shoulders as she went to work. She watched how Brooke responded to every stroke of her tongue, how her chest rose and fell erratically amidst her moans when Taylor dipped her tongue inside of her. How her right calf wrapped around Taylor's back to hold her closer. How Taylor could feel tremors throughout Brooke's body, giving an indication that she was close.

With her mouth still latched to Brooke's core, she slipped two fingers inside and felt Brooke clench around her. "Oh fuck," Brooke yelled as her hips rose off the bed.

Taylor pulled her head back and wiped her lips on Brooke's thigh before she leaned up to hover over Brooke. "You taste like heaven by the way," she said as she continued to move her fingers in rhythm to the bucking of Brooke's hips.

"Taylor," Brooke moaned as she threw her head back on the pillow and gripped the bed sheets beside her. "Right there. Don't stop."

Taylor had no intention of doing that. Not now as she made Brooke yell out in ecstasy. Not nearly three hours later when they were still discovering each other's bodies. Maybe not ever. She could really get used to doing this all the time.

Chapter Eight

Brooke laid awake staring at her ceiling. Her phone screen just informed her that it was four-twenty-four in the morning. Taylor's head nestled into the nook of her neck reminded her that they had roughly just spent the past three hours having sex.

Her body was still vibrating like an electric current as her mind processed the fact that she possibly just had the best sex of her life. Over the years, past memories faded but what still stood out didn't compare at all to what just transpired. No one had ever gotten her so aroused before and created an insatiable need that despite multiple orgasms, she just couldn't get enough. She didn't recall even feeling that with Jaclyn during all of their years of being together. Brooke tried to tell herself that it had simply been a long time since she had good sex and that it didn't mean anything more than that. Deep down she knew she was kidding herself. And she knew that it was fated to not last.

In the dark, she looked up at the ceiling where there was a lone brushstroke of paint that was slightly brighter than the rest of the white ceiling that clearly was a touchup to some mark that was left by a previous tenant. It was silently reminding her of herself. How she had also patched herself up a bit and to the naked eye, you'd never know that she was now a self-conscious and insecure woman. It was something she tried to keep hidden as much as possible, but if you looked close enough, or on the right angle with light reflecting in, you'd see the truth. She was just like the mis-matched brushstroke.

Taylor lightly exhaled in her sleep, moving Brooke's eyes off the ceiling to the woman beside her. Brooke wished there was more light in the room so she could see her and memorize all of her features. What if they were never in this position again? What if she never got to touch or hold this beautiful woman again? She'd need to ingrain Taylor into her brain. The brown beauty mark on her cheek right near her dimple. The curve of her lips when she smiled. The way her eyelashes curled naturally without the need for mascara. The way her skin felt against Brooke's body. Brooke sighed as she the thought about the rest of Taylor's body and how every part of her was attractive. Especially everything on the inside. If Taylor had any paint brushstroke blemishes in her personality, Brooke had yet to see them. But then again it took Brooke eight years to see Jaclyn's true colors.

Brooke shook her head to try to rid herself of these worrisome thoughts running rampant in her mind. Right now, all that mattered was that she had an amazing night and an amazing woman beside her. The rest she could deal with after a cup of coffee.

As sunlight peered into the room at the edges of blackout curtains, Taylor rolled over onto her side to find Brooke already awake lying beside her reading a book. How a woman could look that good after waking up was something Taylor didn't know if she'd get an answer to, but she didn't mind not knowing. Just as long as she got to experience it firsthand again.

"Hi," she said groggily. Her voice felt a bit hoarser than it typically did in the morning, quite possibly from all the sounds that left her mouth last night. "You look really hot in glasses." Brooke was wearing brown Wayfarer glasses that coupled with the book, made her look like a sexy librarian. She could probably convince people to have a love of reading with just one smoldering look.

"Hi," Brooke said with a smile as she placed a bookmark on her page and moved the book to her nightstand.

"So, last night *did* happen," Taylor said with a smile as she realized this was real life. "I kind of thought I might have dreamt it."

"I have no idea what you're talking about," Brooke playfully said as she turned onto her side and rested her head on her hand propped up by her elbow.

"You mean we didn't have incredible sex for hours?" Taylor asked in disbelief.

Brooke bit her lip as she seemed lost in thought. She took her glasses off and placed them on the nightstand. "Did we? Maybe you can show me again now to jog my memory."

When she licked her lips, Taylor pounced onto her into a devastating kiss. The hours prior were just a taste of what could come the more time they spent together – time that Taylor vowed would include making Brooke moan and tremble at her touch, just like she was doing again now. Morning sex had never felt so good.

"Do you remember now?" Taylor asked as she snaked her hand back up Brooke's body.

"Uh huh," Brooke replied as she pulled Taylor back towards her for a deep kiss. "Do you want to go get some brunch? I seem to have worked up an appetite."

Taylor nodded, too hypnotized by Brooke's kiss to formulate words until she remembered the condition of her clothes crumbled on the floor. "Can I borrow a shirt?"

Brooke nodded as they continued to kiss and she wrapped her hands in Taylor's hair. "Maybe a shower first?"

Taylor groaned in response as Brooke dragged her to the bathroom and she reminded Taylor of all the sensations her body had encountered hours prior that she never wanted to forget.

Over the years, Taylor had worn plenty of articles of clothing owned by girls she was dating. Shirts. Sweatshirts. Beanies. Boots. Yet none of them compared to the simple heather gray t-shirt of Brooke's that she was currently wearing. The soft fabric against her skin was making her think about how Brooke would look in it. How the dip of the V-neck would be touching her breasts. Those breasts that looked ever better with nothing covering them. It was all she could think about while looking over the menu before she started to think about last night all over again, including Brooke's apartment. Her questions over the life Brooke leads and the life she had. Which led her to unwelcomed thoughts about Jaclyn.

"Can I ask you something personal?" Taylor questioned as soon as they placed their orders.

Brooke laughed softly as she sipped her coffee. "I think we surpassed personal last night."

"Okay, but this is like emotionally and mentally personal, not just physical," Taylor said with a new softness in her voice. She was aware that what she was going to ask might be inappropriate, but it had been on her mind for two weeks and the sooner she asked it, maybe the sooner she could understand what could possess someone to leave Brooke. There had to be a reason. *Right?*

Brooke leaned back in her chair with a quizzical glare. "Now I'm scared."

Taylor looked into Brooke's hazel eyes and took a deep breath, hoping she didn't fuck it all up and ruin their perfect night and morning together with curiosity. "Did you really not know that Jaclyn was cheating on you?"

"Wow," Brooke said as she quickly broke her gaze off of Taylor. "I was not expecting that."

"I just want to know everything about you," Taylor quickly shared why her mind had taken her to that place, hoping that Brooke could understand why she wanted to know and that it wasn't coming from a negative place. "Including the painful things because everything shapes everyone."

Brooke brushed a strand of hair behind her ear. Taylor already picked up on the fact that this was a bit of a nervous habit for Brooke, and the last thing she ever wanted to do was make her nervous. “I mean, you could have started with something a bit easier like my favorite color or favorite song to sing at karaoke.”

“I’m pretty sure your favorite color has to be green because it brings out your eyes like crazy and you look so good in it and now I really want to go do karaoke with you and find out.”

Brooke smiled as she lifted her eyes off the table and Taylor felt her anxiety over the question start to disappear. “Green *is* my favorite color, and maybe you’ll get to find out my song one day.”

Taylor couldn’t wait for that day. She loved karaoke, especially when she had a duet partner for the 80’s hit “Don’t You Want Me” by The Human League. Brooke probably liked that song too. “And what about the answer to my original question?”

A deep sigh escaped Brooke’s lips before she answered immediately. “In hindsight, all the signs were there. The late nights working. The way she started to disconnect from me. But I didn’t want to see it at the time because I loved her and thought she loved me.”

“How did you find out?”

Brooke scoffed to herself as she clutched her ceramic mug. “When your wife tells you she’s pregnant and you don’t have a penis, you kind of know.”

“Holy shit,” Taylor said softly in disbelief and shock. This was not what she was expecting to hear. “She was already pregnant?”

Brooke nodded lightly. “Yes. My life became a true soap opera.”

Taylor extended her hand across the table to hold onto Brooke’s arm. “I’m so sorry, Brooke. I didn’t ask to open up wounds or anything I was just curious about what happened.”

“I didn’t see the signs, that’s what happened,” Brooke said simply, as she momentarily grazed her hand over Taylor’s on her arm. “And I allowed myself to be more vulnerable and blindsided than I ever could have imagined.”

"She's a fucking bitch," Taylor said firmly. "I mean seriously, A – cheaters are terrible to begin with but B – you are incredible. What the hell could this man have that you don't?"

"Sperm." The sadness in Brooke's eyes revealed the disappointment that she couldn't provide that for Jaclyn. Maybe even for herself. "She decided she wanted kids but not with me. I believe the words "normal family" were thrown in my face amidst our divorce. My wife, who had only had long-term relationships with women, suddenly decided she was pansexual and wanted a baby, which is all fine and dandy, but a hell of a time to figure that out."

Brooke could say she was over it and had moved on, but the wounds were clearly still there festering under the surface. Understandably. Did anyone truly recover from that type of betrayal? If they did, it certainly took longer than two years to completely forget. Taylor didn't know if she'd ever be able to forget something like that.

"I'm sorry," Taylor repeated herself. "Did I mention she's a fucking bitch?"

Brooke laughed as she sipped her cup of coffee. "You did, but I don't mind hearing it again."

"She's a fucking bitch," Taylor playfully repeated. "One more time for good measure."

As they continued their brunch, the topic of Jaclyn was dropped and they were able to enjoy light conversation talking about the couple next to them that abruptly left after the man said the woman shouldn't order a Bloody Mary. For a while, it felt nice to talk about complete strangers and come up with reasons for their fight rather than discuss anything too personal.

"Don't move," Taylor said as she quickly lifted her phone and pointed the camera towards Brooke who was illuminated by the sun behind her, like an angel perfectly placed before Taylor at this table. "You're literally glowing right now."

Brooke followed her orders and looked towards the phone with a slight smile on her lips as Taylor took the picture. "You are so beautiful," Taylor gushed as she looked at her phone and then back up at the woman across from her. "I really mean that."

Taylor felt herself melt every time Brooke blushed. For some reason, knowing she had an impact on the older woman made her feel proud of herself because it seemed like a sign that Brooke could actually like her too. That this wasn't just some crazy physical attraction – it was a deeper bond. "You're even more beautiful," Brooke said softly, not dropping her gaze.

This woman was going to be dangerous. Taylor was sure of that. There was no way she wouldn't be able to fall head over heels for Brooke Lewis.

Chapter Nine

Brooke couldn't believe she succumbed to this. She was forty years old and she just spent thirty minutes scrolling through Taylor's Instagram feed. Now that she had access to the private account, she felt like an entire new world was available to her. Sure, she knew how Taylor looked and acted now, but this opened up a lens into the past. She was able to see photos of Taylor with her friends out to dinner, having drinks, posing with random street art. There were insights into her family life and the type of things she liked to document and share with the world.

But it was the photo from last year of a young woman with blonde hair kissing Taylor that had her most fixated. The caption simply had a yellow kissing face emoji but the comments said it all.

"I love you so much"

"Couple goals!!"

"Hottest. Couple. Ever."

It was evidently her ex-girlfriend and she was in enough photos to show that their relationship lasted long enough. She was cute and nothing like Brooke, physically. Where Brooke took great strides to be polished and sophisticated, Taylor's ex, Stella, appeared edgy and carefree. Although, it was kind of funny to Brooke that this girl really loved mom jeans which should have been a sign of her own generation if TikTok didn't steal that. If Stella was a reflection of the type of girl Taylor liked, Brooke was far from it. She also hated mom jeans and TikTok.

Would it be weird for Brooke to like the most recent picture of pizza on Taylor's page? It would certainly be better than the one five years in the past she was looking at moments ago. A like would be acceptable now, right? They did have sex. They talked every day since. And it was a good-looking pizza.

Brooke sighed in frustration over how she was already second guessing and analyzing everything. Taylor was so lively. Constantly going out and documenting her life like every other millennial. Brooke felt boring in comparison. Her Instagram was mostly full of vacation photos and food. She wished Taylor wouldn't see the photos of her and Jaclyn that she didn't have the heart to delete. She had purged her account to erase their wedding photos feeling like it was an unpleasant reminder of her past life but Jaclyn was still there and now Taylor would see her and all her evil glory.

Would Taylor judge Jaclyn the same way Brooke was judging every woman in a photo with Taylor? The problem here is there were so many. Either Taylor had tons of friends that were girls or lots of girlfriends. At some point she'd probably find out the truth and where she stood in that mix.

Saturday mornings were Taylor's favorite part of her week. She usually slept in and let her body recharge as she slowly started her weekend. On this particular Saturday morning, she was up earlier than she would have liked but she laid in bed completely content, even though she was still exhausted. The previous week had kicked her ass between her two jobs and her desperation to squeeze in Brooke when she could. Yet, despite how tired she still was at seven-seventeen in the morning, she was happy.

For the first time in a long time, if ever, she was truly completely happy. She had a job she enjoyed. An apartment in New York City to herself. A comfortable savings and diminishing student loan debt thanks to her hours at the bar. She had hope for the future. She was optimistic. She was excited. It might have been the mind-blowing sex she had over the past week that was pumping up her endorphins. Whatever it was, it was enough to get her out of bed before eleven and ready to start her day.

She decided to make it a productive Saturday by starting her day at the gym to blow off some steam and focus on her own well-being. She walked around the Barnes & Noble in Union Square perusing for a new book to read. She wound up leaving the store with three books before going to the local farmers market where she picked up some flowers to place in her kitchen. She was *that* happy.

When she got home, she sat cross-legged on her bed with her laptop in front of her. She had been ignoring the movie on her television across the room for the past ten minutes as she fell down an internet rabbit hole. She wasn't exactly sure what compelled her to search for "how to date an older woman" but now she was on her fourth article catered to young men on how to woo an older love interest. It was absurd, Taylor knew that, but she was intrigued and curious and couldn't look away.

Apparently, all Taylor had to do to impress Brooke was be assertive, not talk about age, be on time, and not drink beer. That last one seemed a bit peculiar and sexist, but chances were Taylor would avoid drinking beer around Brooke for quite a while anyway. It always made her feel bloated and that was not how she wanted to feel, or look, so early in whatever it was that they were doing.

Taylor threw herself back against her pillows and wondered why she was suddenly so nervous. Brooke seemed to like her, that's all that truly mattered. So what if they were ten years apart? It didn't bother Taylor. In fact, if she stopped to think about it, she found it extremely sexy. Brooke was mature and knew what she wanted. Taylor just hoped that she was what Brooke wanted as well. She couldn't fake that or con the system by reading articles written by men for men as if they knew what it was like to be with a woman at all. None of them encountered a woman like Brooke who was truly one of a kind.

When her phone dinged beside her, she quickly picked it up hoping it was Brooke replying to the photo she sent her earlier of graffiti someone put on a construction site that said "Brookelyn" over the arches of the Brooklyn Bridge.

Ariana [3:37pm]
TayTay! Eddie is being lame and bailing on a concert tonight. Do you want to come w/ me and Michelle?

There was no sense in staying at home reading articles that would only mess with her mind more. She agreed to go and jumped out of bed to get in the shower.

After the concert, Taylor found herself inside the packed Cubbyhole bar. Of course, a night out with Ariana would leave them at one of the remaining, and smallest, lesbian bars in America. Taylor was usually Ariana's wing woman, and vice versa. It was a friendship that, despite starting out when they matched on a dating app, always remained completely platonic. They liked to think that they were a perfect duo, a Taylor Swift and Ariana Grande combo, that just wasn't meant to be romantically involved.

Thinking about their Halloween costume from a few years ago when they dressed up as the songstresses was the only thing helping Taylor remain calm in this moment when she wished that they had chosen somewhere else to go on a Saturday night. The bar was overly crowded and extremely hot, which wasn't difficult since it was practically the size of Taylor's studio apartment. Taylor pulled off her hoodie and wrapped it around her waist leaving her in just a tank top, desperate for some relief from the barely working ceiling fans up above hidden behind random decorations dangling beside them.

"Hi," the woman next to her said as Taylor struggled to get the bartender's attention. Taylor offered a half smirk before she inched up on her toes and watched the bartender walk away. "You'll never catch his attention that way," the woman beside her noted. As Taylor glanced over at the woman speaking to her, the blonde waved her hand and got the bartender's attention. "What are you having?"

"Two Hendricks and tonic and a Blue Moon," Taylor shared, impressed that the woman managed to help her order their drinks so quickly. Her height advantage surely had to play a role. Taylor wasn't short by any means at five-seven but this woman had a few inches on her.

"I'm Samantha," the woman said as she passed the drinks over to Taylor.

"Taylor."

"Is one of those drinks for your girlfriend?" Samantha asked with a playful smile on her face.

Taylor looked down at the additional glasses in her hands she was struggling to juggle. "No, my friends went to the bathroom."

"Good, then your next one is on me," she said with a smile. There was no hiding the fact that Samantha was relieved to hear that Ariana and Michelle were just friends. She let that become increasingly obvious as Taylor and her friends mixed in with Samantha's friends in the corner of the bar. It was refreshing to have free flowing conversations with other sapphic women, but selfishly, Taylor was mostly relieved to see Michelle talking to someone else.

Things between them had been awkward for a while. After she and Stella broke up, she regrettably got a bit sloppy one night and drunkenly made out with Michelle on the train platform. It meant nothing to Taylor and Michelle seemed to agree but everything changed after that. Michelle became a bit clingy and would jokingly imply that she and Taylor would be a perfect couple, which Taylor didn't believe to be true at all. Taylor felt like Michelle was waiting for a chance for something to happen again and Taylor didn't have the heart to reiterate the fact that they were only ever going to be friends. She already tried that and told her she wasn't looking for anything serious hoping she'd get the hint.

As Taylor got distracted thinking about her friend and past mistakes,

Samantha began to move closer and Taylor realized this wasn't just a friendly encounter either. "Can I take you out sometime?" Samantha asked, confirming her suspicions.

Taylor bit her lip as she tried to figure out what to say. Brooke was technically not her girlfriend. Yes, Taylor liked her a lot. Yes, they had sex. But they hadn't discussed any of it, which was partially why Taylor was so intrigued on tips to make it work. Going out with someone else felt like a betrayal. Both to herself and her own desires, but also to Brooke. New York was a huge city but could still be so small. After all, they had experienced that first hand just by how they met. What if Brooke saw her out on another date? Would that be the end of what they just started? Would Taylor even want to entertain dating anyone else? She knew the answer was no.

"I just started seeing someone," Taylor settled on, which was also news to Ariana across from her who she hadn't told about Brooke out of fear of jinxing it. Only Liam knew about Brooke so far and she would have preferred to keep it that way until she knew exactly what it was they were doing.

Samantha looked defeated before smiling. "Of course you would be." She tapped her glass against Taylor's. "If it doesn't work out maybe I'll see you back here."

Taylor felt like the universe was playing a bit of a trick on her to keep her on her toes. Two months ago, she swore off dating apps and said she wanted to meet someone with substance. Then she met Brooke who seemed too good to be true. Checking all her boxes. Making her feel things she didn't even know she could feel so quickly. And now, here was a cute girl that in any other situation she would have taken up on her offer for a date. She could have had substance too, but as soon as Taylor blinked, there was someone else's face behind her eyelids.

Taylor smiled softly in response as she pulled her phone out of her back pocket, feeling the vibration on her butt cheek.

Brooke [11:02pm]
I should request the bridge and borough be renamed after me

Brooke [11:02pm]
Sorry it took me forever to reply. Had a crazy day. Hope you enjoyed your Saturday!

Taylor looked at her phone and wanted to resist the urge to reply right away. She knew Brooke was busy today but she wondered what she was doing. What else went on in her life that she had no idea about? Although, she was technically out at a bar getting hit on by a stranger. She was no better.

Taylor [11:05pm]
It's better now that I'm talking to you

Taylor [11:06pm]
You definitely deserve landmarks to be named after you

"Wow, you're corny," Ariana said as she leaned over Taylor's shoulder as she read the text message. "Who's Brooke?"

Taylor locked her phone and slid it back into her pocket. "I'm not talking about her right now."

Ariana laughed and raised her brow as she took a sip of her drink. "You might not be talking about her for too much longer if that's how you flirt."

"Funny," Taylor said sarcastically before she turned away to sip her gin and tonic. She could feel Michelle's eyes burning into her side. She no longer seemed too invested in the woman talking to her now that there was potentially something going on with someone named Brooke.

"You're really not going to tell me anything about this mystery woman?" Ariana persisted, fortunately in a much quieter voice than before. "The one that has you turning down a date with a cute girl?"

"No," Taylor said quickly. "It's new and I don't want to jinx it."

"Jinx it?" Ariana said with a laugh. "Damn, you have it bad."

Taylor gently pushed her friend. She *knew* she had it bad. It was almost embarrassing – which was exactly why she didn't want to overshare about Brooke just yet. It could end as quickly as it started. "Please don't tell anyone yet," she said softly. "Especially," Taylor stopped and her eyes slowly moved towards Michelle's direction.

Ariana nodded in understanding and wrapped her arm around Taylor's shoulders. "I won't but only because I want them to see you squirm at the mention of her name." Ariana's eyebrows rose in a devilish smirk. "Brooke."

As predicted, a blush crept across Taylor's face. There was no point in controlling it. She wouldn't want to even if she could.

Chapter Ten

Brooke lost track of how many times she and Taylor had sex over the last two weeks. There was the night on her couch. In Taylor's shower. In both of their bedrooms, multiple times. In a quite spacious bathroom of a bar. She felt like a teenager that had just discovered what sex was and had an insatiable desire that she couldn't get enough of, and she wasn't the only one. Taylor was also initiating their spontaneous hookups and for every moment Brooke felt horny, Taylor confirmed that she felt the same.

Their passionate outbursts had left more than one hickey on Brooke's body that she had to discretely cover up at work. Taylor informed her that she wore hers proudly saying she'd rather have a hickey from Brooke than not. Brooke crossed her legs at the thought of the large mark that Taylor left on her inner thigh last night and the sensations she was feeling inches away from it simply from reading Taylor's text messages.

Taylor [12:57pm]
You know lunch isn't the same when the only thing I want to eat is you

Taylor [12:58pm]
You're ruining everything for me. Every meal. Every pair of underwear

Taylor [12:59pm]
What are you going to do about it???

Dad [12:59pm]
Mom isn't doing well. Can you come down again this weekend?

The latest text on Brooke's screen changed her mood instantly. Her mid-day playful texting with Taylor came to an abrupt halt when her father reminded her of where her priorities needed to be. She placed her phone down and turned back to her laptop to book a Friday afternoon Amtrak ticket as she got her mind out of the gutter.

Brooke [1:15pm]
I reallyyyyyy hate to interrupt this convo but I just found out that I have to cancel our date on Saturday. My dad needs me to come down to DC #onlychildproblems

Taylor [1:21pm]
Damn. Who's going to take care of the ache between my legs now?

Sex and her sick mother should not be mixed into the same conversation, let alone the same sentence.

Brooke [1:23pm]
Come over tonight. I can take care of that for you

Taylor [1:25pm]
I'll bring dinner. You can be dessert ;)

Brooke was in the middle of throwing a load of laundry in when Nina called. Brooke texted her hours ago about the latest turn in her mother's health and the sense of dread that was already seeping through her mind. After she filled her best friend in about her impromptu weekend trip to DC and her plans for the rest of the night, Nina asked the question Brooke was avoiding. "Are you going to tell Taylor about your mom?"

Brooke stood upright as she processed the question that was posed to her as if she hadn't given this any thought before. It had been on her mind for weeks now as she questioned how to casually mention that her mom had stage three cancer without making it something stressful or off-putting, as horrible as that sounded. "No. Why would I?" She knew she should, but deflection was all she knew how to do now.

"I mean you're dating, aren't you?" Nina asked rhetorically. "She should know what you're going through. You'd expect the same kind of honesty from her, wouldn't you?"

"Yeah," Brooke sounded as she sat down on the edge of her bed. "But I don't want to scare her off with so much heaviness when we're having such a good time right now."

"Right. The best sex of your life, how could I forget?" Brooke could imagine the dramatic eyeroll that surely accompanied that statement. "If you want that sex to last you need to be honest. It's not like you to hide things and I mean hello, hypocritical much? Jaclyn hid a relationship from you, you're hiding your mom from Taylor."

Brooke knew what her best friend was trying to tell her but she couldn't bring herself to admit it right now. She didn't want Taylor to see the darker side of her life; too afraid it could shatter the fragile thing they were building – whatever it was. "I'm just protecting myself. I mean what thirty-year-old who can have whoever she wants would want to settle with a divorced forty-year-old with chronic migraines and a dying parent?"

When Nina didn't say anything in response, Brooke glanced at her phone to see if they got disconnected. They hadn't. Nina seemed to be carefully choosing her next words. "If she cares about you and wants more than just sex, she won't care about any of that and would only be more supportive. Any decent human would and I imagine she must be one too for you to even be interested."

"I don't want to take any chances right now. I'm happy for the first time in a long time and I really like her," Brooke admitted aloud for the first time. "I know we probably don't have a real future together but why do I need to end it before it starts?"

"Jaclyn really fucked you up. This isn't like you."

"Thanks for the support," Brooke oozed in sarcasm. "Tell Jayson I understand why he spends his Sundays out watching football to get away from you."

"Fuck you, that's all your fault because you got him those free tickets and opened Pandora's football box and now I have to suffer."

Brooke laughed as she imagined her friend actually being furious over that as she loathed football. "I love you, too," she said as she glanced at the time and told Nina she had to go.

Taylor would be there in an hour and she wanted to jump in the shower and get ready. Instead of telling Taylor why she was going to DC, she focused on the nourishment she got from dinner and the woman wrapped up around her in bed.

In the corner of a crowded wine bar on a Saturday night, Taylor looked at her friends around the table and felt like she was disconnected from them. She had spent weeks talking to them pretending her life was status quo when it had actually been far from that. After the group had all given recaps of what was going on in their lives, it was Taylor's turn and not even the liquid courage had prepared her for this revelation.

"I met someone," Taylor announced, hoping that would satisfy their update request after seeing some of her friends for the first time in almost a month. During that time, she had kept Brooke to herself, with only Liam and Ariana knowing about their dates and their incredible sex. She didn't want to be superstitious, but unlike previous relationships, she also wanted to do everything right this time around. She didn't want to jump the gun; she didn't want to get distracted by their physical chemistry and overlook the incredible woman she was getting to know. And she definitely didn't want her friends to undermine any of it either or overshare in the peanut gallery.

"So, that's where you've disappeared to, huh?" Hayley asked without missing a beat. Her blonde bob moved with her face as she smirked in Taylor's direction. "Underneath someone else?"

"Not just someone else," Taylor said as an uncontrollable lopsided smile crept on her face and words started to pour out of her mouth. "An amazing woman. I mean at first, I was insanely attracted to her but five minutes into talking to her I already knew it was more than just lust." She paused her gushing to take a sip of her wine, finding that realization to be a lot for her to process. When she first saw Brooke, she *was* acting on attraction. Now Brooke's physicality wasn't even the top reason she liked her – but it really didn't hurt. "She's so freaking smart and witty and successful. We can talk for hours and then have sex for just as many. It's such an insane connection."

When she stopped talking and looked up, she saw all of her friends staring back at her with furrowed brows. "What's the catch?" Hayley asked as her blue eyes seemed to question everything about what Taylor just shared.

"What do you mean?"

Melinda jumped in to say, "There's gotta be a but coming. Nobody is perfect."

"She is," Taylor said proudly before pausing. "But-"

Her friends knowingly looked at one another like they had been waiting for this which is why Taylor was hesitant to share the information in the first place. It really didn't matter, nor did it change anything about Brooke or Taylor's growing feelings for her. "But she's forty and divorced and I think a bit self-conscious about it."

"Does she have kids?" Melinda asked with a curious look on her face. "Taylor, the step-mom?"

"No," Taylor replied, briefly squashing the thought about how she wouldn't even mind if Brooke had a child already. "Her wife said she didn't want kids and then cheated on her with a man and had a baby with him."

"Damn," Jessica said softly. "That's gotta mess someone up."

Taylor sensed that it did more than Brooke let on, not that she blamed her. Who would want to discuss their trauma with someone they were having fun and sex with? Taylor just hoped it would come up eventually; it seemed important for them to talk about it more to unpack the betrayal. Much more important than any breakup that Taylor had been through, or ever wanted to experience.

"Are we going to see what this mysterious woman looks like?" Melinda asked. Taylor pulled out her phone and went to the photo she took of Brooke the morning after they had sex for the first time. She was absolutely stunning without an ounce of makeup on her face. This would likely be her favorite photo of the woman for a long time.

Hayley grabbed the phone out of Brooke's hand and started to zoom in on Brooke's face. "That's one sexy woman."

"See!" Taylor said as she took her phone back and looked at the photo and smiled thinking about that morning, and the hours they enjoyed prior to that. Thinking about Brooke made Taylor miss her, despite how clingy that may have made her seem. She hadn't heard from Brooke in ten hours and it was definitely ten hours too long.

Taylor [8:43pm]
Out for wine with friends but wish I was with you instead. Hope alls ok with the rents!

“Are you girlfriends or casually just dating?” Hayley asked to bring Taylor back to the conversation at the table.

She wished she had an answer to that question but it was something that was a blur to her, and gave her more anxiety than she would like to admit. Whenever she dated in the past, things seemed to naturally progress and she never really worried about where she stood in the woman’s life. This felt entirely different. “I don’t know. We haven’t really talked about it. It’s only been a few weeks I don’t want to scare her off or anything but I’d give anything to be her girlfriend.”

Melinda reached over and squeezed Taylor’s forearm. “Tell her. She’s older and probably a lot more into clear lines than blurs. I fucking hate that at twenty-nine, I can’t imagine it at forty.”

Taylor nodded but knew she wasn’t ready to enter that vulnerable territory just yet and part of her wanted Brooke to be the one to do it. She was the one who seemed to have reservations about their age initially, but at the same time if she asked it would show she’s mature enough. Instead of figuring out what to do, Taylor ordered another glass of wine and waited for a reply on her phone.

Brooke spent most of the day crying in secret. All signs and doctor reports were leading to nothing promising. The cancer was spreading and overall, Mary was in bad condition and having a rough time with the radiation, as expected. Mary wasn’t feeling positive about anything and that’s what led Brooke to spend the last three hours reviewing her mother’s will and ensuring that her wishes were still documented properly.

“I’ll come down every weekend,” Brooke said to her father when they were alone in the kitchen after Mary went to sleep. “You can’t do this alone.”

“You can’t put your entire life on hold, we don’t know what will happen," Oscar tried to rationalize. He was always the calmest in the family. "The doctor said there would be good days and bad days, let's not get ahead of ourselves now."

"It doesn't matter. I don't want to miss out on time with her and be here for you."

Her father shook his head in disagreement. "I know how busy you are with work and starting to date again." He paused before he smiled. "You never told me how that was going. It's been almost two months, no? Nina's date a week goal?"

Brooke forced a smile. Talking about dating with her father felt so foreign. They hadn't had a conversation like this in over a decade. "I stopped going on those."

Oscar removed his eyeglasses and placed them on the table. "Already? Why?"

As she processed the fact that she deleted the annoying dating app from her phone and had been consumed with thoughts of only one person, she realized that she was subconsciously putting all her eggs in one basket. Albeit, it was a beautiful, lovely basket. "Because I met someone."

"Brooke!" He exclaimed as his hand slapped the table gently. "Finally, some good news. Tell me everything."

How Brooke got so fortunate to have such loving and accepting parents was something she'd never take for granted. She knew they were more of the exception than the norm but it made her love them even more. Ever since she came out to them in high school, they had been nothing but supportive. They went to Pride parades with her and continued to go in DC even when she wasn't around. They were just as heartbroken when she got divorced because they viewed Jaclyn as another daughter to them and loved and accepted her just the same.

"Her name is Taylor. It's still all very new and terrifying."

"Don't be scared of love. I'm sure Taylor is not Jaclyn. Even her name is nicer."

Brooke laughed but couldn't feel it in her soul. If Jaclyn's immaturity at three years younger was a sign of what's to come, what would ten be like? "She's turning thirty soon," she said softly, almost embarrassed.

"So what? I'm seven years older than mom."

"I'm scared," Brooke admitted, feeling relieved to get this weight off her chest to someone else other than Nina. "I'm too old to get destroyed yet again. I want to be with someone who wants a real future. A marriage that will last. A family," she stopped as a tear fell from her eye as she felt her resolve start to disappear. "I'm scared to set the stage for what I want in the future because I don't want to scare her away and stop being happy in the present. And I'm so happy when I'm around her."

Oscar got up from his chair and stood behind his daughter to wrap his arms around her. "This is exactly why you cannot come here every single weekend. You need to nurture your present for your future. Be with her. See where things go."

"I don't think I can handle more heartbreak," Brooke said softly as she leaned back into his embrace. There was only so much she could take.

He kissed the top of her head before he sat back down across from her. "You're the strongest person I know. You'll be okay, but most importantly, you'll give yourself some happiness that you truly deserve."

Brooke tried to process his words but it was still difficult to accept. She was terrified and that feeling would surely overpower everything else, even the happiness she felt from the green-eyed beauty back home.

When she finally dragged herself up to bed shortly after her father's pep-talk, Brooke looked at her phone at the text that came in two hours ago and felt that reminder of just how much was on the line.

Brooke [10:31pm]

I would much rather have been with you having wine today

Taylor [10:49pm]
Everything ok?

For a moment, Brooke contemplated whether she should tell the woman she wanted to keep dating and having sex with that her mom is dying. It was the right, and normal, thing to do. Until the doubt started to creep in. Did she really want to give Taylor yet another reason to step away from her and all the serious things that she represented? Or worse, have Taylor stay with her temporarily out of pity and guilt rather than actual desire?

Brooke [10:53pm]
Had to help with some paperwork. My parents are terrified of PDFs

Taylor [10:54pm]
Mine too! Well only the ones where their electronic signature gets used. My dad thinks he's committing fraud if it doesn't match his real one

Brooke genuinely laughed for the first time all day. Her dad was bothered by the same thing. Maybe they weren't so different and far off after all. But she wouldn't take that risk and overshare just what was going on. After all, she didn't really know what was happening either.

Brooke [10:55pm]
Same! I'm glad I'm not the only one who has to deal with this

Taylor [10:56pm]

I can be on demand tech support if you need it. I won't even charge you my hourly rate

Brooke [10:57pm]
I love a good discount

Taylor [10:59pm]
When are you coming home?

Brooke [11:00pm]
Tomorrow night

Taylor [11:00pm]
Are you free during the week to hang out?

Brooke wanted nothing more than to see Taylor again, but she knew what the week ahead held. She also knew what sending the next message would entail but she'd take that chance anyway.

Brooke [11:04pm]
I'm pretty sure I'm going to have a week of hell at work but I'm most likely getting free suite tickets to see Billy Joel on Thursday at the Garden. Do you want to come?

Taylor [11:05pm]
Um yes!

Brooke [11:06pm]
Are you even old enough to know who Billy Joel is?

Taylor [11:07pm]

Of course. Olivia Rodrigo mentions him on Déjà vu

Brooke [11:07pm]
Wow...

Taylor [11:08pm]
Jk. I know him because they had a whole episode of his songs on Glee. But it sucked because there wasn't enough Santana in it

Taylor [11:09pm]
JK! Not about the Santana part. I need you to know that I am a Santana stan... I hope you understand

Taylor [11:10pm]
... of course I know Billy Joel! My dad loves him. He's going to be so jelly that I'm going

Brooke [11:10pm]
I'm relieved. And I fully support and understand your Santana admiration

Taylor [11:11pm]
I'm glad we got that out of the way. I'd hate for that to drive us apart

Taylor [11:11pm]
11:11! Make a wish

Taylor [11:12pm]
I can't wait for Thursday

Brooke stared at her phone and realized neither could she. The smile on her face from something as simple as Taylor's silly texts was enough evidence that she was catching feelings, despite how much she was reticent to. This was the first time she smiled all day and had hope for the future. She also made a wish that she and Taylor actually worked out, despite not really believing in making wishes.

> **Brooke [11:13pm]**
> Me either. I also promised my best friend a ticket. I hope that's okay
>
> **Taylor [11:14pm]**
> More than okay. Even though I only care about seeing you :)

Feelings were sticking more and more each minute.

In the morning, Brooke woke up with a new sense of purpose. Maybe it had something to do with the fact that despite how sad she was, she drifted to sleep thinking about Taylor and what could be. As she walked into the kitchen to fix herself a cup of coffee, she found herself humming a certain pop star's song about car rides to Malibu. She felt like a middle-aged woman in the suburbs in that moment and the realization made her smile a bit because in a way she kind of was, as terrifying as that was. The sound of the Nespresso machine roaring to life distracted Brooke as she watched the brown liquid fall into the mug to provide the much-needed caffeine boost she needed to get through the day.

"You're up early," Mary said as she walked into the kitchen and smiled at her daughter. "I miss the days when I had to wake you up at one in the afternoon to make sure you were alive."

Brooke smiled at the memory. She couldn't remember the last time she slept that late. It probably had to do with the fact that she definitely didn't party like she used to when she was younger. Mary's hands were shaking as she went to grab a coffee pod and Brooke handed her mother her untouched cup instead. "Sit, I can fix breakfast."

"I'm not hungry," Mary said as she accepted the mug and sat down at the kitchen nook with her lineup of medication in front of her.

"You can't take pills on an empty stomach," Brooke informed her. The idea of the child becoming the parent was one that was on her mind a lot lately.

The bottles rattled as Mary started to open up her prescriptions and line them up on a napkin. "I'll have toast then. Can you handle that?"

Brooke smirked back at her mother before she grabbed the loaf of bread on the counter. "I'll have you know I'm an excellent cook now." After Brooke stopped crying over preparing meals for one and decided to give her Uber Eats account a much-needed break, Brooke started to find cooking therapeutic and kind of fun. Even if she was eating alone most of the time.

"I know," Mary said before she washed down her first pill with a drink of water. "You've come a long way from your Easy Bake Oven days."

Brooke wished she was still at the age where she could pop some batter into a pink machine and be overjoyed at the somewhat stale cake that came out. Those were much simpler times and days than what she was dealing with now. When she was seven, she never had to think about how to prepare for her mother's death. She barely even knew what death was, and she wished she never had to find out. Wouldn't life be better if you never knew it ended?

Every child expects, and hopes, to outlive their parents when they begin to understand life but when the time begins to approach, how do you even begin to accept that? Do you reflect back on all the good memories over the years or do you focus on the things you should have done?

"I can practically hear you thinking over there," Mary said to bring

Brooke's focus back on the toaster she was staring into.

In a spur of the moment decision, she decided to try to enjoy every last moment they had together. She didn't want to have any future regrets. "Do you want to go take that trip to Rome and see the Colosseum and the Vatican?"

When Mary didn't respond, Brooke finally turned around and saw her mother staring at her with a blank expression on her face. "A farewell tour?"

"Mom," Brooke grunted in frustration before the bread popped up and momentarily startled her. "I'm serious. You always wanted to do it. Let's go."

Mary seemed to ponder the idea for a moment before she started to laugh to herself. "You in the Vatican? You might burst into flames from self-combustion."

"Hilarious," Brooke said with an eye roll as she grabbed the butter and started to spread it across the lightly toasted bread. "Maybe I'll finally help the priests come out of the closet."

Mary stopped laughing and sighed deeply. "Now let's not get crazy," she started. Brooke placed the plate in front of her mother and sat down across from her, gripping her coffee as she looked at her mother's sad eyes. "You know I can't make a trip like that."

Deep down Brooke knew that. She was just desperately hoping for a way to create new memories with her mother before it was too late. They should have taken that trip together years ago. She never thought they would run out of time. "How about a fun weekend in New York with me? We can go see *Funny Girl* on Broadway."

Mary laughed again and Brooke struggled to see what was humoring her mother even if it warmed her heart to see her smile. "You don't like Lea Michele."

"But I love you," Brooke countered with a smile. She wondered what Taylor would have to say about that Broadway production based on last night's conversation. "Or we can go see something else."

Mary placed her hand on her daughter's and squeezed it tightly. "Let's go."

A weekend in New York together seemed small and trivial compared to a week in Italy, but Brooke would take it. It was another chance to show her mother a good time and create memories. "I'll arrange it with dad."

"He's going to be thrilled," Mary said sarcastically. "Remember when we saw *Phantom* and he fell asleep?"

"I think we all fell asleep," Brooke admitted before she took a sip of her coffee.

Mary swallowed her last pill and held her toast in her hand before she stopped to look back at her daughter. "I love you, Brooke."

For some reason, hearing the words felt different today. "I love you too, mom."

While Mary ate her toast, Brooke silently willed herself to not cry. She vowed to make it through the day and get back on the train to New York later that afternoon without having another emotional breakdown. Easier said than done.

Chapter Eleven

Indifferent. That's how Brooke felt about Billy Joel summed up in one word. While she enjoyed a bunch of his classic songs, attending one of his concerts wasn't necessarily high on her must-see list. Nina, on the other hand, was a huge fan of the Long Island crooner and was the most excited about Brooke's work perk of getting tickets to one of his shows, even though she had already seen him in concert twice. She was almost as equally excited as she was to meet Taylor.

Any reservation and anxiety Brooke had about introducing her best friend to the woman she was dating was erased the moment the two met and became inseparable. Whether they were both trying to impress the other, or just naturally seemed to connect, didn't matter. Nina and Taylor hit it off and talked and joked non-stop before the concert started as they downed free glasses of wine and appetizers. If Brooke was concerned about either of them drinking too much, or Nina oversharing, she didn't express it. She just sat there smiling to herself that two people that meant something to her were getting along, all in the name of the Piano Man.

"I'm gonna go to the bathroom and get my dad a shirt," Taylor said as she stood up and smiled at her date before she walked away. Brooke's eyes followed her out the door. She wasn't used to missing someone's presence like this; it was absolutely terrifying and exciting.

"Taylor is *so* nice," Nina said to catch her attention and bring her gaze back to her best friend a seat away. The way she emphasized the words was evident to Brooke that she had more to say. After all, it was the first time they had a moment alone in two hours and Nina wasn't one to keep her thoughts to herself.

"She is."

"Taylor is gorgeous *and* sexy," Nina continued.

Brooke repeated herself. "She is."

"Taylor is *extremely* into you."

"Just spit out whatever you're trying to say," Brooke said in frustration at her best friend tip-toeing around the point.

Nina smiled and slowly sipped her glass of wine. "What I'm trying to say is take off the damn training wheels and just go for it."

Nina had always been Brooke's greatest cheerleader and critic if she was veering off course. It seemed like she was ready to play one of those roles now again just like she had for the past two decades. "I am," Brooke said sheepishly.

"You're not. You're guarded. She's practically throwing herself at you and gives no fucks about anything in this venue except you. Loosen up. Accept that yes, she's almost thirty but she wants *you*."

Taylor popped back into the suite unexpectedly, sending a silence over the women. Brooke panicked thinking she overheard any of Nina's scolding but the sweet smile on her face directed at Brooke didn't reveal any concern. "I forgot my wallet like an idiot."

As Taylor rummaged through her purse for her wallet, Nina whispered in her friend's ear. "Because she was too busy looking at you."

"I'll come with you," Brooke said as she stood up from her seat, trying to listen to her friend's advice. The last thing she wanted was to be perceived as cold and disinterested; the complete opposite of the truth. Taylor's wide grin at the simple act was enough to melt any ice that Brooke was putting around herself in this moment. Not that she even realized she was doing it to begin with.

They walked to the luckily empty merchandise booth where Taylor contemplated which shirt she should get her dad and whether she should get one for herself as well. In her hesitation, Brooke stepped up to the counter and got three shirts, including a matching one for herself. Maybe after tonight she would be a Billy Joel fan as well.

"You know, as cute as it is to match clothes," Taylor said as she wrapped her arms around Brooke's waist, "I kind of like it when we wear matching birthday suits instead."

Brooke laughed and dragged Taylor back into the suite where she, as Nina would later remind her, was a lot less guarded. She laughed. She sang. She drank. She wrapped her arms around Taylor. She let herself feel free and enjoy the presence of the woman that was putting oxygen into her lungs.

"I want you just the way you are," Brooke whispered into Taylor's ear as the same lyrics played behind them. Instead of responding with words, Taylor tilted her head and kissed Brooke deeply. A kiss that Brooke hoped expressed how she felt as well. A kiss that neither of them stopped long after the song finished, completely forgetting about Nina beside them, the other guests in the suite, or the performer on the stage. It was the best concert Brooke had ever been to.

Taylor really hated working weeknight shifts at the bar. Not only was she already exhausted from her real job during the day, but she knew in advance how tired she would be the following day. It was bad enough when she got assigned a weeknight shift, but it was even worse when she willingly took one. Such as tonight when she offered to cover for her coworker, Gene, who was going to the Brooklyn Nets playoff game with his brother. She hoped this would be a favor she could cash in on in the future, especially now when she really wanted her weekends to be open. When she got this second job months ago, she did it to accrue savings quickly but the fact that it helped her not feel so lonely was just an added bonus. Now she had much better things to do in her spare time.

"Oh my God, Taylor?" A woman's voice shrieked from across the room, breaking Taylor's train of thought about how much she was dreading working tonight.

The bartender picked up her head as her eyes landed on a blonde that was getting out of her chair in the corner of the room. This wasn't just any blonde – this was Stella Moritz, her ex-girlfriend, stepping towards her with a giant smile on her face. Of all the bars in New York City, what the hell was she doing here?

"Oh my God, I can't believe it," she continued to gush as she stepped towards the bar. "You're a bartender now?"

"On the side," Taylor admitted, feeling slightly ashamed that her ex could think she lost her job or gave up her decade-long career aspirations. As if her life fell apart without Stella in it. She really regretted picking up this shift. Gene truly owed her now.

Stella didn't seem interested in why she was a bartender, but it didn't surprise Taylor. She always cared about herself more than anyone or anything. "It's so good to see you."

"Yeah," Taylor sounded, not sharing the same sentiment. Since they broke up, Taylor accepted that their tumultuous relationship was purely due to their incompatibility. They initially dated on and off for a few months and when Taylor pressured Stella to be monogamous, she agreed, but then began to resent Taylor for stifling her. It should have been evident that Stella wasn't ready for a relationship but Taylor misread all the warning signs and it led to months of a hot and cold relationship before she eventually pulled the plug.

"How have you been? What's been going on in your life?" Stella asked as if they were old friends trying to catch up instead of ex-girlfriends.

Taylor didn't even know what so say about the last six plus months of her life. Obviously, a lot had happened. She matured. She knew what she wanted both professionally and personally. She had some other insignificant relationships, if she could even call them that. And now she had Brooke. Putting Brooke in the same category as everyone else felt like a massive mis-categorization – she was nothing like anyone she had dated previously. "Been busy focusing on work mostly," she started to buy some time. "Still paying off those MBA loans. How about you?"

"I got a new job in fashion merchandising and have been traveling a lot." Taylor knew all about that. She saw Stella and her new girlfriend posting photos from their travels and looking like they had rehearsed and edited each post until it was worthy of being on social media. It seemed exhausting.

"That's great," she said as she saw the other woman enter the bar and look around before her eyes landed on the blonde between them.

"Are you seeing anyone?" Stella casually asked.

Before Taylor had a chance to respond, Monica approached Stella and wrapped her arms around her waist. "Hey babe," she said before planting a kiss on her cheek.

Stella smiled and leaned into her embrace. "Mon, this is Taylor." For some reason the fact that Stella didn't refer to her as her ex-girlfriend stung. Did Stella really care so little about her and their shared time together that she was reduced to just Taylor? Or did Monica already know all about her, or at least Stella's version of who she was? It was quite possible that Monica had no idea Stella used to date Taylor – she could have adopted an entirely differently persona over the past several months. Taylor wouldn't be surprised if she had.

"What's up?" Monica said in Taylor's direction with a sense of indifference.

"I grabbed us that table in the corner, I'll be right there," Stella said as she motioned for Monica to go to their table while her feet remained planted at the bar. "We've been dating for five months."

"Good for you," Taylor said as she looked around to see if anyone needed a drink. "Your waiter will be over to your table soon."

"I'd rather you serve me," Stella said with what Taylor would have perceived as flirtation if she didn't know better.

"You'd have to sit at the bar for that," Taylor announced, hoping that would be enough to sway her ex to stay at the table that had more comfortable seating. To her surprise, Stella walked over to Monica and told her they were moving to the bar. Part of Taylor wondered if Stella just enjoyed the idea of having Taylor serve *her*. As if she was less than her. The thought alone made her aggravated more than she should have allowed it, but she had feelings at the end of the day.

She contemplated making them both bad drinks, but she didn't want to look like a failure at making espresso martinis either. After all, that was obviously the reason why they came here. Someone posted on TikTok that the bar made good coffee cocktails, which was Gene's masterpiece, so tonight they'd get the substitute. Kind of what Taylor felt like in this moment.

Her angst at the unexpected guests was what led Taylor to take her break outside of the bar. She couldn't unwind in the back of the bar knowing that Stella was sitting there with her new girlfriend, taking photos of cocktails she had made as if that was all Taylor was. An old flame and a bartender.

She walked into the tapas restaurant she had her first date with Brooke at and ordered two empanadas to put something in her stomach. The thought alone of Brooke sent a smile across her face and automatically improved her mood. She took a picture of the inner décor and sent it off in a text.

Taylor [7:47pm]
Coming here isn't the same without you

Brooke [7:53pm]
That was a great first date

Brooke [7:53pm]
Working on a Wednesday?

Taylor [7:54pm]
Covering for my coworker and hating it

Taylor bit her lip as she contemplated whether or not she should send the next message. She didn't want to overshare but for some reason she was compelled to be fully transparent with Brooke, even if it was about something that some might deem off limits, especially so early in a relationship.

Taylor [7:54pm]
My ex is here with her new gf. Taking photos of cocktails and laughing obnoxiously

Brooke [7:55pm]
What is it about your bar??

Taylor [7:55pm]
Seriously! It's only okay when you show up

Brooke [7:56pm]
Do you want me to?

Taylor froze with her phone in her hand. "Two chicken empanadas," the hostess said aloud, catching Taylor's attention. She quickly grabbed her food and then went back to her phone to re-read Brooke's text. Why would she do that if she didn't care about Taylor and wanted to have some sort of stake in the ground? It gave Taylor more energy than it should have.

Taylor [7:57pm]
Are you serious??

Brooke [7:57pm]
If you want. A little revenge can be fun

Taylor warmed up to the idea quicker than she would have expected. She just needed to make sure that Stella didn't leave and there was only one way to do that: free drinks.

Taylor [7:58pm]
Come. But hurry up!

Brooke [7:58pm]
You know I'd rather take my time ;)

Taylor stifled her laugh as she ran out the door and back in the bar. Luckily, Stella and her girlfriend were still sitting at the bar talking. "You ladies doing okay?" she asked as she walked up to them.

"Great," Stella said with a smile.

"Don't go anywhere, I'm going to make you a drink I think you'll like."

Taylor scarfed down her empanadas in the back of the bar and then whipped up two French 75's. They were simple drinks from a cocktail perspective, but their bar used extra tall flutes that Taylor knew would fit right in to Monica's Instagram and TikTok aesthetic.

Fifteen minutes later, Brooke walked through the door and just like every other time, Taylor felt her breath catch in her throat. She still seemed to be dressed in her clothes from work and the presence she carried was intimidating. Taylor certainly didn't look that good in a blazer, jeans, and ankle boots.

"Hi," Brooke said as she sat in a vacant seat that happened to be one away from Monica.

"What are you doing here?" Taylor asked with a smile, trying to pretend that she didn't concoct this plan. She wasn't desperate or trying to make her ex jealous. *No, not at all.* This was all Brooke's idea.

"I thought I'd surprise you and take you home," Brooke said simply as she reached across the bar to place her hand on Taylor's hand. That action was enough to finally catch Stella's attention.

"You cease to amaze me," Taylor said playfully despite how genuine it was. Brooke had been nothing that she ever experienced before and wasn't someone she ever wanted to stop being surprised by.

Brooke tossed her hair over her shoulder as if she knew the two women to her left were very obviously staring at her. "I aim to please," Brooke said when her eyes fell back on Taylor. "Can you make me a martini, babe? Extra dirty."

Heat rushed throughout Taylor's body. *Babe*. Brooke had never referred to her with any term of endearment phrases before. Was this all just part of the role she was playing? Or did she mean it? Taylor didn't know but she became fully aware of the fact that she wanted Brooke to call her "babe" more often. And she certainly wanted her to use the phrase "extra dirty" more as well. That was oddly arousing even if it was just olive juice.

"Of course," she said when she finally had the strength to speak and remember that she was working and had a role to play herself.

She stepped away and started to make Brooke's drink as she kept her ears perked to hear if Stella or Monica said anything to Brooke but they both seemed to be stunned into silence when Taylor turned around and found Brooke on her phone and the other women quietly looking at their cocktails.

"Extra dirty, just how you like it," Taylor announced as she placed the drink in front of the woman she was dating. They were dating, right?

A tint of blush crept across Brooke's pale cheeks. "Thank you."

Taylor nervously looked between Brooke and Stella and felt like she needed to address the elephant in the room. After all, she wanted Stella to know for a fact that Brooke was hers. Even if they were technically playing pretend in a way.

"Um," she cleared her throat as she tried to find the right words to say. Her hesitation perfectly aligned with the awkwardness she would really feel if her current and past lovers unexpectedly crossed paths at the bar. "Brooke, this is Stella."

Brooke played her role perfectly and looked over at the couple waiting for more context of who she was to Taylor but nothing came. Instead, she extended her hand towards Monica and said, "Nice to meet you."

It was such a perfect burn that Taylor had to restrain herself from not jumping across the bar and kissing her senseless. She didn't want to assume that Brooke knew who her ex was, but even some light snooping on her Instagram account would have confirmed that it was the blonde. Either Brooke didn't care to look or she was pretending that Stella's existence didn't matter.

"I'm Stella," the blonde said as she stretched her hand across her girlfriend. "This is my girlfriend, Monica."

Watching the two of them shake hands felt like an out of body experience. Clearly Taylor had been picked up by aliens tonight and this was some bizarre scientific experiment playing out in her mind. There was no other explanation for the alternate reality she was living in where Brooke and Stella were exchanging pleasantries.

"How do you know Taylor?" Stella asked when she let go of her hand.

Brooke glanced back towards Taylor and raised her lips in a smile. "We're dating. How do you two know each other?"

A beat of silence filled the air before Stella finally answered the question. "We used to date." Their entire relationship demeaned to just "used to date" status. It should have stung but Taylor didn't really care. She was only focused on the present and the future.

"Oh!" Brooke exclaimed. "Wow, I picked a popular night to come here." She looked at Taylor to try to add to their coverup but the bartender was still coming to terms with the fact that this entire interaction was even happening. And that Brooke confirmed they were dating.

Taylor cleared her throat and stepped back towards the bottles lining the wall behind her. "Not what I was expecting on a Wednesday," Taylor confirmed.

Brooke turned her attention back to Monica and Stella and started to talk to them as Taylor stepped away to make sure her other customers were still being taken care of. For a moment, she forgot she even had a job to do. Her tips would probably reflect that tonight but the payoff she was getting from watching Stella's very obvious jealousy seep through was something that outvalued any money tenfold. Brooke was pouring on the charm and talking about everything that Taylor found fascinating about her. Her job. Her travels. Her interests. It was alluring to say the least.

When Brooke got up to go to the bathroom, Taylor picked up her empty martini glass and caught Stella staring at her. "You're dating *her*?"

"Yes," Taylor confirmed. She didn't want to know what the accusatory tone was meant to imply, nor did she really care.

Stella shook her head in confusion. "I haven't seen her on your Instagram or anything." The admission was enough satisfaction for Taylor. Stella looked. And now she knew what she was missing out on.

"I don't need to post for it to be real," Taylor said mostly as a dig to Monica. "She's the one who took me to see Billy Joel last week."

"Yeah, because she's like forty," Stella scoffed. What was said as an insult was something that didn't even bother Taylor.

"She's perfect, that's what she is," Taylor declared.

"She's beautiful," Monica found her voice, sending a shocked look across her own girlfriend's face. "Do you think she could help me get some publicity work? I'm an Influencer."

Of course Monica would make this about her. She and Stella were doomed. Neither of them would care about the other at the end of the day. "She's got a pretty stacked client list."

Monica nodded but when Brooke sat back down, she didn't have the courage to ask her for help. Maybe she was intimidated, or maybe it had something to do with the scowl that was plastered on Stella's face. When they finished their drinks and asked for the check, Brooke waved her hand to catch Taylor's attention.

"It's on me," Brooke declared.

She should not have been paying for Stella's drinks. That was not part of this plan but luckily Taylor didn't have to be the one to say that. "No, you don't have to do that," Stella said quickly as she dug in her bag for her wallet.

The look that came across Brooke's face was not one that Taylor had seen before. If she had to place it, it was somewhere between devious and satisfied, and judging by the words that followed, Taylor knew Brooke did not play games. "Consider it payback," she started. "Thank you for not being right for Taylor to send her to me."

Monica's jaw dropped at the dig before she stifled a laugh. She didn't even seem to be bothered at the stab at her current girlfriend.

"That's not necessary," Stella said coldly.

"Babe, the check please," Brooke repeated. "And can we leave soon?"

Taylor nodded as she placed the bill in Brooke's hands. The fact that she was paying for four drinks for complete strangers just to prove a point told Taylor all she needed to know. Brooke did not half-ass anything.

"Thank you," Monica finally found her voice. "For the drinks and conversation." She was clearly still sucking up.

"It was nice meeting you both," Brooke said with a smile.

Stella looked at Taylor and frowned. "It was good to see you again, Tay."

Taylor wished she could have said the same. She didn't have any lingering feelings for her ex-girlfriend by any means, but it stirred up something inside of her that she didn't like. Feeling like she wasn't good enough. Feeling like there was something wrong with her to make them incompatible. It took her a while to realize that sometimes two people just weren't meant to be and that was that. "Get home safe," she replied before looking at Monica. "Nice to meet you."

Monica smiled softly, still seemingly unfazed by a run-in with an ex-girlfriend. As she turned away and Stella followed, Taylor shifted her gaze onto Brooke who was staring back at her with an unreadable expression on her face. "Thanks for coming," she said meekly as she grabbed Stella and Monica's glasses to clean up.

Brooke remained silent until Taylor turned back around to face her. "How do you feel?"

It was a question that the bartender wasn't prepared for – she was expecting some passive aggressive comment about lingering feelings for Stella or something about her appearance. Then Taylor remembered that Brooke was much more mature than anyone she ever dated. Despite it being her idea to one-up Stella, she wasn't going to take stabs or be jealous. Unless she just didn't care enough to be jealous.

"I feel really relieved that you came," Taylor admitted. "I didn't think I could waste any more brain cells talking to them."

Brooke smiled softly and leaned back in her chair. "There's only so much TikTok I can handle in one conversation."

"Same," Taylor said with a reciprocal smile. "It all made me feel stupid for even being with someone like Stella to begin with."

"We live, we learn," Brooke said nonchalantly. It made Taylor think about Jaclyn and how burned Brooke was. Breaking up with Stella was nothing in comparison to a divorce. She couldn't imagine how it would feel to run into an ex-wife unexpectedly. Or even worse, how it would feel to be the new partner and experience it first-hand.

"You ever have an awkward run-in with an ex?" Taylor asked to deviate the topic off of herself.

Brooke lifted her head as she seemed to be lost in thought. Taylor's eyes were drawn to her neck and she could almost feel the way Brooke's body would react when she would place kisses along the exposed skin. "When I was younger, but I really do my best to leave the past in the past."

An unshakeable thought entered Taylor's mind. She never wanted to be part of Brooke's past. She needed to find a way to remain next to this woman for as long as possible. She was no Stella. She was incredible.

"I'm working until twelve," Taylor announced to stop her racing thoughts. "I should have told you that earlier. You can head home if you want."

"If you're up for it, I'd like you to come home with me," Brooke said without missing a beat. "So better make me another drink."

Taylor couldn't control the smile that crept across her face. Brooke wanted to stay and spend the night together. "Extra dirty?"

"Filthy," Brooke said with a wink. This woman would surely be the end of her one way or another.

Stella [11:24pm]
Your girlfriend is kind of a bitch

Taylor laughed out loud when she finally opened her phone to look at the text that came in over an hour ago. She walked out of Brooke's bathroom to the bedroom to show her the message, not even thinking about the way girlfriend was thrown around. Girlfriend. *God, that sounded so nice.*

Brooke smiled and shrugged. "She's not wrong."

"You're my bitch though," Taylor said without thinking before Brooke's wide eyes revealed that she said more than she intended, and possibly insulted her in the process. "I mean you're not a real bitch, but like, even if you are I don't mind."

Brooke grabbed her to pull her down on the bed. "Just kiss me."

Taylor complied and let her lips tell Brooke just how grateful she was for her. Not just for what happened tonight, but for the past two months. As she fell asleep in her arms, it was the happiest she had been on a Wednesday in a long time.

Taylor [8:13am]
She's mine and that's all that matters

It truly was.

Chapter Twelve

Taylor [7:53pm]
Kon'nichiwa! Can I take you to my fav Japanese restaurant Friday night?

Brooke bit her lip in thought. Could she re-arrange the plans with her parents and let her mother and father have a romantic meal together on her expense? Of course. But she wanted to enjoy every hour her parents were in New York. This was her idea and her wish to have these memories together.

Guilt started to trickle in that she was about to tell Taylor her parents were in New York and she had no plans to introduce them. How could she? Taylor would then know her mother was sick and that would send their relationship down the path she was terrified to explore.

Brooke [8:18pm]
My parents are visiting this weekend and have taken up all my time

Taylor [8:20pm]
It's sweet how close you are with your parents. Even though I'm sad I won't see you

Taylor [8:21pm]
Or have sake and the best sushi rolls

More guilt packed onto Brooke. While she always had a good relationship with her parents, the only reason she was seeing and talking to them as much as she was now was because Mary was sick and they didn't know how much time they had left together. Previously, she could go a week with barely talking to them aside from some text messages. Now a single day didn't go by without a phone call checking in. If only she had done that more frequently over the years she might not feel as guilty as she did now.

Brooke [8:20pm]
Are you free Sunday night? I'm sure I'm going to need something good to end the weekend on

Taylor [8:21pm]
And what's that??

Brooke knew she'd be putting herself on the line but she sent the following text anyway not caring about the implications. It was true after all.

Brooke [8:23pm]
Just being around you. That's enough to make everything better

Taylor [8:24pm]
And here I was thinking you might only be using me for

my body...

Brooke laughed to herself. She could just imagine Taylor saying that aloud, oozing in sarcasm with a playful smile on her face. *God, I love her smile.*

Brooke [8:25pm]
I do like your body too. A lot

Taylor [8:25pm]
Me too

Taylor [8:25pm]
I mean I like your body

Brooke [8:26pm]
You know what else I like?

Taylor [8:26pm]
What?

Brooke [8:27pm]
When your body is on top of mine

Taylor [8:27pm]
I really like that too. I can almost feel you under me now

Brooke [8:28pm]
What would you do if I was?

Taylor [8:28pm]

I'd kiss you first

Taylor [8:28pm]
Caress your tongue with mine and make you moan

Taylor [8:29pm]
Then trail my lips down your chest and suck on your nipples

This escalated in ways Brooke didn't expect although she was the one who started the conversation looking for Taylor to be the distraction she needed.

Brooke [8:29pm]
I love when you do that

Brooke [8:30pm]
Keep going

Taylor [8:30pm]
I'd drag my tongue lower and lower and then grab your thighs and throw them over my shoulders

Brooke [8:30pm]
I'd be wet and ready for you

Taylor [8:31pm]
You taste so fucking good

Brooke [8:31pm]
Don't stop

Taylor [8:32pm]
I'd slip my finger inside and feel you clench around me

Brooke couldn't stand texting right now. She needed to hear Taylor's voice. She called her on speakerphone and dropped the phone beside her in bed as her hand slipped between her legs.

"Fuck, Brooke. Are we really doing this?" Taylor's voice was a bit breathless on the other end of the line and it spiked Brooke's arousal even more.

Brooke swallowed hard, trying to suppress just how turned on she was from a few text messages. "Doing what?"

Taylor was initially quiet before she spoke again. "Am I the only one touching myself right now?"

"No," Brooke said softly as a moan escaped her lips at the visual of Taylor touching herself in bed. "I am too."

"Let me come over," Taylor pleaded. "I need you."

Brooke's eyes rolled back in her head as she felt her body start to tense up. "Yes," she sounded. "But I can't stop now."

Taylor groaned and Brooke worked harder, faster, in pure desperation of being in need of a release. She needed to come now, there was no other alternative. She listened to Taylor's pants echo throughout the bedroom and felt her chest tighten before her body started to tremble.

When Brooke came, she closed her eyes as she listened to Taylor's release on the other end of the phone. She couldn't believe she just sexted and had phone sex and was about to have Taylor come over and continue things in person. Who was she?

"I'll be there in a half hour," Taylor said before hanging up.

Brooke stared at the ceiling in confusion. She wasn't this person who had an insatiable sex drive. A person who couldn't physically get enough of someone else. A person who wanted to give in to her desires all the time. Or was she?

Two days later, Mary stared out of Brooke's window looking down Ninth Avenue as she clutched a cup of tea. Brooke had been quietly watching her mother for the past five minutes before she announced her presence by sliding up beside her. "Looks like a nice day out," Brooke said feeling relieved that they would have sunshine and good weather for their day out together.

"How are you affording this apartment?" Mary bluntly asked, like a typical mother, when she turned around to look at her daughter. "Are you sure you're doing okay?"

A sigh escaped Brooke's lips as she looked at the city moving down below. "I'm perfectly fine, mom," Brooke started, trying to find the words to calm her mother's qualms when she should only be worried about herself. "I jumped into my last apartment because I needed a new place to live and now I'm living where I deserve."

"It's not a question of deserve. It's a question of money. This seems like a swanky New York City building and it's nicer than your apartment with Jaclyn. That's all."

It was definitely an upgrade, but so was all of Brooke's life post-divorce. She might have gotten cheated on and lost her wife, but she got promoted at work and started living her life for herself for the first time in a decade. "I promise you that I'm doing fine," Brooke reiterated. "If I wasn't, you'd be the first to know."

"Now that's a lie," Mary said with a light chuckle. "You'd tell your father anything before me."

That was only true now that Mary was sick. Prior to that, Brooke would always share things with her mother first. She felt fortunate enough to have a mother that was not only a great parent, but a confidant as well. Now, Brooke confided in her father when everything with Mary felt like walking on eggshells. There was a reason why only Oscar knew about Taylor.

"That's not true," Brooke said as she ran her fingers through her hair. "Are you ready to head out?"

Mary nodded before she glanced at her daughter with furrowed brows. She reached out and adjusted the hair that Brooke had just moved to expose a dark mark on Brooke's neck. "Do you have a hickey?" Mary almost shrieked.

Brooke felt heat rush to her face in an uncontrollable blush. *Fuck*. She wasn't thinking about her hair that had been perfectly placed to cover the mark that Taylor left on her neck that even four coats of cover-up couldn't mask completely. Eighty degrees was also too hot to wear a scarf. "Oh no, I uh, burned myself with the curling iron yesterday," she tried to lie as she moved her hair back across her neck.

"What's her name?" Mary asked with a knowing smirk.

Brooke rolled her eyes as she walked away from her mother, knowing she was certainly confirming the presence of a woman rather than the lack of her existence. "Dyson."

"Dyson doesn't use heat like that," Mary followed up as she trailed behind her daughter. "You taught me that."

Brooke pretended to be busy on her phone in hopes that her mother would drop the inquisition into her personal life.

Brooke [12:33 pm]
I hope you know that my mother just saw the hickey I told you NOT to leave!!

Taylor [12:35pm]
I didn't really hear you telling me to stop

Brooke [12:36 pm]

I did!

Taylor [12:36pm]
Since when does "fuck me" = "stop"?

Taylor [12:36pm]
Because I've def been using it wrong then

"Are you texting the Dyson?" Mary inquired. "Your face is redder than when I saw your hickey."

"Jesus Christ, mom," Brooke said as she locked her phone feeling like she was caught in a losing battle. Not ready to tell her mother the truth, she pretended nothing was going on.

"Dad is going to get hangry if we don't get to brunch soon."

"Deflection," Mary announced as she looped her arm through her daughter's. "You learned that from him."

As they descended the elevator and met Oscar downstairs after his walk around the neighborhood, the family went to brunch and began their touristy New York City weekend together.

Brooke [3:11 pm]
I don't think "fuck me" and "stop" should ever be used in the same sentence

Brooke [3:11 pm]
At least not with you

Taylor [3:15 pm]
Agreed

Taylor [3:15 pm]

Will make sure that's not the case tomorrow

Mary watched Brooke with knowing eyes. A mother's intuition was surely playing a role but there was no sense in disclosing the truth now, especially when this weekend was supposed to be all about bonding together. Brooke put her phone away and focused on her parents the rest of the day despite the fact that part of her heart had already become consumed by someone else.

Chapter Thirteen

Brooke sat at her desk staring out the window instead of her computer screen that kept flashing with new notifications of messages and emails. She was reflecting on how she worked hard for the last twenty-years to get to where she is now. The fact that her career was equivalent to two-thirds of Taylor's life wasn't something she overlooked either.

Ever since she was in college, she pushed herself harder and harder. She was at the top of her class graduating Summa Cum Laude. She had three internships before she even graduated. She worked hard in her early twenties and when everyone else was out getting blackout drunk on Fridays, she used that time to put in a few extra hours at work to prove she was worthy of advancing, all while getting her Master's degree. She never wanted being a gay woman to hold her back, even though that was a notion and pressure her therapist would later tell her she applied to herself.

"Hey, you got a minute?" Derek asked as he appeared at her door. He was Brooke's assistant, even though she hated the idea of having one. She had known too many people with assistants who acted like they were better than everyone else – she was definitely not that kind of boss.

"Of course," she said as she waved him in to her office. It's not like she was actually getting any work done now when she was lost in her thoughts.

"I was going through the calendar and noticed you're working remote Thursday and Friday but Andy Weissman is coming in person for the meeting."

Brooke exhaled softly. That wasn't a meeting she wanted to take over Zoom. She preferred to be there in person and be a force that Andy couldn't talk over and mansplain the way he was notorious for doing every time he got in a room with anyone. "See if he'd be available to reschedule for next week when I'm in otherwise tell him to just join via video."

"Do you think it's a good idea to reschedule? He's been pretty adamant about renegotiating terms for his clients."

Of course Brooke knew that. And despite how much she disliked Andy on a personal level, this was business and she needed his clients to stay at their agency. Losing one of his brands or up and coming celebrities would be a huge loss, but Brooke couldn't put her personal life on hold. Work had to come second.

"I can't come in Thursday. I'm taking my mom to get some important cancer scans done and I have to be there."

"Oh Brooke, I'm sorry. I didn't mean to overstep like that."

"You didn't," Brooke said softly, "I'm just letting you know I need to prioritize that this week and possibly some other days coming up."

"I completely understand." Derek had a look on his face that Brooke knew was a combination of sympathy and concern. It was a look she appreciated yet hated because it reminded her of just how bad the situation she was in actually was. Why was it so easy for her to tell someone she worked with and not the person she was sharing a bed with? Brooke knew it was because Derek's knowledge of her mother would have no impact on whether or not he stayed in Brooke's life.

"While you're in the calendar, can you get me a plus one for next week's gala?"

A playful grin spread across Derek's face as he sat down in a vacant chair across from his boss. "Are you seeing someone?" Despite being in a work environment, a blush crept across Brooke's face. "You totally are! Details!"

Derek was gay, and it was the only reason why Brooke even entertained telling him about Taylor. It felt safe, comfortable even. She hated office gossip but it was too difficult to deny the butterflies she felt in her stomach. "Maybe," she settled on. "But can you let me know if it's possible before I ask her?"

"I'm going to make it happen just so I can meet the mysterious woman that has you blushing like a school girl."

Derek bounced out of her office and within forty-five minutes, he already had an answer for her: she was set to bring a date.

Brooke didn't know if bringing Taylor as her date to an event like this was the best idea, but she found herself wanting to have Taylor there with her. They could enjoy some free lavish food and drinks and spend time talking about all the ridiculous outfits people would be wearing. At least that's what she and Derek did the year before.

Brooke [11:14am]
I have to go to a work gala next Friday where everyone dresses up and schmoozes but there's free drinks and food

Brooke [11:14am]
Do you want to come with me?

Taylor [11:27am]
First Billy Joel. Now this. What's next??

Brooke laughed to herself before she started to worry that her so-called dates were just work perks that she was using as a way to spend more time with Taylor, not that she seemed to mind.

Brooke [11:29am]
I'll have to try to top that next time

Taylor [11:30am]
...

Taylor [11:30am]
I'm sorry I'm now stuck in a loop thinking about you on top of me

Taylor [11:30am]
And it's really hot

Brooke [11:32am]
Maybe we can make that a reality

Taylor [11:33am]
After the party. Because I am totally coming with you

Taylor [11:33am]
And then coming for you

Heat rushed to Brooke's face and just as she was about to respond, she noticed Derek standing in the doorframe with his arms folded across his chest. "Total school girl!" he said with a smirk.

She couldn't even deny it, not like she'd want to.

On the train down to DC on Thursday, Brooke thought about how she was spending more time on Amtrak than she ever imagined. Growing up in DC, she always thought she'd stay local and work in politics. She quickly learned while at Georgetown that political publicity was not something she wanted to spend her life doing. Battling scandals and targeted ads from opponents with views she didn't share seemed exhausting. She knew that life would drain her in every capacity. She didn't necessarily expect to work primarily in entertainment publicity either, but after years of climbing the corporate ladder and working ridiculous hours, she found herself exactly where she wanted to be.

She always found a great sense of comfort from being in control of the narrative; of shaping her clients to say and do appropriate things at appropriate times so the message could be well received. The irony was never lost on Brooke that she didn't have the same approach to her personal life. Sure, she always wanted everything to be perfect but she knew as much as she could try to control situations, she could never control a romantic partner. She wouldn't even want to and she would never want a partner to do that to her either. If she had been a sliver of the persona she was at work, chances are her marriage might not have failed because Jaclyn would never have stepped out of line. But then again, everything happens for a reason.

As Brooke watched the trees pass by the window, long ignoring the work waiting on her opened laptop, her mind drifted to Taylor, as it had been a lot lately. She was the furthest thing from in control around her. Mentally. Emotionally. Physically. She had no idea what she was doing as she was constantly gravitating to the woman she still couldn't understand why was choosing to be with her. Was Taylor just playing her? Using her for a physical partner until someone younger came around and swept her off her feet? Should Personal Brooke be more like Work Brooke and set barriers and expectations to protect herself and keep Taylor in-check? The more she thought about it, the more she didn't want to keep Taylor in-check. She wanted her to be authentically herself. Yet, she knew she could keep herself in-check by holding on to her vulnerabilities.

On this trip to take her mother for another round of tests, Brooke decided that Taylor would never know about Mary's sickness until absolutely necessary. This had to be something she dealt with alone and if Taylor left her along that journey, then at least she would know it was because of herself, and not her family situation. Not that that would be any easier to process. Now that Brooke found Taylor, she never wanted to lose her.

Chapter Fourteen

When the Friday of the gala rolled around, Brooke was applying lipstick in her bathroom mirror as Taylor's name appeared on her ringing phone. A sense of worry crept into her mind that Taylor might be canceling at the last minute. This was the first time she had a real date to an event since Jaclyn. This was a big deal to her; a step in the right direction of opening herself up and allowing the possibilities of a relationship begin to bloom, and with that came waves of insecurity. "Hello?" she finally answered before it went to voicemail.

"I just want to make sure you were serious that this was a dressy event and I'm not going to walk in all fancy and everyone else is in jeans," Taylor said breathlessly. "I once believed someone when they said it was a costume party and I walked in dressed like Lara Croft and I was the only one dressed up."

Brooke smiled as she sensed Taylor's slight panic across the line. At least she wasn't the only one who seemed to be nervous about tonight. "I'd like to see pictures of that. But I promise you it's a fancy event. I'm already in my dress so at the bare minimum you won't be alone."

"Okay, good," Taylor said amidst a sigh. "I have to finish getting ready but I'll see you there at seven!"

She immediately hung up and Brooke smiled at her dark screen. Something about Taylor was just so genuine and carefree that Brooke had to remind herself that she was real. And tonight, she was her date. Who would have thought?

Brooke waited outside the venue so that she and Taylor could walk inside together. She alternated looking at her phone and smiling at people she knew that arrived and were walking up the carpeted steps to check in with the hosts guarding the front door. Brooke normally hated these types of events ever since the divorce. She felt like she was on her own without someone to turn to and escape conversations. Without someone she could dance with and enjoy top-shelf drinks with for a fun night out.

Having Taylor there with her was more of a big deal than she let on, but she didn't want to apply any more pressure to the evening than she already had placed on herself on wanting everything to be perfect.

Taylor [6:58pm]
1 block away!

Brooke took a deep breath and put her phone back in her purse as she awaited Taylor's arrival. When Taylor's Uber pulled up and the door opened, the first thing Brooke saw was all leg. The high slit of Taylor's dress rode up as she maneuvered out of the car and she stepped out to meet Brooke's eyes across the sidewalk. Her eyes that were surely comically wide as she took in the sight of Taylor in a long black gown with a plunging neckline for days. She was beyond striking and breathtaking; far more elegant than Brooke had ever seen her before. They needed excuses to dress up more often so Taylor could showcase this old Hollywood glamour look more often.

"Is this okay? I really didn't know what to wear." Taylor's nerves were evident by her eyes darting down to her dress as her eyebrows furrowed in doubt. "I can run home and change and be back in like a half hour."

"You look absolutely stunning," Brooke interrupted as she reached out to place her hand on Taylor's arm.

Taylor bashfully looked Brooke up and down before she stepped closer. "Not as stunning as you." In her royal blue dress, she might have been brighter in color, but she would definitely not stand out as much as Taylor. She was going to be a showstopper inside and for that Brooke beamed before she gently closed the gap between them to bring a soft kiss to Taylor's lips. She hadn't touched those lips in nine days and all she could think about was how much she'd rather just go home and be alone than walk around the party.

"Shall we?" Brooke asked as she held her hand out and Taylor slipped her hand inside of hers. It was the first time they ever truly held hands, excluding that night in Stonewall dodging the crowd, and Brooke enjoyed it more than she should but she couldn't control herself. Derek was right. She did feel like a schoolgirl holding hands with her crush as if it was the most serious thing that had ever happened in her life.

And maybe it was. Maybe this was the sign that Brooke needed that Taylor was the woman that made her weak in the knees and blushing non-stop. She tried to hide her feelings as they walked around the lavish event space and downed glasses of free champagne but it was hard to hide something that was bursting at the seams looking for a release.

Derek caught a glimpse of them and started dramatically fanning himself when Taylor wasn't looking. Brooke blushed even harder and did everything in her power to keep Taylor as far away from him as possible because he didn't have a poker face and would be quick to overshare. It was up to Brooke to reveal her feelings, not her overzealous assistant. But tonight wasn't about that. It was about networking and having this beautiful woman to return back to. The latter was definitely the most important to Brooke.

Taylor watched Brooke own the room. She was polite and courteous to everyone who approached her and then noticeably firmer with people who she told to call her next week to discuss projects. The way she composed herself and held onto her mostly full glass of champagne was practically a work of art and everywhere she went people were looking at her and admiring her. Just as much as Taylor was.

As a spectator, Taylor found herself questioning how Brooke was single. Obviously, she knew about Jaclyn and how devastating that breakup was to experience. Yet, how come no one swept Brooke off her feet like she deserved since then? She was an incredible woman and judging by how everyone looked at her when speaking to her, including both men and women, it was evident she was capable of having countless suitors.

Brooke's laugh entered Taylor's ears and she couldn't help but smile at the sound. Or when Brooke looked over her shoulder and smiled softly in her direction before turning her attention back to someone else. It was then that the notion of other people started to scare Taylor. She knew she wasn't seeing anyone else but what if Brooke was? What if they had just been casually dating and having sex but she was also doing that with someone else?

They hadn't had a conversation that truly defined what they were to each other even though Taylor felt pretty confident Brooke wasn't the type of woman who dated or slept with multiple people at once. When would she even have the time? Or was that why she was sometimes unavailable?

"Sorry about that," Brooke said as she returned to Taylor's side at the table. "I promise our next date will be just us without distractions."

A lopsided smile moved across Taylor's face. Brooke was already thinking about their next date. Was she doing that for everyone else under her spell? "Do your thing. It's kind of hot watching you in action and I'm like your trophy wife."

The second the words left her mouth she regretted them. Both because she was implying being her wife and because it could have implied that she didn't mean anything to Brooke other than a pretty young thing on her arm. She didn't want to be *just* that at all. Brooke didn't seem to be phased by the statement as she laughed and took a sip of her champagne. "Is that so?"

Before Taylor had time to reply, another man appeared at the table and hugged Brooke as he said it was good to see her again. Taylor didn't appreciate how he held Brooke in his arms for longer than necessary and how his eyes seemed to scan down to her chest without any decency before his eyes traveled over to Taylor.

"Miguel, this is Taylor," Brooke said before stopping short of adding any additional clarity around who she was.

"Nice to meet you," he said as he extended his hand for her to shake. "Do you work with Brooke or another agency?"

Taylor knew she looked like a deer caught in headlights as she lightly shook his hand. She didn't know what to say. Who was she to Brooke? Especially at a work function. "No, we're just friends." The f-word tasted like venom on her lips. Maybe it was that poison playing with her mind to make her feel like she sensed Brooke slightly wince at it as well.

"She's a great friend to have," Miguel said with a smirk as he dropped her hand. "I've tried to get her to be my girlfriend but she refuses."

Gross. Brooke seemed to agree as she rolled her eyes in response. "I'm going to tell Adriana."

"You know she wouldn't mind," he said with a laugh. "She has a crush on you too."

Brooke deviated the conversation by asking about his wife and their kids as Taylor silently stood by listening, and still judging the way Miguel looked at Brooke. When he suggested they grab drinks soon, Taylor hoped that Brooke's 'sure' was just her being polite and that she wasn't actually going to spend time with this man.

"I think I've had enough schmoozing for the night," Brooke said almost exhausted as she looked over at Taylor once they were alone again. "Did you eat enough? Do you want to stay longer or head out?"

Taylor barely ate, but it was mostly due to her own racing thoughts and anxieties over the woman staring back at her. She seemed to have focused more on all the passed appetizers and champagne rather than the meal stations in the corner of the room. But she wasn't there to dive into all the calories, she was there simply to be Brooke's date. "I did. We can go whenever you're ready."

Brooke took Taylor's hand in hers again and guided them out of the party without going back to say goodbye to anyone.

"Do you want to come over?" Brooke asked Taylor when they walked onto the street. Her phone was clutched in her hand seeming to wait to order a car when Taylor decided she couldn't go on in this gray area anymore. She needed to put a stake in the ground and see what happened.

"I do, but first I want you to know that I'm not seeing anyone else." The words came out more forcefully than she anticipated but the surge of confidence she gave herself couldn't be contained. "I haven't since the day we met."

Brooke's hazel eyes lifted off her phone and up to Taylor; a perplexed expression painted on her face. "Okay."

"Are you?"

It felt like years had gone by as Taylor waited for confirmation that she was the only woman Brooke was dating. "Of course not."

Relief washed over her that one hurdle was already overtaken. She didn't have any other competition. She was the only woman in Brooke's life. "So, we're exclusive? Are you my girlfriend?"

Taylor's heart fluttered when Brooke smiled at her – that smile that could warm her soul on the darkest of days. The smile that she wanted to call hers. "Do you want me to be?"

"I do. I hated saying I was your friend inside."

"Me too," Brooke said before pulling her in for a scorching kiss. There in the middle of 53rd street, their relationship transgressed into something with meaning. Something both of them longed for more than they wanted to share.

"Take me home," Taylor said softly when Brooke pulled back. It was oozing in desire, and Brooke looked at her with hungry eyes before she ordered a car and then returned her hand to hold Taylor's where it remained clenched the entire car ride. For something they hadn't done before, Taylor couldn't get enough of feeling Brooke's palm pressed against her own.

When they got back to Brooke's apartment, it became even more evident that they weren't friends. Something changed within Brooke the second they got on the elevator in her building. Or maybe it changed in Taylor, she wasn't even sure. All she knew was that Brooke had her pinned against the elevator wall and was kissing her like her life depended on it. Taylor simultaneously felt like the ride to the seventeenth floor was far too short and yet also couldn't wait to get inside where they could have true privacy.

A pool of heat soaked Taylor's underwear the minute she stumbled backwards through Brooke's front door and Brooke was back on her in desperation. Their purses were dropped on the hallway bench but neither of them bothered to take their shoes off as they moved in sync further into the apartment.

Without hesitation, Brooke trailed her hand up the high slit of Taylor's dress to gain access to dip into her underwear. "You're so wet," Brooke growled in astonishment as her fingers moved against Taylor's slick folds.

"Fuck," Taylor grunted the second her back slammed against the hallway wall and Brooke dived in, moving her fingers like a skilled violinist strumming the most delicate part of Taylor's body.

Between still being in her heels and what Brooke's hand was doing between Taylor's legs, Taylor was quickly struggling to maintain her balance. She tried to arch her back and lean on the wall for support that she was desperately in need of as she grew closer to a release.

"Should I stop?" Brooke playfully teased in Taylor's ear, seeming to catch on to her girlfriend's struggles.

"No," Taylor said breathlessly. "Please don't stop."

Brooke didn't stop, but she slowed her pace to simply torture Taylor.

Drawing gentle circles around the bundle of nerves she needed to be touched the most. She could feel herself float into ecstasy at how much she enjoyed Brooke dominating her right now. Even if she could barely stand on her own.

When two fingers unexpectedly moved inside, Taylor groaned and wrapped her left leg around Brooke's waist. She was quite literally fucking her against the wall but Taylor wanted more. She *needed* more. And she needed gravity on her side. "Island. Now," she said as she lowered her leg and pushed Brooke backwards to the kitchen.

Brooke's immaculate and clean apartment came in handy when Taylor sat on the cleared island, her legs dangling over the edge as she pulled her dress up higher over her waist. Brooke didn't miss a beat as she pushed Taylor's legs apart to pull her underwear down before she lowered herself to Taylor's core.

"Fuck, Brooke," Taylor moaned as she grabbed the back of Brooke's head to keep her close. She couldn't believe that Brooke was literally crouched down between her legs on the kitchen island while still wearing a dress and heels. This was something straight out of porno and the second Taylor had that thought, she lost control.

The orgasm that followed was hands down the strongest Taylor ever had in her entire life. It now pushed the first time they had sex into second place; a feat Taylor wasn't sure would ever be possible. It had to be the build up at the party. The declaration of feelings. The passion when they burst through the door. The explosion of it all now. She *really* liked having a girlfriend.

"I will never look at a kitchen island the same again," Taylor said breathlessly as she laid back and sprawled her arms out on the marble countertop.

Brooke laughed as she walked to the fridge to pour herself a much-needed glass of water. "I'm going to need one in every apartment I ever live in."

Taylor turned her head to look at Brooke slowly drinking water. Her previously perfect up-do was now a disheveled mess from Taylor's hands being tangled up in it. Just when she thought Brooke couldn't get any sexier, she had to go and upstage herself yet again.

"Come here," Taylor beckoned. She craved Brooke right now in ways she couldn't even properly formulate in her mind, let alone with words. So instead, she just simply declared it. "I want you to sit on my face."

Brooke spit out the water she was in the process of drinking. "On the island?"

Taylor nodded and extended her hand. "I want you to think of me doing this to you every time you're in this room."

Taylor almost expected Brooke to say no to her extremely bold and blunt request. It was one thing to do this comfortably in bed, but it would be another to have to put weight on knees against marble. Brooke didn't seem to be bothered by the idea as she slowly unzipped her tight dress and let it pool to the floor. She stepped out of it and kicked off her shoes before she pulled down her underwear and Taylor realized she got more than she bargained for. Forget the island, she would never be able to look at a kitchen the same again now. Every kitchen would never compare to Brooke's where she got naked and climbed on top of Taylor on the island.

Instead of getting in the position Taylor requested, Brooke hovered over Taylor and kissed her deeply. Taylor didn't think she could ever possibly grow tired of these types of kisses and the way Brooke's lips and tongue moved in perfect sync with hers and ignited waves of desire within her body.

"You're so amazing," Taylor said into her mouth. "The things you do to me. You're like a drug and I'm addicted."

Brooke moved her lips to Taylor's neck as she intertwined their hands against the island. "Drugs are bad."

"You are so fucking good," Taylor clarified before she grew tired of talking. She needed to show Brooke how she felt. She needed Brooke to feel just as good as she did – love stoned. She started to pull and push

Brooke's body upwards until she got her right where she wanted her with her knees surrounding Taylor's head.

Taylor slowly brought her tongue to Brooke's core and shivered at the discovery of just how wet Brooke was. Taylor loved knowing that Brooke got turned on from pleasing her, and now she was going to drink it all in and devour her.

Never had a vision been more arousing than having Brooke hovered over her in the middle of the kitchen, completely naked and moaning in pleasure as her body rocked back and forth on Taylor's mouth. It was enough to make Taylor think that she could get off again just from the sight and sensation alone without even being touched herself.

"Taylor," Brooke sounded amidst a moan as she tossed her head back and clutched at Taylor's breast which was still unfortunately covered by her dress. "I'm going to come," she announced before her body rode out a trembling orgasm.

It was everything Taylor ever wanted.

When Brooke collapsed her body on top of Taylor's she kissed her tenderly, a much calmer pace from their frantic strides mere moments ago. "Best girlfriend ever."

Taylor certainly agreed.

Chapter Fifteen

Brooke forced a smile like she had been doing all afternoon. Having cups of wine handed to her certainly helped, even if it only masked the pain in her chest and her heart. Screaming five-year-olds were on the loose and they certainly didn't care about the uncomfortable reminder that Brooke was childless, or the migraine she had from their voices. And maybe the wine, but she couldn't let go of it now.

"Why did you invite me again?" she asked her friend, Beth, when she slid into the empty seat next to her, wiping a bead of sweat off her forehead as she raised her sunglasses.

"To remind you you're so lucky to not have kids," Beth said innocently.

That was the angle Brooke presented to most people. That she was content without children so she could focus on her own relationships, and lack thereof, amidst her career and travel. Only Nina and her parents knew how much she wanted to have kids and how much she had suppressed that in the name of love. "And because I haven't seen you in forever. At least today we can hang with Nina."

Brooke glanced over at Nina chasing her own son who was on a sugar-induced rampage. Maybe there was a benefit to being child-free. Or maybe Brooke should just hope for a girl. "You can barely catch your own breath let alone hang out," Brooke joked.

Beth sighed and downed the remainder of her beer in three long gulps. "I know. I really miss the nights we could splurge on charcuterie and wine and watch *Sex and the City* re-runs."

"We can still do that," Brooke reminded her. "You'll just have to go home after and not sleep on my couch."

"Or next to your toilet," Beth added with a headshake at the memory of one night that uncharacteristically got out of control. "Speaking of toilet, I need to do a bathroom check."

Beth placed her hand on Brooke's shoulder before she walked off to ask the children if anyone had to go to the bathroom. Brooke glanced at the scene and got up to refill her cup before she sat down on the blanket she brought and started to apply sunscreen. If she was being subjected to this children's party in the park on a scorching hot June Saturday, she could at least try to get a tan in the process.

"You know most people participate in parties, not lay out on a blanket like a supermodel." Even with Brooke's eyes closed she could tell Nina was standing over her, probably with her hands on her hips.

"Kids these days can take better pictures than us," Brooke said as she opened her sunglass covered eyes and confirmed Nina had her hands on her hips, scolding her like her own children. "They could make me Instagram famous."

Nina studied Brooke's face before she sat down beside her. "You're upset, aren't you? I told you to just stay home."

Brooke sighed and closed her eyes again. She could live without having this conversation today, maybe ever. "I'm not. I'm an adult. I know how to handle my emotions."

"Liar," Nina pushed. "It's okay to be sad. But seriously, imagine if you and Jac had a kid and then she did that to you?"

"Thanks for the daily reminder of things I'd like to forget." Truth be told, Brooke had been relieved that things panned out as they had. She couldn't imagine being divorced and having to share custody with Jaclyn. That felt like torture – both for herself and their child. Jaclyn was never going to be a good mother, at least not the version of herself that Brooke had been exposed to. She loved her routines and herself too much to care for another living being. It's the same reason why they never got a dog which Brooke also wanted. In hindsight, Brooke didn't get quite a few things she wanted and now it might all be too late.

Nina patted her hand on Brooke's thigh, stopping all the wandering thoughts in her mind. "You can always take mine. I'd gladly trade you my kids for a night of romantic dinners and sex like you're having."

Brooke rolled her eyes. "With Taylor? Do I need to be worried?"

Nina laughed and wrapped her arm around Brooke. "Oh, don't get jealous. You know that one time in college was enough lady loving for me."

"One?" Brooke questioned sharply. "You and Amanda were like a three-time thing."

"Only once was I not almost black out drunk," Nina defended herself. The memories might have been twenty years old but they still felt like yesterday and managed to make Brooke feel warm inside that the good times would always outweigh the bad.

"Mommy!" Nina's son yelled out. "Theo stole my ball!"

Nina groaned in frustration. "Seriously. Please take them for a night. Babysit them with your girlfriend and give me a break."

When Nina returned to her son, Brooke pulled out her phone and sent a text to Taylor hoping for an excuse to head out of the party early, without having to return to her apartment alone on a Saturday afternoon.

Brooke [2:13pm]
Any chance you're free and want to grab a drink?

Taylor [2:22pm]
Actually grab a drink or is this code for something else ;)

Brooke [2:23pm]

We could start with a drink

Taylor [2:24pm]
I wish I could but I have plans. I just wanted to know on a scale of 1-10 how much I was going to regret having them now

Taylor [2:24pm]
It's a 78

Brooke laughed to herself and laid back down on her blanket as she started to feel the disappointment creep in that she wouldn't be seeing Taylor today after all. There was never any expectation of that, but as the waves of loneliness and childlessness crept through her mind, right now all she wanted was to be around the one person that made her feel nothing but joy. Every single time.

Brooke [2:25pm]
Only a 78?

Taylor [2:26pm]
More like 782856508242390

Taylor [2:26pm]
And now I'm going to be thinking about you even more than I already was when I'm supposed to be focusing on my friends!

Brooke felt the same way right now. Although, it was about five-year-olds and their frantic parents.

Brooke [2:28pm]
Have fun and don't think of me

Taylor [2:28pm]
Impossible

At almost ten o'clock later that night, Brooke's phone rang beside her on the couch. "Brooke! Hey!" Taylor yelled the second her girlfriend answered. "Are you home?"

"Yeah."

"Good because I'm outside."

Brooke's eyes flung open wide. She was wearing sweatpants and a New York Mets t-shirt, a far cry from how she wanted Taylor to see her. Despite Taylor seeing her at her most vulnerable, naked or makeup-free, somehow the idea of her seeing her in casual loungewear made her nervous. She couldn't help but feel frumpy but there was no time to change her clothes when the knock on her door announced her girlfriend's unexpected arrival.

Brooke ran her fingers through her hair to at least provide some additional volume to her loose waves before she opened the door. Judging from Taylor's loud, slurred speech on the phone, and the very glossy look in her eyes now, it was obvious that Taylor was drunk. She swayed towards Brooke and wrapped her arms around her tightly. "I hope it's okay I just showed up," she said into Brooke's neck. "I really wanted to cuddle."

Brooke smiled as she held Taylor in her arms, finding the way Taylor meshed into her something that she'd never grow tired of. Whether or not she was wearing comfortable clothes suddenly didn't matter. All that mattered was how she felt in this moment.

With her apartment door still open, she finally pulled away and let

Taylor inside. "Do I have to be the big spoon again?" she asked with a smile. She'd happily always be the big spoon because it meant she got to hold Taylor.

"I can be the big spoon tonight," Taylor said as she kicked off her shoes and walked into the living room to sit down on the couch. She looked up at the ceiling and sighed deeply with her eyes closed. Brooke could sense that something wasn't right and it didn't seem to be solely because of alcohol.

"Is everything okay?" Brooke nervously asked as she sat down beside her.

"I drank too much," Taylor stated the obvious. "Mimosas at brunch. Then prosecco. And then a couple pickleback shots."

Brooke couldn't remember the last time she had a shot. Now that seemed like something an entirely different person would do, or something she'd only rely on in an extreme situation of emotional turmoil. Not a typical Saturday night after mixing liquors.

"How about some water and something to eat?" Brooke asked as she got up to walk to the kitchen knowing Taylor was going to need something to hurt less in the morning. Before she could walk to the kitchen, Taylor grabbed her hand tightly to pull her back.

"Why haven't you asked to meet my friends?" Taylor asked as she looked up at Brooke.

The words stopped Brooke in her tracks. She wasn't sure if this was just Taylor being drunk or if something bigger was brewing under the surface but either way, it hit close to home. "Why haven't you offered?" she countered back. The thought had been on her mind and it occasionally made her assume that Taylor wasn't too serious about their newly labeled relationship status.

"I," Taylor started before stopping abruptly and furrowing her brows. "I don't know. I kind of thought you might not want to."

"Why would I not want to meet your friends? I'm your girlfriend."

Taylor lifted her head off the back of the couch and found Brooke's eyes. "I've only met Nina so I started to think you were embarrassed to be with me or something. Are you embarrassed? Do you not like me? Because I like you."

Brooke sat back down beside her girlfriend and looked into her dazed eyes. She might have been drunk, but she was an honest drunk and Brooke found it endearing. She was being vulnerable. Maybe Brooke wasn't the only one that was scared of the fragile nature of their relationship. Maybe for every fear Brooke had, Taylor had a similar one. Maybe they should talk about these things instead of being afraid of finding out the truth and popping their bubble. Brooke took a deep breath and chose honesty. "I like you a lot. And I'm not embarrassed to be with you at all, but I am a little nervous to meet your friends. What if they don't like me? What if they think I'm too old for you?"

Taylor rolled her eyes as her head followed the movements. "I literally was bombarded today with questions about you. Everyone wants to meet you to know that I'm not making you up."

Brooke smiled and took Taylor's hands in her own. "I'm pretty real. You can touch me and find out."

Taylor squeezed Brooke's hand and smiled in return. "I know, but seriously I sat there talking about this smart, funny, incredibly gorgeous woman who sets my body on fire and takes me to free parties and concerts and cute dates who I allegedly met randomly at the bar. It's too good to be true and I kind of need to show you off."

Brooke felt her heart flutter at Taylor's description of her. It was everything she had hoped she'd be to the woman who she felt the exact same thing about. "Let's go out with your friends," Brooke said simply, feeling her anxiety start to disappear. It didn't matter what Taylor's friends thought of her; all that mattered was what Taylor felt.

"Really?" Taylor squealed, as if she almost expected Brooke to say she didn't want to do that. That made Brooke even more disappointed because at some point, she must have given off that impression.

"Of course. Plan it."

A huge smile spread across Taylor's cheeks before she threw her arms around Brooke's shoulders and held her tightly. "I'll take that water and snack now," Taylor said in her ear. "And a kiss."

Brooke leaned in and brought their lips together before she walked to the kitchen. She didn't have too many hangover prevention options at the moment but landed on some bread and cheese, hoping that would be sufficient for the alcohol absorption.

Taylor was fast asleep on the couch by the time Brooke came back. The alcohol and profession of feelings must have knocked her out. Brooke nudged Taylor awake and led her to bed where as promised, Taylor was the big spoon for a change.

Brooke had never been so nervous to meet the friends of someone she was dating. Not her first girlfriend's back in college. Not Jaclyn's. No one else except Taylor. She knew that she was a good person and people should be able to see that, but friends were always quick to be critical and judgmental. Especially the younger they were.

Meeting Taylor's friends was terrifying because all she could think about now was her age. And it wasn't even a big deal. They all knew she was forty and that they were ten-years apart. No one batted an eyelash over Brangelina's twelve-year gap. Although they didn't end well so maybe that wasn't the best comparison.

Now as Brooke stood outside of the apartment building where Taylor and her friends were on the roof for an evening of barbeque and cocktails, she remembered what it felt like to be young and entering into these situations for the first time. Or how she judged boyfriends Nina or any of her other friends dated. Or how her own girlfriends were judged. She should have been prepared now – she had years of experience on her side, yet she was terrified.

She wished she told Taylor to meet her earlier so they could arrive together, finding herself a bit anxious to walk into a crowd without the comfort of Taylor beside her. *Now who's the immature one?*

She took a deep breath and pushed open the rooftop door to the sound of laughter and music on the other side of the building. She stepped over the concrete divide and heard the voices start to quiet down as they processed that the final guest had arrived.

"Brooke!" Taylor cheered as she bounced over to her girlfriend. "You made it," she said with a lopsided smile as she threw her arms around Brooke's shoulders. It was obvious that Taylor was a bit tipsy; also evident from her flirtatious texts scattered with uncharacteristic typos an hour prior. Day drinking was always dangerous, which Taylor should have learned a week prior when she drunkenly showed up at Brooke's apartment and had a hangover to deal with the day after.

"I made it," Brooke said as she accepted the sweet kiss on her lips.

"I can't wait to show you off," Taylor cooed as she laced their fingers together and dragged Brooke towards where her friends were sitting. Feeling Taylor's hand in her own gave Brooke all the strength she needed to overcome her fears now. Taylor made her feel like anything was possible, even the harsh criticisms from a group of late twenty somethings.

"Everyone, this is Brooke," Taylor said as she beamed back at her girlfriend with a proud smile on her face. "Brooke, meet everyone."

Brooke very quickly learned just who everyone was. There was Jessica, a graphic designer and her tattoo artist boyfriend, Max. Ariana who worked as a book editor and kept her eyes on Brooke longer than she felt comfortable at times. Melinda who had the bluest eyes Brooke had ever seen that periodically would get exposed when she lowered her sunglasses to stare at Brooke. And then was Hayley, who proceeded to talk Brooke's ear off for the next twenty-five minutes about topics ranging from what Brooke's favorite book was (*Wuthering Heights*), romantic comedy (*Notting Hill*), and what she considered the greatest song of all time ("Bohemian Rhapsody"). Brooke didn't know if she passed whatever test Hayley was giving her, but considering the smile on the young woman's face, she sensed she did pretty good.

When Hayley finally took a break from her inquisition, Taylor got up and grabbed Brooke's hand to lead her towards the makeshift bar. "Is it just me, or are your friends staring at me?" Brooke asked as Taylor refilled Brooke's cup with rosé.

"They are," Taylor said simply without any concern. "The early first impression results are in and I've heard the words hot, magical, smart, sexy, and wife material thrown around."

Brooke laughed nervously, mostly at the last description. She was glad that Taylor's friends had that first impression of her, but all that mattered was that Taylor agreed with them all. "Wow, I'm flattered. Who said what? Maybe I should pursue being with them."

Taylor placed their cups down on the folding table and turned to look at Brooke. Her eyes were slightly glazed over but they had a mischievous sparkle to them. She placed her hands around Brooke's waist and pulled her closer so their bodies were flushed together. "Are you trying to make me jealous?"

"Not at all," she said playfully.

Taylor nodded and licked her bottom lip. "You can't pursue them because you're *my* hot, sexy girlfriend."

"I am," Brooke said softly as she gently pushed Taylor's hair out of her face that the breeze was blowing across her eyes.

"Get a room!" A voice yelled out from across the roof. Brooke knew it was directed at her and Taylor but that didn't stop her from leaning in and kissing Taylor to the chagrin of the crowd. Brooke pulled away with a giggle before she picked up their cups and walked back to the sofa with Taylor attached to her waist.

All of Brooke's worries steeped in insecurity about being judged by Taylor's friends for being older and divorced went out the window, or off the roof, the moment they sat back down with the group and Brooke finally relaxed. She was able to enjoy herself and have fun, rather than get caught up in her own thoughts. All of these new people she met were extremely likeable and friendly and only seemed to want the best for Taylor, as did she.

Chapter Sixteen

Brooke silently drove Mary home from the hospital where she had her latest CT scan. Worry and dread sat in the backseat of the sedan as well and seemed to drown out the music on the radio. Mary would usually loudly sing along to any Fleetwood Mac song, as would Brooke, but right now "Dreams" didn't feel the same. Thunder was all Brooke could hear inside her mind. Another migraine inching forward to match the pain in her chest.

When they pulled into the driveway and Brooke turned off the ignition, Mary put her hand on her daughter's forearm to stop her from opening the door and getting out of the car. "I'm sorry," she said softly.

Brooke raised her eyes off the steering wheel and looked at the woman sitting beside her. "For what?"

Mary's eyes were glassy when she lifted her head to meet her daughter's gaze. "For everything. For not listening to your pleas to quit smoking. For pretending it would be okay. For telling you to be a daughter, not a parent."

Brooke swallowed hard. She knew this was difficult for her mother who was equally as stubborn as she was loving. She hated to admit she was wrong. It's part of the reason why Brooke thought she was typically quick to admit she was wrong; she never wanted to be like her mother in that sense. "I just wanted you to be healthy."

"I know," she said amidst a sigh. "And I want you to know that I love you so much."

"Mom, stop," Brooke interrupted her, feeling like this was a conversation seeded in dread about the future. It was the conversation they had been tip-toeing around for a few months now but that didn't mean Brooke wanted to have it either. "I know that."

Mary shook her head and squeezed Brooke's arm harder. "Let me talk," she said before she exhaled sharply. "I know sometimes I've been hard on you but I've always known you were going to become this incredible woman. I'm so proud of you."

Hearing her mother say this across the car console hurt Brooke even more when all she wanted to do was jump over and embrace her to stop this conversation. To be cradled in the arms she was raised in and might be soon deprived of ever experiencing again.

"I might not survive to see your next success or marriage or meet your children but I know you'll be amazing at everything," Mary continued.

Tears fell on Brooke's jeans, freely falling from her eyes. This conversation was so unexpected, so raw, that it was breaking her apart. It was shocking that they had made it this far without having a talk like this, which meant that something had started to change within Mary as well. "Don't say that," Brooke said softly. "You'll be around for everything."

Mary's glance out the window told Brooke everything she needed to know. Her mother's body knew she wouldn't be around for too long and it's not like within the next few weeks Brooke would get a new job, married, or have a baby. Mary would likely miss out on all of those milestones and to Brooke, that was more heartbreaking than her not experiencing them to begin with.

Her mother always wanted to be a grandmother. She told Brooke this countless times during her twenties and thirties. She wanted a little angel to spoil and take to Disney and get excited to come to grandma's house. It was something Brooke could picture seeing happening behind her eyes. And then she selfishly deprived her mother of that joy by marrying Jaclyn. Sure, Brooke also said she didn't want kids because she was also being selfish. She wanted to focus on her own career and take lavish vacations without added responsibility. She chose her own fun with a woman who convinced her they didn't need kids to have a happy marriage and life, and then she screwed her over by going and having a baby anyway.

If Brooke listened to the part of her heart that wanted a child to call her own, one that would adore their grandmother, then her own mother wouldn't be sitting here reflecting on all the things she was going to miss out on. All the things that Brooke never managed to give her. "I regret marrying Jaclyn," Brooke said to offer her mother an olive branch to know she wasn't the only one with regrets. "I was clouded by love and fun that I didn't realize how much I was hurting by not having kids."

Mary turned her head back and grabbed her daughter's hand. "You had to marry her," she started. "You were so in love and maybe you needed that breakup to reset your priorities. Everything happens for a reason."

Having your wife cheat on you and get pregnant wasn't something that Brooke thought happened for a valid reason aside from a devastating cruel joke.

"It's not like I'm in a good position to have them now," Brooke tried to rationalize. "Geriatric pregnancy and all."

Mary laughed and for a second it was startling but then comforting to Brooke's ears. "For a brilliant woman, sometimes you are so dumb. Did you not see the hospital we were just at? Science is on your side. You can have a surrogate. You could adopt. Or you could marry a hot young thing."

Brooke raised her brow at her mother's last statement and the playful smirk on display on her face. "Dad told me you have a new girlfriend. Why didn't you tell me?"

Brooke deviated her gaze over to the console to avoid her mother's questioning eyes. She thought back to the weekend they spent together in New York and how Brooke avoided bringing Taylor up because she felt it was too fragile to share. Like it was information better suited for her father given everything else that was going on. "I didn't want you to get your hopes up. It's only been three months."

"Three months is not three weeks," Mary exclaimed. "And judging by that hickey on your neck, it's been going well."

Brooke blushed and gave up trying to fight it. Her mother knew and there was nothing she could do about it. She wasn't a seventeen-year-old hiding a hickey and a secret lover; she was forty and had a girlfriend. Which also seemed a bit old to have exposed marks left like that. "She is the Dyson," Brooke said with a light laugh.

Mary patted her daughter's thigh, wiped her cheeks and opened the car door. "Now, I want us to go inside and not tell your father about this little cryfest confessional but you're going to show me this woman and tell me everything."

Putting aside how emotionally raw Brooke felt in this moment, she followed her mother's orders. Her father was blind to their slightly bloodshot eyes as he was engrossed in a documentary on TV while Brooke told her mom everything about Taylor.

Mary gushed over Taylor's appearance and said she didn't care if that made her vain; she only wanted a beautiful woman beside her beautiful daughter. It was everything Brooke could have asked for and more, except she wished they all had more time together. Forever would be nice.

Fourth of July weekend was full of invitations for Taylor. Jessica and Max were having another barbeque on her roof. Ariana was renting a car and driving out to Jones Beach. Hayley was going to Brooklyn to watch the fireworks. After much deliberation, Taylor decided that she would go with Hayley. Watching the fireworks seemed like a fun and simple way to celebrate, even if a lot of alcohol was involved earlier in the day.

The last time Taylor watched the fireworks was the first summer after she moved to New York with Liam. That year she vowed to do every possible touristy thing New York had to offer. She went to the Statue of Liberty, the top of the Empire State Building and One World, she saw Broadway shows, and took cheesy photos in Times Square. The only thing she didn't do was venture there for New Year's Eve to watch the ball drop. She had to draw the line somewhere.

Watching the fireworks this year felt fitting. She was just as in love with New York as she was seven years ago when she and Liam moved across the country. Except now Liam was an ocean away not even celebrating the Fourth of July. But Taylor knew the real reason she was enjoying New York was because of Brooke.

Brooke ignited a new sense of adventure and curiosity inside of her. She was exhilarated at discovering new places with her. Trying new restaurants or bars. And even the places she had already been, she found herself enjoying them even more because of her girlfriend. She felt like her entire life had been rejuvenated in every possible way.

A shrill scream coming from Hayley's mouth beside her startled Taylor out of her thoughts. "Why are you screaming?" she questioned as she sat up.

"Jessica just texted us. She's engaged!"

Taylor grabbed her phone and was shocked to see the photo their friend had sent them. A new shiny ring was located on Jessica's left hand with an accompanying text that said, "Does this ring make me look engaged?"

"Who would have thought Independence Day would be romantic to become dependent," Taylor joked.

"Don't be a bitter bitch," Hayley said with a laugh. "They set off their own fireworks."

Taylor looked at the photo again and drowned out Hayley discussing the shape of the pear diamond. Taylor couldn't focus on it because she was having conflicting thoughts of her own. Was she a bitter bitch? Of course not. She was extremely happy for Jessica and Max. They were her friends. They were a good couple. Yet somehow it made her feel less than and she couldn't understand why.

Taylor was never a believer in the *need* to get married. It would be nice if it happened but she could also be with someone and not need the government to validate their feelings and love. But maybe that was the immature side of her that focused on patriarchy over personal passion. Maybe she was growing up too because the idea of getting engaged seemed exciting. She wanted to share a photo like Jessica did and have her friends scream in excitement. She wanted to show off an engagement ring and have people know she was with someone she loved. Her materialistic side said she'd definitely want a bigger ring than Jessica had, but then part of her kind of liked the idea of being the one to propose to someone. To shock her girlfriend with a ring. To make her feel how much she loved her. And then get a ring of her own, of course.

As Taylor looked back down at her phone and the insistent text messages coming through the group chat, she saw one appear from Brooke.

Brooke.

How nice would it be to marry Brooke? To have a partner that is so breathtakingly beautiful and not have it be the most important thing about her. Brooke was genuinely kind. She was caring. Compassionate. Smart. Sophisticated. Funny. Successful. Okay, maybe the last one was a bit of a bonus but imagine the life they could have together? Would that ever be in their cards? Taylor had no idea what could happen in one month let alone a few years but she secretly hoped for it. Even if she knew she'd never tell anyone else she felt this way. Including Brooke. Not yet.

Brooke [9:12pm]
You can't get more patriotic than 4th of July fireworks in DC!

Below was a photo of explosions of light illuminating the Washington monument. Taylor selfishly wished she could have gone with her for the weekend. It would have been fun to be there for that and even more exhilarating, and nerve-racking, to meet Brooke's parents. Taylor wasn't sure what Brooke was up to in her hometown. She had been back down there a few weekends already since they met and she didn't get the vibe that anything was wrong but it almost felt like Brooke was working a second job or living a double life. Maybe she was.

Taylor [9:13pm]
That's beautiful. I'd be really happy to be an American if you were president

Brooke [9:13pm]
Hahaha we haven't even had a female president yet. Let alone a lesbian one

Taylor [9:14pm]
That would be hot though. You'd look sooooo good in a power suit

Brooke [9:15pm]
Are you trying to tell me you're into role play?

Taylor [9:15pm]
Now that you mention it...

Taylor [9:15pm]
But no. I was just thinking you'd make a good politician. Ever consider it?

There was a delay in Brooke's response and Taylor wondered if she struck gold.

She used that delay to congratulate Jessica on her engagement and join in on the plots for what her engagement party should be like.

Brooke [9:19pm]
Hell no! I'd never survive public scrutiny like that. And I like having some free time for a life

Taylor knew it was a stretch but at least she asked.

Taylor [9:20pm]
Any chance you want to use some of that free time on me tomorrow when you get back? I can make you dinner, Madam President

Brooke [9:21pm]
Okay but my secret service will have to come

Taylor [9:21pm]
That sounds kinky

Brooke [9:22pm]
Lol be careful tonight. People drink more than they care about democracy

Taylor [9:22pm]
Yes, Madam President. I'll see you tomorrow!

"Hello!" Hayley yelled at Taylor, "I've been talking to you for two minutes and you didn't even pick your eyes up off your phone!"

"Sorry," Taylor blushed as she locked her phone and put it away. "I was talking to Brooke."

"Did you tell her you want to get engaged?"

"What?" Taylor shrieked. She didn't mean to actually yell but somehow the accusation struck a nerve.

Hayley motioned to her phone and Taylor grabbed it to read the group text chat she had been ignoring.

Ariana [9:20pm]
Ten bucks says Taylor is next

Hayley [9:20pm]
Omg yasssssss!!

Jessica [9:21pm]
But who would propose to who?!

Jessica [9:21pm]
I think it'll be Brooke

Hayley [9:22pm]
No way! It'll be Tay. I'm literally looking at her right now drooling onto her phone talking to her

"You're an asshole," Taylor said with a rushed breath. "We should be focusing on Jessica and her engagement. Please and thank you."

"You didn't deny any of it," Hayley stoked again before the first fireworks setoff in the night sky. A colorful burst of beauty that came at the right time to avoid continuing the conversation.

Taylor didn't confirm or deny because she didn't even know the answer herself.

As soon as Brooke got off Amtrak back into Manhattan, she jumped on the train to Taylor's apartment. There was a sense of desperation overtaking her as she counted down the minutes until she could feel safe in Taylor's arms. After the conversation with her mother on Friday and over the weekend, Brooke found herself craving her girlfriend for a sense of purpose. For an anchor to keep her grounded, and yet help her soar in the clouds full of joy and happiness at the same time.

"Hey," Taylor said with a giant smile the second she opened her door. "You're right on time, I'm almost done making dinner."

"It can wait," Brooke said as desire took over and she grabbed Taylor and kissed her deeply as they stumbled backwards towards Taylor's bed. In moments like this, Brooke really liked how convenient everything was in Taylor's studio apartment. They could move from the door to the bed in a few steps without needing to break their lips apart.

"Whoa, easy tiger," Taylor said with a laugh when she finally broke her lips free. "What's gotten into you? Was it me calling you Madam President?"

Brooke laughed as she leaned back on Taylor's lap and allowed her mind to catch up to her libido. "Sorry, I just had this insane desire to kiss you."

Taylor leaned up and kissed her sweetly. "I really like it, but I'm going to burn the apartment down if you don't let me get up."

Brooke rolled over and allowed Taylor to sprint towards the oven. As she sat there looking at Taylor maneuver around the small kitchen, she couldn't help but feel warm at the idea of how nice it would be to one day live together. To cook meals together. To come home to an apartment that included the woman that had gotten under her skin in all the right ways. When Taylor declared that dinner was saved, Brooke stopped thinking about things that would likely never happen. Instead, she got up from the bed and let Taylor serve her a delicious meal.

"I found out today that I have to head to LA for work next week," Brooke shared, already finding herself saddened by the fact that she'd go a week without seeing Taylor. There was a reason why she shouldn't check her work email on a Sunday.

"Oh yeah? Maybe you can go meet my parents."

Brooke almost choked on her red wine as soon as her mind processed what Taylor suggested. She had mentioned that her parents moved out to California a couple of years ago, but she never thought Taylor would suggest that she *meet* her parents. Not now. Not ever. That was what people in a serious relationship did. Were they there now? It wasn't just in Brooke's mind? "What?"

"My parents live in Santa Barbara. When are you coming home? Maybe I can go out to visit and we can have a mini vacation." When Brooke didn't respond, too shocked and suddenly nervous to speak, Taylor looked up and clearly saw the baffled expression on Brooke's face. Brooke told herself to respond, to blink, to do anything. Yet she remained frozen. "I'm sorry, that was really presumptuous of me. Is that too soon?"

If Brooke was being honest with herself, she would have accepted how happy it made her to hear Taylor say she wanted Brooke to meet her parents. That was a massive step in a relationship and showed that Taylor was serious enough about her to introduce her to her parents. It was the actual action of *doing* so that terrified her into a comatose state. What if Taylor's parents thought she was too old for their daughter? What if they looked down on her for already being divorced? What if they simply didn't like her? Despite Taylor's closest friends seeming to like her, Taylor's parents could be a complete game changer.

"Maybe," Brooke said as she tried to rationalize a reason for why she shouldn't meet them. She couldn't say it was because she didn't want to introduce Taylor to her own parents yet either. "It's only been like three months since we started dating."

Brooke hated the way Taylor's face fell upon hearing her words. That was not her intention at all but it was reality. Taylor's green eyes darted towards the table as her shoulders slumped in the chair. "Shit, I'm sorry. I didn't mean to make this awkward."

Brooke extended her arm across the table to place her hand on Taylor's forearm, hoping some physical contact could lessen the blow. This was a blow, right? Brooke wasn't just imagining this reaction because she wanted some sort of confirmation that Taylor truly cared about her? "That's just a big deal. I mean I feel like I just met your friends and now I'd be meeting your parents. You know?"

"Yeah, totally, you're right. I wasn't thinking clearly," Taylor said as she abruptly got up to start cleaning off the table.

Panic spread across Brooke's body. Taylor was obviously hurt and disappointed all because Brooke was putting a divide between them out of fear. Fear that only she seemed to have. She got up and wrapped her arms around her girlfriend's waist to try to salvage the situation the best she could, if she could. "But if you want to go visit them and then spend the weekend together, I'd be open to that."

"Oh yeah?" Taylor asked as she turned around in Brooke's arms.

"Yeah."

"And what are we going to do all weekend?" Taylor asked with a raised brow, removing all traces of sadness that were present moments ago.

"Sightsee and do things," Brooke said with a playful smile as she placed a light kiss on Taylor's lips.

"What kind of things?" Taylor asked with Brooke's bottom lip between her teeth.

As Brooke started to deepen the kiss, she pushed them towards Taylor's bed in the corner of the room. "Let me give you a sneak peek."

Deflecting the conversation, and the insecurities she had, with sex, wasn't Brooke's proudest moment but she didn't know how else to react. She had just spent seventy-two hours with her parents researching potential hospice options and worrying if that was the last time she'd see her mother alive. How could she realistically go and meet Taylor's parents now when she was so emotional? The sight of Taylor with her mother might shatter Brooke and all the protective barriers she tried to build up would come crumbling down. Even if she knew she should let them fall and see if Taylor would catch her.

Chapter Seventeen

Taylor landed at LAX with a giant smile on her face. She was exhausted since she decided to take a flight out of New York at six o'clock in the morning to get into town as early as possible, but even the lack of sleep couldn't keep the grin off of her face. She was surprising her parents at home today and come tomorrow, she'd be with Brooke for their first vacation together. Not even the idea of rush hour traffic and having to catch up on work once she got to Santa Barbara could ruin her mood.

When Taylor's parents decided to move from Phoenix to Santa Barbara five years ago, Taylor felt disappointed that her childhood home would be gone. That she'd never have a place to return to where she could reflect on memories. Until she quickly realized that Phoenix wasn't home – home was where she and the ones she loved were at any given moment. New York was her real home now and when she'd spend time at her parent's new house, she'd be just as comfortable since she was in their company.

Taylor [9:32am]
I just landed. Can't wait to see you tomorrow!

Taylor moved from her text messages to her GPS and started to guide her rental car out of the parking lot. She opened the windows to let the California air fill her lungs. It was hot, but it was invigorating. The last time she went on a vacation was in February when she and some friends had rented a house in Vermont and Taylor spent most of the time sitting by the fireplace reading and drinking wine. She wasn't interested in going skiing with everyone else but relished in the quiet time alone away from everything else in her life.

It was kind of ironic that despite being ten years younger, Taylor liked to spend her free time in the same way as Brooke did. She didn't need to go out to clubs and loud bars to have fun. Sure, she did enjoy that frequently, but she could be just as content with a good book or binge-watching TV shows from the comfort of her couch. Or Brooke's couch. She was really getting used to spending time at her apartment and feeling like she belonged in the older woman's life. It felt so natural. So genuine. So unexpected.

When Taylor stopped getting lost in her thoughts, she focused on driving as she sang along to Britney Spears' entire *Circus* album. By the time she pulled up to her parent's house, she was wide awake and ready to burst into the house dancing. As she parked, she laughed to herself at the small, but noticeable, Arizona Diamondbacks garden gnome her father had clearly tried to hide near a bush. It was shocking that her mother hadn't thrown that in the trash yet. Not only did she hate garden gnomes, but she also hated baseball.

Taylor grabbed her carry-on suitcase and walked up the driveway to ring the doorbell with her phone in her hand to record her mother's reaction once she opened the door.

"Taylor!" Louise yelled before she covered her mouth in shock. "What are you doing here?"

"I came to surprise you," Taylor said as she stopped her video and engulfed her mother in a tight embrace.

Louise pulled her daughter back to study her face before looking over her shoulder towards the street. "Is everything okay?"

"Yes, mom," Taylor said quickly, knowing her mother was quick to jump to conclusions and probably thought that her youngest daughter showing up unannounced must have meant something bad happened.

"I'm spending the weekend in LA so I thought I'd come see you."

Louise closed the door and wrapped her arm around Taylor's shoulders as they walked in the hallway. There was more decor on the walls compared to the last time Taylor visited. Previously empty beige wall space now housed a large abstract painting before some family photos. Including ones Taylor wished never saw the light of day again. "What's in LA? I wish you told me; I would have had lunch ready for you."

Taylor took a deep breath as she moved her bag out of the hallway and looked around for her father. She had hoped that today would be one of the days that he worked from home and she could have surprised him as well. "My girlfriend is in LA."

Louise stopped walking and turned around to look at her daughter. Taylor wished she was still recording her mother just to capture the confused look on her face. She hadn't told her parents about Brooke yet, not because she was embarrassed by any means, but because she was treading lightly. She didn't want to burst the perfect bubble they were in but was willing to throw the caution away on this trip. "You're dating someone in LA? Long-distance?"

"No, she lives in New York," Taylor confirmed. "She had to fly out for work and I decided to come too."

Louise nodded along as she stared at her daughter, her pupils finally returning to a normal size as relief set in that Taylor wasn't preparing for potential heartbreak in a long-distance relationship. "You didn't tell me you were seeing anyone."

"I'm telling you now," Taylor said with a playful smile as she sat down on the couch. "Where's dad?"

"He's in the office today. Should be home around five." Louise folded her arms across her chest before she continued her train of thought. If there was one thing Louise was, it was predictable. She never dropped a subject until she found out all of the necessary information and could come to terms with moving on to a new topic. "Is your girlfriend coming over?"

"No, I'm meeting her in LA."

When Louise didn't respond, Taylor looked up to see her mother looking at her with the same look she had grown accustomed to her entire life. When she was younger, she and her sister had nicknamed it "The Shook Look" because it always seemed to accompany some firm statement or accusation that would leave them both struggling to answer. It was usually used when they were in trouble, like the time Harper hid beers in the fridge or when Taylor snuck out to meet a girl she met online and her mother watched from the front window. This was not one of those moments and despite not doing anything wrong, she knew her mother was displeased.

"She's a couple of hours away and not coming here? That's a bit weird, do I need to be worried?" And there it was. The displeasure.

Taylor knew her mom would find it strange that Brooke wasn't coming over, even if she didn't know Brooke existed until mere moments ago. Her mother liked to be in the know about everything, and if there was one thing she always instilled into Taylor growing up, it was proper manners. To Louise, not coming over was probably as insulting as showing up to someone's house without bringing something for the host. The ultimate insult.

"No, it's just kind of soon, ya know?" Taylor tried to rationalize, even though she struggled with the concept herself. She wanted Brooke to meet her parents. She wanted Brooke to know she cared about her and was serious about their relationship. And she wanted everyone she came across with to know the same as well. "We've only been dating a few months and I don't want to get ahead of myself or anything and introduce you all."

Louise nodded along, processing the words as The Shook Look started to slowly fade away. "You introduced me to Katrina after two weeks of knowing her. You broke up with her the next week."

Taylor would never make that mistake again. She vowed never to introduce anyone to her parents unless it was serious. That's exactly why she didn't have any hesitation in asking Brooke if she wanted to meet her parents. Three months might have been a bit premature for introductions but she knew her feelings for the woman were real and deepening daily. "Yes, and I've learned my lesson," Taylor tried to prove herself. "She is no Katrina but I want to do this all right. Maybe next time you come to New York we can all go out to dinner."

Louise finally released the pressure on her daughter as she nodded in understanding, even if she was just pretending. "Do I at least get to see a photo of this mysterious woman that has you flying across the country?" Louise asked as she walked into the kitchen. "You want a coffee?"

"Sure," Taylor said as she got off the couch to follow her mother before she sat down at the kitchen table and pulled out her phone to see Brooke's text reply.

Brooke [11:37am]
I'm counting down the hours

Taylor suppressed her smile as she scrolled through her photos and pulled up the one she took of Brooke two weeks ago when they went to Brooklyn and spent the day walking along Brooklyn Bridge Park without a care in the world. Taylor couldn't control the smile on her face as she thought about their laughs when they went on the carousel like they were kids. It was a picture-perfect moment.

Louise put on her glasses to grab ahold of the phone that Taylor had just turned around and placed in front of her. "Oh Tay, she's beautiful." Hearing her mom say that only made Taylor feel even more proud that Brooke was her girlfriend. How did she get so lucky? She wasn't sure but she didn't want it to ever run out.

For the next hour, mother and daughter talked about Brooke and everything that was going on in Taylor's life back in New York.

Louise didn't bat an eyelash at Brooke's age or the fact that she was divorced. Afterall, Harper was already on her second husband. Louise was fascinated by Brooke's job as a publicist and when her father came home from work, he was equally as impressed when he received his Billy Joel shirt. He even inquired if Brooke could get them tickets in the future – a request Taylor hoped she'd get to cash in on because it meant they would still be together in the future.

Taylor took a picture of her and her dad wearing their matching shirts and sent it to Brooke.

Taylor [7:18pm]
The only thing missing here is you!

Brooke zoomed in on the photo on her phone screen. Taylor looked utterly adorable in her concert t-shirt and the smile on her father's face showed just how happy he was. A pang of regret coursed through Brooke's body as she thought about how selfish and cold it was for her to say no to meeting Taylor's parents. If the tables were turned, she'd see this as a huge red flag in the relationship and now she was intentionally giving Taylor reasons to doubt her feelings about her. She sighed and tried to find a way to lessen the blow the best she could.

Brooke [10:29pm]
I'm so exhausted that I would totally ruin that adorable photo if I was there

Brooke [10:30pm]
I hope your dad liked the shirt and I hope your parents

don't think I'm some sort of monster for not being there with you

Taylor [10:43pm]
I'm pretty sure they are obsessed with you

Taylor [10:43pm]
I mayyyy have spent a lot of time talking about you and how awesome you are

Taylor [10:44pm]
My mom also thinks you're beautiful. Like mother, like daughter

Taylor [10:45pm]
Ew that sounded weird. I TAKE IT BACK!

Brooke burst out laughing in her hotel room. There was always a sense of comfort and ease that came from talking with Taylor, even in silly text messages like this. No matter what, Taylor was guaranteed to bring a smile to her face.

Brooke [10:47pm]
She has good taste at least!

Taylor [10:48pm]
Anyway... wanna see baby Taylor photos?

Brooke [10:48pm]
You mean from last year?

Taylor [10:49pm]
Hysterical. I don't know why you didn't pursue standup comedy!

Before Brooke could reply, a series of photos popped up on her screen. All framed photos of Taylor over the years. Taylor in a pink tutu at what she assumed was a dance recital. Taylor and her family at the Grand Canyon. Taylor and her sister with Mickey Mouse at Disneyland. Taylor graduating high school and college. Her heart clenched as she zoomed in on every image. Taylor went from an adorable child to a cute teenager to a gorgeous woman.

Brooke [10:53pm]
Awww!!! You were so cute!!!

Taylor [10:53pm]
WERE?

Brooke [10:54pm]
Send me a pic of you now and I'll let you know what I think

What Brooke received was not what she was expecting. She figured Taylor would send her a silly selfie with a cheeky grin. She was not expecting a photo that was taken at an angle that showed her lying in bed wearing a camisole top pulled down just enough to leave little to the imagination and her legs tucked underneath her, very clearly only wearing her underwear. As she looked at the photo and felt her breath start to get caught in her throat, another one came in with Taylor puckering her lips towards the screen.

Taylor [10:56pm]
Thoughts?

Brooke [10:58pm]
You are so beautiful and incredibly sexy

Brooke [10:58pm]
And definitely still cute

Taylor [10:59pm]
Uh huh. Now where's my pic??

Brooke ran her fingers through her hair nervously. She didn't want to not deliver a photo, but she felt like she looked horrible. She had just taken a shower and she wasn't wearing any makeup on her very tired and puffy face. She was wearing a hotel bathrobe; a far cry from Taylor's satin camisole and underwear. She took a deep breath and started to take numerous photos trying to be equally cute and seductive, if that was even possible.

Taylor [11:04pm]
You are truly the most beautiful woman I've ever seen

Brooke found herself stunned at the declaration, despite the fact that Taylor had told her this before. She struggled to think it was real, thanks to the mountains of insecurity that Jaclyn had dumped on her.

Brooke [11:06pm]
You should look in the mirror more often then

Taylor [11:07pm]
I can't wait to look at you in person tomorrow

Taylor [11:08pm]
Gonna go to sleep now before my mom wakes me up at 6 to go for a walk... she's kind of insane. You're lucky you're missing out

Brooke [11:09pm]
Good luck! See you tomorrow

Taylor [11:09pm]
I'll see you in my dreams first ;)

Brooke replied with a kissy face emoji before she threw her phone down on the bed. She was starting to realize just how in over her head she was.

When Taylor arrived at Brooke's hotel, the first thing she did was wrap her arms around Brooke's neck to kiss her deeply. She couldn't understand why her desire to kiss Brooke so passionately kept happening after not seeing each other for days. This time she wondered if it was their physical distance for most of the week. The feeling that Brooke was so far, and now she was here with her arms wrapped around Taylor's waist, meeting Taylor's desperate kisses move for move. The light moan that escaped her lips was enough to make Taylor's knees weak. "Hi," she said against her lips.

"Hi," Brooke replied as she linked her hands with Taylor's behind her back.

"Is it just me or does kissing you in California feel even better than it does at home?"

Brooke rested her head in the nook of Taylor's neck. "Maybe the sun is getting to you."

"You're getting to me," Taylor said with a smile. "But speaking of sun, when can I finally see you in a bathing suit?"

Brooke laughed and pulled Taylor into her hotel room. "You've seen me naked; I didn't think a bathing suit would be as appealing."

Taylor couldn't help but look forward to it because the mental vision she had of Brooke in a bathing suit was arousing. Solely because she knew exactly what was underneath. She tried to shake the inappropriate thoughts out of her head as she looked out the hotel window and collected herself. "Everything about you is appealing," she admitted. "Especially if less clothing is involved."

Brooke wrapped her arms around Taylor's waist from behind as she leaned her face against the side of Taylor's. It felt really nice for Brooke to only be an inch taller than Taylor, if that even, to let her perfectly mold up against Taylor's body. In this moment, Taylor felt whole. She never thought that a partner should "complete you" because that would imply that she was broken. She felt whole because for the first time in a long time, she felt a part of herself come alive that previously was dormant. Brooke wasn't the missing piece of her, she just held the key to open up the locked doors.

Taylor spun around in her arms and looked into Brooke's hazel eyes. The specks of yellow and orange popping more than usual from the sun reflecting off the window. "Do you know what I've always wanted to do in LA?"

"What?"

"See a movie at the Grauman's Theatre and pretend I was there for a movie premiere."

Brooke smiled and tightened her grip around Taylor's waist. "You would. We can do that."

"Really? You're okay being in LA and of all the things we do, we go to the movies?"

When they had discussed what they wanted to do for their forty-eight hours in LA together, neither of them had strong preferences. Brooke said she just wanted to spend time together and Taylor, well, she had been too focused on the idea of the vacation to actually think about what to do. Mainly because she knew she had to see her parents first and open up about her relationship status.

"I told you I didn't care what we did," Brooke said sweetly as she pushed Taylor's hair behind her ear. "I'm just happy we're here together."

"Me too," Taylor echoed, ignoring her heart pounding in her chest. This moment felt oddly heavy. The doors that had been opened were now pulling her in on an exploration of the areas previously hidden and what all the writing on the walls actually meant.

"I did make us reservations at The Beverly Hills Hotel, so we need to get going there first."

The Beverly Hills Hotel, which Taylor had casually mentioned she wanted to eat at in hopes of seeing a celebrity. The two times she had been to LA, neither Liam nor Harper wanted to go there to eat and Taylor had missed out on her chance. "You remembered," she said softly.

Brooke didn't seem to think anything of it; that naturally she would have listened to Taylor and made sure she took her where she wanted. "Of course I did," she said with a smile. "You can look up movie showtimes while we're in the car." She placed a soft kiss on Taylor's lips before pulling away to get ready to leave the hotel. She was completely oblivious to how dumbfounded Taylor was, rooted in the same spot understanding just how much she cared about Brooke.

"You're amazing," she finally found the words to say.

"So are you, babe," Brooke replied with her signature beautiful smile.

Babe. Taylor still hadn't gotten used to that word. Or used to Brooke in general. She made a mental note that she needed to remind Brooke just how much she meant to her at every possible moment. But for now, they had an entire day together to enjoy lunch, walking around Rodeo Drive and looking at Beverly Hills mansions like tourists before ending the day watching a movie. She might not have been in a gown or walking a red carpet, but Taylor felt like a million bucks. All because of the woman beside her.

On Saturday, the couple went to the Santa Monica Pier before they took a ride out to Malibu and went to El Matador State Beach. Taylor finally got Brooke in a bathing suit just like she wanted and Brooke relished in how desired she felt just seeing Taylor look at her in admiration and with a touch of lust.

When they came back from going in the water and were drying off, Taylor sat between Brooke's legs on a towel as they gazed out at the ocean. The sounds of children squealing in the distance were the only noises they heard aside from the waves crashing against the shore. It was completely peaceful and Brooke couldn't help but run her hands up and down Taylor's arms enjoying the embrace of her leaning back on her.

As the sky started to turn a shade of orange that you'd only see in paintings, Taylor jumped up to take a photo. Brooke watched Taylor staring at the sunset through the rock formation in front of her. In this moment, she truly didn't know what was more breathtaking: this natural marvel and the orange sky or the woman trying to capture it on her phone. Brooke quickly decided it was Taylor, especially when she looked over her shoulder to beckon Brooke closer for a selfie. With her arms wrapped around Brooke's shoulders, she took a photo of them with the sunset behind them.

"I'm so happy I met you," Taylor said with a lazy smile as she looked into Brooke's eyes.

Brooke felt that immensely. In fact, she felt too much for the woman beside her. All of the feelings started to bubble to the surface and her mind very quicky caught up to what was being processed. *I love her.* Brooke tried to quiet the voice in her head by placing a soft kiss to Taylor's lips, which Taylor naturally caught on camera.

"Best picture ever," Taylor said softly as she looked at them on the screen. It felt almost too good to be true. In what universe would Brooke be so fortunate to have found love again? And with a woman ten years younger than her that slipped her phone number with a check at a bar while she was on a date. This was something you'd see in a movie or hear about from a friend who has all the luck in the world. Brooke was never that person.

As Taylor laced their hands together to walk back to their towels, Brooke started to wonder if her luck was changing or if it would quickly run out. Only one of those options was possible and she was terrified of finding out which would be victorious.

Chapter Eighteen

Three days later, Brooke nervously sat at a wine bar waiting for Nina to show up. She was already fifteen minutes late, which was uncharacteristic for her best friend, and that led Brooke to down her glass of Pinot Noir quicker than she even realized. She was too distracted on scolding herself for her feelings and for all of the mistakes she had already made, and all the ones she was capable of still making. She needed someone like Nina to tell her that she couldn't make another because she didn't know if she'd ever be able to recover.

By the time Nina settled in to the vacant seat, apologizing for a meeting running late, Brooke was on her second glass of wine. As she swallowed another sip, she felt the words foaming at her mouth begging for a release. It was shocking that she was able to keep them inside for as long as she did. "I'm in love with Taylor," she announced without any build up and context.

Nina looked across the table without changing her expression at all. She was so still that Brooke didn't even think she heard her until she finally spoke. "Tell me something I don't know."

"What?" Brooke questioned.

"I've known for weeks," Nina stated as if this wasn't some major revelation that had been keeping Brooke up the last three nights and completely distracted during the day. "Maybe even since the first month you started dating but I knew you needed to figure it out yourself."

"You're full of shit," Brooke scoffed as she picked up her wine glass to down the contents. Getting the words off her chest wasn't helping alleviate the tension and anxiety of their existence. "I've liked her all along, obviously, but I only just realized I loved her in LA."

Nina rolled her eyes dramatically. "It doesn't matter when, it just matters that you do. And what are you going to do about it?"

That had been the question keeping her up at night ever since she got back into her apartment. Her apartment that felt so cold and lonely without Taylor there. The suffocating reminders of how much she felt and how much she wanted but was too afraid to confess. "I'm not going to tell her if that's what you're asking."

"So, let me get this straight. You're going to not only lie to her about your mom but now lie about your feelings," Nina mocked. "Some girlfriend you are."

When Nina put it that way, Brooke didn't like how it sounded, even if it was the truth. She felt like she wasn't lying about her mom or about her feelings, she was just avoiding it completely. That wasn't any better. "I just can't tell her now. It's way too soon and I don't want to scare her away. And what if she doesn't feel the same?"

Nina rolled her eyes over the rim of her wine glass. "She looks at you like you're the center of her universe. I'm sure she feels the same."

"Not taking that chance," Brooke said quickly as she waved her hands in front of her. "I will take another glass of wine though." She flagged the waiter and ordered another drink she knew she'd regret in the morning.

Nina silently stared at her best friend; eyes full of judgement that Brooke knew very well. She thought that Nina might tell her she was making a mistake being with Taylor, that she was only setting herself up for heartbreak. Instead, she was met with the complete opposite. When Nina finally took a long sip of her wine, she placed the glass down and leaned on her elbows to grow closer to her friend. "Can I ask you a serious question?"

"Of course."

"What did you honestly think was going to happen?" Her tone wasn't as accusatory as Brooke was expecting, but it was full of curiosity. "You're her *girlfriend*. Were you expecting to just never have any deep feelings or let things progress past that stage? Forever girlfriends that don't fall in love? Or did you just plan on breaking up at some point?"

Brooke wasn't thinking, that was the problem. She was blindly following her heart that had latched onto Taylor and never wanted to let go. She wanted to bury herself deep in the sensations of happiness every time Taylor's name appeared on her phone. Every time she saw her face. And God, every time they connected physically. If she could bottle up how she felt when Taylor touched her, she was sure it could be studied to cure ailments all over the world. Maybe even provide world peace. Maybe.

But along with those sensations came the deeper feelings. The ones she could no longer deny. The ones she wished didn't happen but there was no controlling them. She was in love. And it surpassed the physical. Taylor made her happy just by existing. She never wanted to lose her now that she had her yet she knew she would.

They never had serious conversations about the future. Yes, Taylor was the one who wanted clarity on whether they were girlfriends. Yet, Brooke felt like that was an easy stepping stone. When she was thirty, she met Jaclyn and also wasn't thinking about getting married and a future mere months after meeting. That all came two years later before it came crumbling down. And maybe they shouldn't have gotten married to begin with.

"I kind of pretended the feelings weren't there all along," Brooke softly admitted. If there was anyone she could share that with, it was Nina. "I'm scared. I don't want to lose her."

"You'll only lose her if you give in to fear," Nina countered. "No one dies from love or heartbreak either. Don't forget that."

"What if this is just a summer fling for her?" Brooke asked, feeling herself falling down the rabbit hole. "What if she doesn't really care about me?"

"You technically met in spring in April. You've transcended seasons." Nina wore a smug smile as she took a sip of her wine. "And I'm pretty sure she cares about you a lot. She wanted you to meet her parents. She flew across the country to spend a weekend with you. I can't even get my husband to drive upstate for the weekend with me."

Brooke sighed deeply. She knew she was looking for excuses to run. She was scared. *Terrified.* To finally have something and realize you might lose it was devastating. She was fully aware that she was acting like the immature one in the relationship at this point and was using Taylor's age as a scapegoat to not have to own up to how she felt and how hard she had fallen. Ten years ago, Brooke wouldn't be panicking like this. Ten years ago, she hadn't known what it was like to have your entire life turned upside down at the expense of someone you loved.

Brooke glanced up at her best friend and wondered when she became the source of rationality in her life. This was the woman that thought taking Irish car bomb shots was a good idea. The one who bounced from bad boy to bad boy in college and beyond. The one who regardless of her crass attitude was the most honest and genuine friend she ever had in her life. The one she'd turn to now, too ashamed to admit her feelings to any other friend who simply wouldn't understand Brooke's insecurity and the damage done by Jaclyn.

"I love you," Brooke declared simply, finding it easier to tell her best friend that than the other woman she loved, in a much different way.

"I know that but you need to tell the person you're *in* love with," she emphasized. "Unless you're finally in love with me too. I might be willing to leave Jayson for you."

Brooke smiled and felt some of her fears start to disappear. "We'd be terrible together and you know it."

"Yeah, considering I'm straight," Nina said with a laugh before her face grew somber. "I'm worried about you, Brooke. You seem like someone who's going to fuck up because they're trying so hard to be perfect and control everything."

That was certain. If anything went wrong, it was likely going to be Brooke's fault. And despite knowing that, she didn't know how to prevent it. "Do you really think I have a real second chance at true love?"

Nina placed her hand on Brooke's on the table. "You'll never know if you don't try."

Brooke sighed and worried how many missteps she was going to have along the journey, but she had to start somewhere. It's what prompted her to pull out her phone and let her heart, and the wine, guide her.

Brooke [8:05pm]
I miss you

Taylor [8:11pm]
I'm flattered but I have a girlfriend

Brooke [8:13pm]
She's really lucky

Taylor [8:15pm]
I'm home if she wants to really get lucky

Brooke [8:16pm]
She really does

Brooke might have realized she was in love with Taylor and used wine to cope, but that didn't mask any of her feelings. She definitely didn't regret anything in the morning, despite how tired, and slightly sore, she was.

Taylor sat at her desk at work with her eyes closed. If she could just zone out for a few more minutes, she knew she'd be able to snap out of the sleep-deprived funk she was in. The past week had finally caught up with her. Working at the bar. Working her real job. Going to LA. And then there was last night's sleepover with Brooke, which she could barely call a sleepover because for some reason, they barely slept. Taylor simply couldn't get enough of Brooke and the feelings were mutual.

"Rough night?" Taylor's coworker, David, asked as he sat in an empty chair next to her. Moments like this really made Taylor hate open floor concepts where people could sit anywhere they wanted. She would have preferred an assigned seat far away from him. Maybe on another floor. Another company would be even better.

David felt like the type of guy that existed in every office that shouldn't. The one who thought too highly of himself. The one who made passive aggressive comments. The one who made a pass at Taylor at a holiday party even knowing she wasn't into men and had a girlfriend at the time. Taylor really hated David.

"Didn't sleep well," she said to hopefully answer his question well enough to get him to move on to a different topic, or stop talking to her entirely.

He loudly pulled his laptop out of his bag to connect it to the monitor. "I had a late night too. I met this hot redhead from Iowa so naturally I had to show her a good time."

Taylor really hated David. "Spare me the details," she said as she looked back at her computer screen and decided she'd much rather work than engage in a conversation with him.

"What's your deal lately? Seeing anyone?" If anyone else asked this question, Taylor would think it was mostly innocent, but she knew that he would likely make some inappropriate comment in the process. Yet, part of her really wanted to rub it in his face that she definitely had a hotter girlfriend than his rendezvous from Iowa.

"Been with my girlfriend for over three months," she said simply.

Out of the corner of her eye, she saw David nod his head along. He surprised her by not asking to see a picture but the only reason he apparently didn't was because their boss, Michael, was standing behind Taylor.

"Hey Taylor, you got a minute?" Michael asked.

She spun around in her chair and erased the exhaustion from her face the best she could. "Of course," she said as she got up and followed him down the hall into his office. A sense of dread started to creep up her spine. Michael wasn't one to have unplanned meetings – could something be wrong? Was she getting fired? Of course, now when everything else was going well in Taylor's life, she'd be thrown for a loop professionally. Maybe it was a good thing she hadn't quit the bar just yet.

"How's your morning going?" he asked. Making small talk also wasn't something Michael was big on which increased Taylor's anxiety level another three notches.

"Pretty good," she said with as much enthusiasm in her voice that she could before having finished her first cup of coffee.

He smiled at her and clasped his hands on the desk. Taylor found herself staring at them looking for any sense of trepidation on his end. "Well, hopefully this will make your day a bit better," he started, sending Taylor's eyes up from his hands to his face. He was smiling now. She couldn't be getting fired if he was smiling, right? "As you know, Kelsey gave her notice last week and after some brief internal discussions, we'd like to offer you her position."

Not fired at all. Promoted.

"The Senior Marketing Analyst role?" she questioned to buy herself more time.

"Yes," he confirmed. "Obviously, it would be a promotion and added responsibilities so I wanted to make sure you're up for it, otherwise we'll be posting the job today."

"I'm interested," Taylor spat out quickly. She didn't even think about the changes the role would entail – she knew what Kelsey did well enough to know that she wanted the job. It was a senior role; it would surely include a pay increase and greater exposure in the company. This was everything she had been working for. It was the reason she pursued her MBA – she wanted to get a leg up on the competition in any way she could. It seemed like things were finally looking up for her professionally after all.

"Excellent," he said with a smile. "I'll let HR know and then we can chat more either later today or tomorrow."

"Great!" Taylor almost squealed before getting some composure over herself. "Thank you for considering me and for the opportunity."

Michael smiled back at her. "Thank you for all your hard work. It's paid off."

Taylor spun out of the room and when she was out of his line of vision, she closed her fists and subtly punched the air in excitement. Whenever good things happened previously, the first people Taylor would contact were always her mom, Liam, and her sister, in that order. Yet as she walked down the hall into an empty office, her fingers involuntarily moved to someone else's name.

"Hey," Brooke said when she picked up on the fourth ring. "Is everything okay?"

Taylor smiled to herself that Brooke immediately thought something had to be wrong for her to be calling before ten o'clock in the morning on a workday when she just saw her two hours ago. "Maybe I just missed hearing your voice," she teased as she leaned back in the chair. "I got so used to hearing you moan and yell through the night that my ears are missing it."

"I hate to disappoint, but I can't deliver on that at the moment."

While that wasn't the reason Taylor called, she couldn't help but feel a little disappointed. It wasn't her fault that Brooke had that effect on her. "That's not why I'm calling," Taylor admitted. "I wanted some career advice."

"Okay," Brooke sounded. "What's going on?"

"I'm being offered a promotion."

"Oh my God, Taylor!" Brooke exclaimed on the other end of the line. "Congratulations! I'm so happy for you."

Taylor started to draw a doodle on a sticky note as the smile on her face grew a bit smaller. She was obviously very excited, but felt a bit embarrassed that she was asking her girlfriend for advice on this topic. She should have known what to do. She shouldn't have to seek advice elsewhere. "Thanks. I just want to make sure I don't get screwed over and I feel like you'd know what to do."

"You mean financially?"

"Yeah. Since they're basically offering it to me, I don't know how to make sure I get a proper salary increase. I'm so used to just switching teams or leaving companies that I've had more leverage but now I'll still be reporting to my same boss."

Taylor heard Brooke typing on her keyboard before she responded. "Are you free at ten-thirty? Can I call you back then and give you all my tricks of the trade?"

"All your tricks, huh?" Taylor flirted.

"Get your head out of the gutter," Brooke said amidst a laugh.

Taylor found that increasingly difficult lately. "Okay. Ten-thirty." As she looked at the doodle she drew, she realized that without even thinking about it, she had drawn hearts around Brooke's name like she was in elementary school. Her own heart clenched at the thought of what her body might be subconsciously trying to tell her – of what she wanted to ignore for more than one reason. "Thank you for helping me," she mumbled softly.

"You know I'd do anything for you," Brooke said without missing a beat.

The black inked hearts stared back at Taylor, almost blinding her vision with their meaning. "And I'd do anything for you too. You're amazing, Brooke."

As silence filled the line, Taylor wondered if she said too much. What started as a panic over a promotion was now a panic over her feelings. Both she should be ecstatic about, yet both had her absolutely terrified.

"You are too," Brooke said softly.

Could she hear Taylor's labored breaths on the phone? Did she know that Taylor had started to sweat? Why was there no air in this office? Someone should really talk to the building about the ventilation system in there.

"I have to jump to a meeting but I'll call you back. Okay?"

"Okay," Taylor said in a higher pitch than she wanted to.

For the next thirty minutes, Taylor sat in the same room sweating while she processed her thoughts and feelings. Could she have been in love with Brooke? Maybe. But she didn't allow herself the chance to figure that out because she told herself of all the reasons why she should *not* be in love. Starting with the fact that it was way too soon. That Brooke gave her no inclination of feeling the same way. That they were still in the early stages of dating. That she was drawing hearts only because she was nervous about discussing salary negotiations with her girlfriend, not because of actual feelings.

By the time Brooke called Taylor back, she had reprioritized herself to only think about work. She listened to all the tips Brooke shared. On how to walk in prepared with a market value analysis of comparable salaries for the same position at other companies. To be prepared to ask for the appropriate percentage salary bump. To have a plan of what she wanted to tackle in the role and her own previous experience as a backup. Brooke was so direct about it all that Taylor wondered how many times she had gone through this experience herself. Maybe there was a reason why she was as high up at work as she was. She surely knew what she was doing. In more ways than one.

Damnit. Taylor bit her lip at the thought. Her mind was drifting again and she was relieved when they got off the phone and she didn't have to listen to Brooke's incredibly sultry voice filling her ears. She shook her thoughts off and focused on work for the rest of the day as she prepared everything she'd need for her next meeting with Michael.

Until she got home. Outside her apartment door was a bouquet of flowers with a card attached.

I know it's not official-official yet but... congratulations! I'm so proud of you!
xoxo Brooke

Good thing these weren't hand delivered by the sender because Taylor surely would have confessed all of her feelings. Not that she had them.

Chapter Nineteen

Taylor found true solace on Brooke's couch. It was a safe space where she could fully unwind from the week, forget about any of her worries, and just find herself melting into the comfortable leather. Or maybe it was the woman that she was curled up next to whose heart she was listening to under her ear. As strange as it sounded to herself, listening to Brooke's heartbeat made Taylor smile. It was a reminder she was alive and present, and hers.

"I've always wanted to move to Europe," Taylor mindlessly said as they watched a corny movie that just jumped across the Atlantic Ocean to France. The rest of the plot was lost on Taylor. She was too busy thinking about how nice it was to have a Saturday night off and do nothing but order in Thai food and lay here beside Brooke. This apartment made her feel like she was on vacation. They might not have been in Europe, but it was definitely a type of paradise.

"Where would you go?" Brooke asked.

"London makes sense since Liam lives there, but I think I'd like to live in Barcelona and live off tapas and wine," she said with a hum as she started to picture it behind her eyes. "Or the Amalfi Coast. Can you imagine waking up to that view every day?"

"It's beautiful there," Brooke declared, "I can totally picture you there in a sundress drinking espresso while you look out at the water."

Taylor could picture it too. And the person handing her the espresso was Brooke. Not that she would dare to admit that. "Have you been?"

"I have."

"What's the most amazing place you've ever been?"

Brooke closed her eyes as Taylor continued to run her fingers through her long dark hair. "Here with you doing that."

Taylor abruptly stopped and gently tugged on her hair. "I'm serious!"

"Egypt," Brooke said after a beat. "It used to be the Maldives but after I went there and saw the pyramids and all the ancient tombs and hieroglyphics, I feel like I had an out of body experience. It was so surreal and fascinating."

Taylor paused in responding, finding herself even more wowed by Brooke. She truly lived an entire life that Taylor never even dreamed possible. She was working two jobs just to be debt free and while she'd been to places like Paris and the Caribbean, she never even thought about the possibilities of being able to go to the Maldives and Egypt, despite how much she would have liked to.

"Where *haven't* you been?" Taylor asked accusatorily. "Maybe that's the question?"

"Iceland and Finland for starters," she answered quickly. "The Northern Lights have been on my bucket list but I haven't made it yet."

Taylor took a mental note. Her friends had been to Reykjavik. It wasn't that far or expensive to her understanding. Maybe with the right planning, and the right timing of the moon phases, she could take Brooke for her birthday to see the Northern Lights. *Definitely getting ahead of herself.*

Taylor shifted her weight to wrap her arm around Brooke to hold her a little tighter. Moments like this made her worry Brooke was simply out of her league. It had nothing to do with age, although ten years of working and going on vacations would give her an advantage in that category, but just on a human level Brooke was ethereal to her.

"Can we just stay here all night?" she finally asked to fill the silence.

"I do have a more comfortable sleeping option," Brooke said as she placed a soft kiss on the side of Taylor's head.

Taylor wouldn't have cared if her arm fell asleep or if she got a leg cramp from being curled up on the couch; all that mattered was that they were together. Feeling like this was terrifying, but not as terrifying as verbalizing it aloud to the one person that could destroy her with a simple rejection.

Halloween was Brooke's favorite holiday. As a child, she loved going trick-or-treating and dressing up. As an adult, she loved going to or hosting parties. It had become sort of a tradition for her and Jaclyn to have annual Halloween parties. Costumes were always required. Over the years their costumes ranged from the silly bacon and eggs to the fun and sexy Wonder Woman and Supergirl.

Pumpkin picking with Taylor would be a perfect date. Brooke thought about how she'd rent a car and they'd drive to New Jersey and get pumpkins. Maybe some apples too. It was something she couldn't stop smiling about as she grocery shopped with the beauty beside her and noticed all the Fall items start to hit the shelves in the middle of August. Running errands on a Sunday had never been so pleasant after a quiet night in together watching TV and cuddling. It felt almost like a routine she could get used to.

"I'm going to make you the best pasta you've ever had in your life," Taylor boasted as she dropped more items in the cart, bringing Brooke's attention back to the store and out of delusions of grandeur.

"Are you practicing for your life in Amalfi?" Brooke questioned, without even thinking about how much she didn't want to know the real answer to that question.

"Yep," Taylor said indifferently. "I'm going to be the best chef there."

As Taylor spun around and started examining the basil in the produce section, Brooke felt her heart tighten in her chest. Was Taylor serious about moving to Europe one day? Did that mean she wasn't really thinking about the future? A future that included her.

She cleared her throat and tried not to have a meltdown in the middle of Whole Foods. Her visions of a life with Taylor were being popped like a needle to a balloon. Just as she expected. "Are you serious about moving?" she found the strength to ask.

Taylor peeled her eyes off the basil and back towards her girlfriend. "I don't know. It's just a dream. Dreams don't always come true."

"Right," Brooke sounded softly.

"I don't know what kind of marketing analyst I'd be there but I could definitely bartend," Taylor tried to rationalize. "I guess I'd also need to learn Italian."

Brooke couldn't respond. She wouldn't know how if she tried. This was everything she dreaded. Taylor's future was never meant to include her. She didn't fit into the plans in Amalfi. She didn't fit into any plans for a future that hadn't yet been figured out. Taylor was still young enough to have dreams and endless options ahead of her.

"You'll figure it out," she finally said before picking up a tomato to glance at it. The red surface didn't hold any answers to the questions floating in her mind.

"Hey, I'm not going anywhere now," Taylor said as she removed the tomato from Brooke's hand. "Who would leave New York when you're here?"

The words should have placated Brooke; it was the confirmation she was seeking after all. Yet, they only ignited her anxiety. She was the afterthought. Staying with Brooke wasn't Taylor's dream. Europe was her dream. And Taylor wasn't going anywhere *now*, but she might later.

"You should never put your dreams on hold for someone," Brooke declared. "Trust me, I know."

"I'm not putting anything on hold," Taylor responded immediately. If Brooke wanted to believe what she saw, she'd see that Taylor was slightly panicked. Judging by the way her eyes softened and how she wrapped her arms around Brooke's waist. "It's just an unrealistic pipe dream. Don't you have any of those?"

Brooke certainly did, but they were still pretty realistic goals. She didn't want to live abroad. She wanted to have a family. "Yeah," she said simply.

"Tell me your dreams," Taylor asked sweetly.

Brooke could have been honest and said her dream was to be a mother, but that would expose her in the most vulnerable of ways that she was not ready for. Especially not now while grocery shopping. Instead, she went with what used to be a dream of hers years ago before she grew up and changed her perspective. "I've always wanted a couple of houses. One in Big Sur. One in the south of France."

"South of France and Amalfi are kind of similar," Taylor said with a smile. "Maybe our dreams aren't so far off after all."

If she only knew just how drastically different they truly were.

"I guess not," Brooke said before pulling out of the embrace. "We should hurry up. I have a feeling this dinner is going to take you hours to prepare."

"It might," Taylor admitted as she started to push the cart. "But I promise it'll be worth it."

When they finally got back to Brooke's apartment and Taylor made an absolute mess in the kitchen, Brooke couldn't even enjoy the meal that was delicious as promised. All she could think about was their conversation from the store and how falling in love with Taylor was a terrible idea. She'd never want the same things Brooke did and the longer Brooke let things linger, the more she was going to get hurt.

Taylor was already passed out in her bed after Brooke took her time cleaning up the kitchen and loading the dishwasher. She was convinced that her thoughts were so loud that Taylor would be able to hear them when she got into bed beside her. Maybe if she could, then Brooke wouldn't have to verbalize them after all.

Chapter Twenty

Brooke sent off another email on her long ride on the A train to the tip of Manhattan. She was meeting Taylor at The Cloisters, which would have excited her on a normal day, but now she was just tired. She was glad she told Taylor she'd meet her there so she could catch up on work now and have one less thing on her mind during their day together.

"You look tired," Taylor said after she kissed Brooke hello. "We could have come another day."

"It's fine, I was up late catching up on work." It was a lie, but she didn't want to raise too much suspicion around another trip down to DC. She had snuck down on Thursday when her father said Mary was having dizzy spells. She came up first thing in the morning to not miss her Saturday date. It would surely be only a matter of time before Taylor started to question just what was happening in DC, or even worse, want to come with her. At some point, Brooke was going to have to tell Taylor the truth, just not today.

"You work too much," Taylor said with a smile.

"Says the girl with two jobs," Brooke countered.

"Temporarily," Taylor clarified. "I think I'll quit by December."

"How much do you make in tips?" Brooke questioned in astonishment.

"I'll have made a big enough dent by then especially with my promotion," Taylor said with a proud smile. "And I think I'd like my weekends fully mine again. You know to have dates and stuff."

Right. Dates. Would they still be with her come December or would Taylor have moved on to someone else? Instead of worry about who Taylor would be with when she cast her aside, Brooke tried to focus on making it up the concrete stairs that didn't seem to end. When she agreed to a museum date, she surely didn't think that included exercise as well.

"How many more stairs are there?" Brooke questioned when she stopped and tried to catch her breath.

"You say that like you're out of shape," Taylor said as she bounced up to the next set of never-ending steps. "I think you have great stamina."

Brooke rolled her eyes at Taylor's flirtatious comment and tried to catch her breath as they walked up another set of steps towards the castle. She was suddenly realizing maybe there was a reason why she never came here in all of her time living in New York. It took too much work. Yet, once they finally arrived, she had to admit that it was charming and worth the effort.

After leisurely wandering around the museum, and finding it hard to appreciate The Unicorn Tapestries' depiction of murder, they walked back outside into the bright light of day. A stark contrast from the Medieval vibes just feet away.

"The gardens are so simple yet beautiful," Taylor said as she mimicked other visitors and tourists taking pictures of the famous brick archways. "Take a selfie with me," she added before she grabbed Brooke to stand in front of her and she extended her arm to take a picture. Brooke smiled when Taylor's lips met her cheek before pulling her down to sit in one of the archways.

As they sat down in the shade in silence, taking in the sights and people around them, Taylor placed her hand on Brooke's thigh, tempting Brooke to hold it. She wanted to but something was nagging at the back of her head today that was making it difficult to fully be at ease.

Maybe it was the look on her mother's face when she said goodbye this morning. Something told her it might be the last time they saw each other. And what was Brooke doing? Leaving her to come here with a woman that might not be a part of her future either.

"Did you know people have weddings in here in that empty room we were just in?" Taylor asked as she looked around. "Feels a little creepy with a crucifix hanging from the ceiling."

Brooke laughed and nodded her head. "I'm sure they charge a hefty fee to be watched by Jesus."

Taylor looked at her girlfriend and bit her lip before she asked a question that never came up before. Brooke obviously was never going to bring it up and Taylor never seemed to care to ask. "Do you ever want to get remarried?"

Brooke found herself mulling over an answer longer than she intended. Right after her divorce, she couldn't fathom the idea of ever loving someone enough to marry them. To trust someone enough to make that vow in hopes it wouldn't be broken. After her therapist first encouraged her to put herself out there again, she had mild hope that was quickly extinguished when she went on one unfulfilling date or had sex with someone that lacked any substance.

She wanted to answer with a "no" because she was jaded but a part of her wanted to answer "yes" because Taylor reminded her that she was capable of loving someone again so much she'd want to spend her life with them. She wanted to say "yes" because she really did want to get married again and wanted Taylor to know that. But she sure as hell didn't want to say she'd like to marry Taylor one day, even if her heart was telling her it's what she wanted. "I don't know," she settled on instead. "I like the idea of it but I'm not sure if it'll actually happen." She didn't want to read into the slight look of surprise on Taylor's face. "What about you?"

Taylor broke her eye contact and returned to looking at her lonely hand on Brooke's thigh. "I don't know either," she said softly. "I mean you need to be lucky to find someone worth being with forever."

"It's forever until you get divorced," Brooke tried to joke.

"Yeah, I mean damn, to love someone so much you marry them and have it fall apart sounds so painful." She paused with open eyes and squeezed Brooke's thigh. "Oh God, I didn't mean that in any negative way to you. I'm so sorry."

"It's fine," Brooke tried to brush it off, despite how much it hurt. Not so much the comment about her own failed marriage, but that Taylor didn't know if she would ever get married. "I guess it's just a sad reminder that love can fade."

"But who would want it to ever fade with you?"

Brooke's heart clenched in her chest. She had been asking herself that question for two years. Now on the precipice of whatever it was she and Taylor were doing, she was reminded that this could also fade. Taylor could grow tired of her the way Jaclyn did. She'd stop seeing her as the fun person to date and have sex with. She'd see her as just another piece of her life that she could live without.

"Do you want kids?" Brooke turned the conversation. She almost wanted Taylor to say "no" so she could cement her hopes for a future once and for all. Get it all out in one conversation so she could go home and cry while she ate a pint of Ben & Jerry's and then regret it all in the morning.

"I think I'd prefer a dog first," Taylor said with an innocent smile. "I've wanted a pug since I was a kid. Maybe a puppy will help me understand how I'd be as a mom."

Taylor wasn't in any position to think about kids. Another reminder of just how far off they were. "Pugs are cute," Brooke agreed as she tried to hide her disappointment. "Maybe cuter than some kids."

"Right?" Taylor said with a laugh. "They just seem so funny and loyal. And they don't talk back."

Brooke didn't even know why she was hurt by Taylor's excitement over a dog instead of a child. She had spent eight years with Jaclyn accepting the fact they would not have kids. The part of her that wanted one was suppressed so deep inside of her she didn't even know it existed until Jaclyn had one of her own without her. She'd give anything to be a mom right now and have a child she could raise and love unconditionally.

"Should we head out?" Brooke abruptly asked, wanting to run away from her feelings and this entire conversation. Despite how much she already loved Taylor, she was panicking that she'd never get her true happy ending in life. Jaclyn stole her chance at it. Now it was just further proof that she was cursed to have fallen for the wrong woman yet again.

"Yeah," Taylor said as she continued to look at Brooke stand up. "Is everything okay? You don't seem like yourself today."

Why does she always notice these things? "Yeah, I just don't want to burn out here," she lied, using the sun on her pale skin as an excuse for any change in her behavior.

Taylor jumped up and wrapped her arms around the exposed skin on Brooke's arms. "I'll protect you."

Despite thinking Taylor would ultimately do the complete opposite and hurt her, she accepted the embrace.

"I'm planning to go home to Phoenix for Christmas. Tell me you'll be at your sister's this year."

Taylor glanced down at her phone before sipping her coffee. She was relieved that Liam was looking at something off camera when she responded. "I don't know where I'll be for Christmas yet."

"Are you serious?" Liam exclaimed as his head spun back towards the phone screen. "I thought the Thompson family calendar was booked years in advance. It's always either Phoenix or Santa Barbara."

Louise made sure that she knew in advance when and where she'd see her children. Unless it was unplanned like when Taylor showed up in July. "It is."

"Taylor Marie Thompson. Is there something you're not telling me. Oh God, Harper isn't getting divorced again, is she?"

Taylor laughed at Liam's usage of her full name and of the idea of Harper and Bryan breaking up. Not that she wanted that to happen

– but it just oddly seemed comical in the moment. "No, she's not. I'll probably be in Phoenix but I'm keeping my options open for now."

As silence overtook the call, Taylor looked back at the screen to see Liam's questioning brown eyes glaring back at her. This was the look she was hoping to avoid. The look that knew Taylor was hiding something; something she didn't want to discuss right now. "Holy shit. You're hoping to spend the holidays with Brooke, aren't you?"

"What?" Taylor snapped, hoping that reaction would show Liam that she was not even considering that as part of the reason why she might not be in Phoenix this year. Except it was *definitely* the reason.

"You've never missed Christmas with the family," Liam noted with a knowing glare. "Even when you dated Diana for two years. Even though you say New York is most beautiful at Christmas-time."

"Yeah, well maybe this year I want to enjoy a real New York City Christmas and be a tourist," Taylor offered. A New York Christmas sounded really nice, but so did a DC Christmas if the option presented itself. She just wouldn't admit that.

"Alone?" Liam was nothing but relentless.

"Sure."

"Uh huh. And where's Brooke going to be? Is her family in New York?"

Taylor didn't want to talk about Brooke's family, mainly because she didn't know too much about them, aside from their previous careers and the fact that Brooke had been traveling to help them – with what, she didn't know. Her lack of insight could be a sign that their relationship wasn't very serious, despite that being the complete opposite of what it was to Taylor. She was serious about everything. "Her parents live in DC but I don't know what they do for the holidays."

"But you sure as hell hope she's doing you," Liam said with a wiggle of his eyebrows.

"Stop with the sex jokes, they're not funny anymore," Taylor found herself snapping. It was uncharacteristic of her to lose her cool but somehow, Liam hit a nerve she didn't even know was sensitive. "Don't talk about her like she's just some toy to me or whatever."

Liam grew silent on the other end of the screen before a wide smile on his chiseled face revealed it all. He knew Taylor's secret. There was no keeping anything from her best friend. Afterall, that's what gave him that title to begin with. "You love her, don't you?"

Confirming it would make it real and despite how much that scared Taylor, she needed to unburden herself. "I do," Taylor said aloud for the first time. It felt good to admit it to someone other than herself. "I really do."

Liam yelled out in a cheer and Taylor shook her head in disbelief at just how loud Liam could be. "Wake up my entire building why don't you."

"You should be shouting it from the rooftops that you're in love!" Liam yelled through the phone. "Have you told her yet?"

"No," Taylor said softly.

"What are you waiting for?" Liam yelled back at her.

That was the million-dollar question on Taylor's mind that lacked an answer. "I don't know if I will yet," she said softly as she tried to collect her thoughts and all of the pros and cons she had mentally listed out in her mind over and over again. "I think it's too soon."

"There is no such thing as too soon. When you know, you know," Liam tried to encourage her. "James told me he loved me two months after we met. At first, I thought he was crazy but I loved him too so I was just as crazy."

"I'm terrified of telling her," Taylor said as she flung herself back on her mattress. "She's been married before. How do I even compare?"

"You don't because there is no comparison," Liam lectured her. "You are not her ex-wife and good riddance because she sounds like a bitch."

"She is," Taylor chipped in.

"And your love for Brooke has nothing to do with her ex. Tell her you love her and go make lesbian babies together." Taylor smiled as she listened to her friend continue to plan out how her life should go. "Your birthday is coming up, maybe she's going to tell you she loves you as her present."

Could Brooke love Taylor back? Maybe. She did look at her with such intense yet affectionate stares that Taylor started to convince herself that Brooke felt the same way. That every time they had sex Brooke was thinking of how she's the one for her. That every handhold and caress was a sign of her feelings. Feelings she just never verbalized.

"I doubt it," Taylor admitted as she thought about how nonchalant Brooke had been when she asked if Taylor had any birthday plans. She asked if she could take her out for the day if she didn't already have plans and it seemed like she would have been content if Taylor already had other plans with her friends. Unless she was just trying to downplay whatever it was she had in mind. "She seems kind of sad lately and I'm a little worried."

The nagging thought had been on her mind ever since they went grocery shopping a couple of weeks ago. Taylor had brushed it off as getting in her head but then when they went to The Cloisters, something still seemed off. Every time she asked if Brooke was okay, she said she was just tired. How much work was Brooke actually doing at night and on weekends to be that tired all the time? But then again, Taylor was also taking up a lot of Brooke's free time and Brooke never seemed to mind. She was still smiling and laughing and being affectionate with her, and that's what Taylor had been choosing to focus on.

"You are the queen of overanalyzing things," Liam interrupted her train of thoughts. "You always go from zero to panic. I'm sure everything is fine."

"You're right," Taylor said, mostly to convince herself. "But that makes me nervous to tell her so I'm going to wait a bit."

"Don't wait too long. You're a terrible liar."

As she ended her call with her best friend, Taylor exhaled sharply. She *was* a terrible liar, and there was no way she could lie about her feelings for long.

Chapter Twenty-One

For the last three weeks, Brooke spent a lot of time contemplating what to get Taylor for her birthday. It was a tricky decision because it was the first time they would exchange gifts for any holiday or occasion. What if Brooke went too big and Taylor was intimidated? What if Brooke went with something smaller and sentimental and Taylor was disappointed? Brooke couldn't remember the last time she had this much indecision over a gift, including gifts for Jaclyn who sixty percent of the time returned what Brooke got her to buy something else. Maybe her dissatisfaction for thoughtful gifts should have been a sign of things to come.

Yet, thirty was a big birthday. It warranted something memorable and Taylor deserved anything and everything. Brooke had mentally crossed off numerous gift ideas including jewelry, designer clothes, a Montblanc pen, and even a pair of Louboutin heels, which Brooke selfishly thought Taylor would look incredibly sexy wearing.

After much debate, she finally settled on an experience. She wanted Taylor to *remember* her thirtieth birthday for what she did, not what she received. This is what prompted Brooke to book them a couples massage and then go have a lavish dinner together at a restaurant Taylor mentioned she always wanted to go to. Brooke could give her a memory and that would surely last longer than any tangible item she could purchase.

Luckily, Taylor seemed to really enjoy the idea of having a birthday experience. They both took the day off from work, which alone seemed to make Taylor happy before Brooke surprised her with the massage. Taylor couldn't stop raving about how relaxed she felt after and Brooke would have felt the same but she was too worried about everything going perfectly at dinner to ensure that Taylor had a good birthday.

Brooke forced Taylor to go home alone and get ready so she could pick her up before their reservation. Taylor didn't know where they were going but she was instructed to dress up. The sense of mystery only seemed to excite Taylor more and bring a sense of satisfaction to Brooke that she managed to make Taylor happy.

When she arrived at Taylor's apartment with a large bouquet of flowers, she felt her heart sink into her stomach the second she saw her girlfriend. Taylor understood the assignment and was simply stunning. As she stood in the doorway wearing an elegant and sexy black jumpsuit, Brooke had to keep herself together and focused on the fact that they had a reservation to get to, but being charged the $250 cancellation fee didn't seem like a waste to have the chance to remove that jumpsuit.

Taylor didn't allow her the opportunity to as she declared that she was starving. The second she saw their Uber pull up to the restaurant, she kissed Brooke hard on the lips before bouncing out of the car. She might have been thirty but it was as if she had all the excitement of a two-year-old who was happy with anything they saw.

The service at the restaurant was impeccable as expected. After all, it was a Michelin star restaurant and the food was outrageously delicious. Not that Brooke could even focus on the chef's tasting menu or the wine pairing because all she could do was look at Taylor smiling back at her. She wanted her to have a memorable thirtieth birthday. One that was better than her own. When she turned thirty, she went to New Orleans for Mardi Gras with some friends and spent the better half of the night throwing up in the hotel bathroom after she had a Hurricane and a Grenade. It was a night that forced her to never drink sugary drinks again.

"Are you having a good birthday?" she found the words to ask when

Taylor batted her eyelashes back at her.

Taylor lifted her leg up Brooke's calf under the table. "The best I've ever had." Brooke wanted to believe it but she was still self-conscious about her ability to actually please Taylor on a deep, emotional level. "Thank you for today," Taylor continued. "The massage, this dinner, just being with you. It's the perfect gift."

Brooke smiled softly and wanted to respond but their waiter arrived with their next course and wine pairing. The conversation deviated off of the serious back to the culinary right through dessert when Taylor blew out her candle as she held Brooke's hand on the table. Their hands remained connected until they got back to Brooke's apartment twenty minutes later.

"Can I be honest," Taylor said as she dropped her bag onto Brooke's hallway bench. "I am so full I don't think I'll even need to eat tomorrow."

Brooke smiled as she gently wrapped her arms around Taylor's waist. "I know how you feel."

Taylor turned around in her arms and rested her hands on her shoulders. "Like I'm so full, I can't have birthday sex tonight full."

Brooke laughed as she placed a kiss on Taylor's forehead. "Might be a good idea to avoid that on a full stomach."

As Brooke started to pull away from the embrace, Taylor pulled her back in, staring eye to eye. She placed her hand on Brooke's cheek and gently caressed it with her thumb. "I hope you know as much as I like the nights we have sex, I also really like just sleeping and waking up beside you."

Words were struggling to stay bottled up in Brooke's throat. Her heart screamed to tell Taylor she loved her and her brain was struggling to keep up. "I like that too," Brooke said softly. The heaviness of this moment and the proximity of their bodies was short-circuiting her system. "I like everything about you. Actually, I," she bit her tongue. No, that was not what she was going to say. *It couldn't be.* In a panic she took a detour at the last second, "I was really nervous about doing everything right today.

I hope this wound up being a good birthday for you."

Taylor smiled and leaned in to press a kiss to Brooke's lips. It was the confirmation she was looking for, even if it didn't verbalize the truth. "I'll take that as a yes?"

Taylor nodded and separated herself from Brooke. "It was the best. I'd show you more appreciation but I better stop before I really regret being so full."

Brooke was oddly relieved they were full, because if they weren't, there was a high chance she would slip out three words during sex which is not how she wanted to tell Taylor she loved her, not that she had any idea how or when she would do it. She had to shake the thought out of her head and try to downplay the level of emotions to be that of just something liked, not loved. She enjoyed being in Taylor's presence. She enjoyed their dinners or walks. Their nights on the couch watching a movie. The days they kissed and cuddled in bed. And obviously, the nights they had sex. She liked it all. She couldn't love it when the person she felt it for didn't seem to be anywhere near the point of having similar feelings.

"Get your hot ass in bed for some cuddles!" Taylor yelled across the apartment.

Brooke got her head out of the clouds of confusion and walked to her bedroom. Cuddling with the woman she liked was exactly what she needed. Even if she knew she loved her.

Taylor stood in front of her mirror holding up a short black dress against her chest before tossing it on the bed to grab a loose green dress instead. She was trying to figure out which one looked better on her and which one felt more appropriate for her second birthday outing. She wasn't sure why she was obsessing over this outfit so much. Her actual birthday was yesterday and she spent the whole day and night with Brooke.

Their dinner was definitely the swankiest meal she ever had on any of her previous birthdays before, or any other night. It was nothing like the Applebee's she was used to as a kid or the bars she'd go to in her twenties. This was a sexy and adult restaurant and it was absolutely divine, even if she only cared about the company. She had spent an hour and a half picking out that outfit, which was currently a wrinkled mess after it was discarded into a ball on the floor of Brooke's apartment. Even though she only held Brooke in her arms as she slept, Taylor had no complaints.

She grabbed the black dress again from her bed and decided this was perfect for a night out to celebrate another year around the sun. She was going to dinner with her friends before going to a bar for drinks and meeting Brooke there. This wasn't anything spectacular, but she knew she'd enjoy every second of it regardless of what she was wearing.

"To thirty and flirty!" Hayley yelled in a toast at the restaurant.

Taylor toasted to it but knew there was no longer any purpose for flirting in her life except for Brooke. During dinner last night when assorted pastries were on the table and Brooke was smiling back at her over the candlelight on the table, Taylor realized she was ready to tell Brooke that she loved her. She was ready to take the risk of not hearing it back because she wanted her girlfriend to know how she felt. How she thought she was the most incredible woman on the face of the planet. How happy Brooke made her. And how much of a relief it would be to not have to carry that secret with her anymore. It would have been a birthday gift to herself to relieve herself of that pressure.

She ultimately chickened out because she was still so nervous about everything. What did being girlfriends with Brooke truly mean? Did that have a different level of sophistication since she was older and already married? Did she believe in taking things slow? Taylor didn't think that was the case, since technically, their relationship moved faster than she would have expected.

The birthday girl laughed to herself at the fact that they kissed on their second date and had sex on the third. That was not what she would have expected looking back at their time together, or getting to know Brooke more. Yet, it was just reflective of the undeniable connection they had. Yep, Taylor was in love and she needed to tell Brooke sooner rather than later and she wanted to make it special. But that's not what tonight was about, it was about having fun.

Tonight's dinner was full of laughs and cocktails with her closest friends and a reprieve from the swirling thoughts in her mind and in her heart. When they got to the bar, Brooke was already sitting in the corner at a booth that Hayley had reserved. Taylor wasn't the first to notice her; Ariana saw her first and practically pounced on her in a tight embrace. Nothing warmed Taylor's heart more than seeing her friends and the woman she loved together.

Shit. She was totally going to tell her she loved her at the wrong moment.

Brooke couldn't help but admire Taylor from across the room as she danced with a couple of her friends to the Spice Girls. It was one of the most endearing things Brooke had ever seen. The passion that Taylor was putting on display during "Spice Up Your Life" was something she hadn't seen from her girlfriend before and it warmed her heart.

"You and Taylor, huh?" Michelle started as she slid in next to Brooke. The blonde wore a mischievous smile that Brooke couldn't quite read. Michelle was the only friend in attendance tonight that Brooke hadn't met before and since Taylor didn't talk about her too often, Brooke felt like she was basically a complete stranger. "I didn't see that one coming."

"Me either," Brooke admitted. In the thousands of possibilities of directions her life could have taken, she never imagined in a million years that the thirty-year-old bombshell bartender on one of her failed dates would be the woman she fell in love with.

"You were married before, right? No kids?" Michelle asked as she took a sip from the paper straw sticking out of her glass.

"No kids," Brooke confirmed.

"Do you want them?"

Brooke wasn't sure why Michelle was digging into her personal life like this but she didn't have any reason to lie. Lying about not wanting kids is what got her into the mess she was in before. "Yeah, I'd like that."

Michelle nodded and put her drink down to look Brooke in the eye with the same mischievous smile on her face that Brooke now understood to be borderline aggressive. "Taylor doesn't want kids. She's always been pretty set about that. She can barely keep a succulent alive."

Brooke had seen the latest succulent that Taylor failed to keep alive, but in her defense, Brooke also couldn't keep any plants alive. She knew she'd have much better luck with a child, if she ever had the opportunity. "Okay," Brooke sounded.

Michelle raised her brow in a challenge. "So, why are you with her then?"

Brooke didn't like the tone that Michelle was starting to take with her. It was hostile and with each statement and question, Brooke felt like she was being pushed up against a wall. At some point, she would be surrounded and have nowhere to run, but until then, she tried to maintain composure for the sole sake of this woman being Taylor's friend. She opted for a tone she would use at work when she was heading into a tough conversation with someone that opposed her viewpoint. It was the only defense mechanism she had at the moment. "I don't know why the details of our relationship are any of your business."

"She's my friend and it's pretty clear you both want different things long term," Michelle said without missing a beat, taking her first swing at Brooke's heart. "You're just a good time to her, you do know that, right? She likes having sex with you and hanging out but it's mostly just sex, nothing serious."

The second swing at Brooke landed hard. If her heart could actually shatter, it would have been pooled in pieces at her feet. Hearing those words said back to her stung in ways she wished it didn't. That wasn't what she wanted to hear, nor was it something she wanted to be true. "I didn't get that impression from her," she tried to lie and hide her own insecurities. Was this actually true after all? Did Michelle know more than Brooke did? She might have questioned their future together, but she truly thought she was more than *just* sex to Taylor. It wouldn't have been the first time she misread the signs. Especially when it was what she dreaded the most.

Michelle placed her hand on Brooke's arm and Brooke hated the condescending look that was on the younger woman's face. It was pure pity. "I'm sure this hurt to hear, but I've been there with her. So, woman to woman, I'm telling you don't get too attached. She's not in this for the long-haul. Someone new will come along and she'll follow. Trust me."

Tears burned Brooke's eyes begging to be released. She wouldn't cry in this bar in front of Taylor and her friends. She *couldn't*. "Excuse me," she said softly as she walked away to the bathroom where she locked herself in a stall and looked at the wood ceiling as tears streamed down her face. Everything she feared was just confirmed to her by someone she never met before. Someone that also had a history with her girlfriend and was speaking from experience.

In this dingy bathroom stall, Brooke replayed her entire relationship with Taylor. Every conversation, every look, every touch. She didn't think she was *just* sex to Taylor, but they sure as hell had a lot of that. Was that why Taylor had to make a point of clarifying that they wouldn't have sex last night? That it was the expectation? Brooke started to question if she confused sex for love at some point. That if it had been so long since she was in this situation that she thought she was in love when she was just clouded by mind blowing orgasms and companionship. She shook her head and knew that wasn't true. Her feelings for Taylor surpassed the physical. She truly loved her. Loved *all* of her. Even the part of her that apparently would never love her back and want to be her future.

"Fuck," Brooke mumbled to herself as she started to pat her cheeks with toilet paper to wipe the tears off her face. She walked out to the sink and dabbed the corner of her eyes with a wet paper towel to clean up her running eye makeup. She couldn't let Taylor see her like this. She had to get through the night and pretend everything was fine. Michelle didn't deserve to win and have an effect on her.

When Brooke walked back upstairs, she went straight to the bar and ordered herself a shot of whiskey. This was an appropriate time to down a shot when she needed something to take the edge off quickly. She cringed as she swallowed the brown liquid and turned back to look towards the dancefloor to see Taylor staring back at her. She was beckoning her to join her but Brooke shook her head from side-to-side. She would have loved to dance with Taylor but the brighter lights in that area of the bar would betray her eyes and reveal her pain. And there was no way she could have fun when she was panicking over her relationship.

Instead, she turned around and ordered herself another drink to have her back towards Taylor who moments later wrapped her arms around her waist. "Do you want to get out of here?" Taylor asked as she rested her head on Brooke's shoulder. "They want to go get hot dogs before going to another bar but I kind of want to go home."

"It's your thirtieth birthday, you should go out and have fun," Brooke said coldly as she awaited the bartender to return with her drink.

"I'd rather have fun at home with you," Taylor said into Brooke's ear with a playful bite of her earlobe.

That's all she was good for, right? Sex and a fun time?

"I know I saw you this morning, but I missed you today," Taylor continued, sending Brooke's heart aflutter. Was that something someone who didn't care about her would really say?

"We can do whatever you want," Brooke said simply, choosing to ignore the statement that was just declared. She couldn't think too much of it, knowing false hope was going to destroy her more than it already had.

Brooke's drink arrived and she quickly took a few sips as she tried to pull herself together. She knew she needed to turn around eventually and that she couldn't hide her face from Taylor. She took a deep breath and spun around in Taylor's arms and saw concerned orbs looking back at her. "Is everything okay?"

Now was not the time Brooke wanted Taylor to be attentive and caring. She couldn't let Taylor see the cracks in her façade around her friends. Brooke was never one for making a scene in public, and the words that were hanging on the edge of her lips would surely result in a scene and potentially a lot of tears. Mostly from her. "Yeah."

Taylor placed her hand on Brooke's cheek before moving it to caress the back of her neck. "You were in the bathroom for a while, I thought about checking up on you. Are you sick?"

"No," Brooke clarified. "I was just getting a little bit of a headache."

"Yet you're drinking more?" Taylor asked with a suspicious raised brow. "You always say no more alcohol when you feel a migraine brewing."

If she was just sex, why did Taylor remember this detail? Even Jaclyn overlooked Brooke's migraines, granted she was the reason why they got so much worse.

"Trying not to be a party pooper," Brooke lied in hopes it would be a good enough answer to get Taylor off her case. In response, Taylor took Brooke's drink out of her hand and took a long sip.

"Hurry up and finish your drink. I want to go home and use that new toy." She smiled sweetly before lacing her fingers through Brooke's vacant hand and dragging her back to the dancefloor where she told her friends they were leaving.

Michelle's eyes darted to Brooke, almost trying to judge whether Taylor knew about their conversation. The fact that Taylor hugged her goodbye was a sign that nothing was wrong, despite how much it should have been for the friend. Instead, everything was wrong for Brooke.

Back in the apartment, Brooke sat on the edge of Taylor's bed trying to quiet her anxiety. Moments prior, she quickly took a shower to rinse off and give herself some privacy to collect her thoughts. Luckily, she managed to get out before Taylor joined her. She needed a few more minutes to compose herself and ensure she didn't fall apart at the seams.

It had been a struggle so far. The entire taxi ride back to the apartment, Taylor was whispering dirty things in Brooke's ear. About how much she wanted to do to her. How much she wanted to show her appreciation for yesterday's birthday festivities. If this was any other night, Brooke would have been dripping in anticipation, and it's not that she wasn't, but she was also distracted. She was hurt. She was scared. Those feelings didn't necessarily pair well with foreplay and sex. How could Brooke be fully invested in having sex right now when she felt like that's all she was to her girlfriend?

A light sigh escaped her lips as she looked up towards the ceiling willing herself not to cry. "Is your head okay, babe?" Taylor asked from across the room.

Brooke quickly diverted her eyes to see Taylor leaning against the bathroom doorframe dressed in lingerie. A red bra that was pushing her already supple breasts up to the point they almost spilled out. An equally as sheer red garter belt with barely-there underwear connected to thigh highs. Any panic Brooke had moments ago was slowly slipping away. She was only human after all and madly in love with this woman. "Jesus Christ," she said as she blinked to ensure that what she was seeing was actually real.

As Taylor stepped towards her girlfriend, it was only then that Brooke realized she was also wearing a pair of heels. In comparison, Brooke had a bathrobe of Taylor's on and certainly didn't look like that. "I know it's technically my birthday weekend but this is a gift to myself," she said with a light chuckle. "I really wanted to see your reaction to me in this. It's what I wanted to do last night."

"You look incredible," Brooke said as she reached out to hold Taylor's hands.

Taylor stood between Brooke's legs and leaned down to kiss her tenderly. Despite whether or not they were taking their time or frantically trying to please one another, the one constant was the tenderness of their kisses. Brooke could always feel it running through her body, giving oxygen to her lungs and always creating desire.

"I meant what I said in the car," Taylor said as she pushed Brooke back onto her bed. "I want to make you scream."

Brooke didn't have time to respond before Taylor pounced on her. She was certainly already working on living up to her promise. Taylor never seemed to not deliver on what she said she was going to do, and that accountability didn't stop in the bedroom either.

Taylor looped her finger in the knot of Brooke's robe and pulled it open. She pushed the silk fabric to the sides so her lingerie covered body could fall flush against Brooke's naked skin. Taylor moved her mouth over Brooke's body like she owned it. As if every centimeter of Brooke's skin was Taylor's and in a way it was. She just didn't know it.

With her knee pressed between Brooke's legs, she applied pressure to each of her movements, trying to get a rise out of Brooke with each pivot of her leg. It was working all too well as Brooke found herself mirroring the rhythm to have greater contact. Taylor removed her lips from Brooke's and began to drag her tongue straight down the middle of her body until she took one slow, long lick across Brooke's clit.

Taylor pulled away far too soon, sending chills down Brooke's body from her absence. Her eyes followed Taylor's movements as she leaned over to her nightstand and pulled out the double-sided strap-on she purchased last week. When she suggested ordering it, she expressed the idea of how erotic it would be to literally fuck Brooke and get fucked at the same time. She wanted the two of them to be completely in sync; to literally be connected in every possible way.

"I hope this works," she said with a playful look on her face as she stared at the hot pink toy in her hand. "I mean, technically, it should, right?" The uncertainty in her voice made Brooke's heart clench. Taylor had yet to understand that Brooke didn't need anything more than just her. Even if this failed to work, she would be completely satisfied and still completely connected to Taylor. "I want you to put it in me first," Taylor said as she handed it to Brooke.

This was not Brooke's first time using a sex-toy, but it had been a long time and now she felt oddly nervous. Everything would have certainly felt different if they were doing this before the conversation at the bar. Before Michelle shattered her and told her what she meant to Taylor. Just sex.

"Okay," Brooke said softly as she turned the toy around so that the smaller side meant to go inside who was on top was facing upwards. She took a deep breath and tried to shake her nerves. She could do this. She *wanted* this. She leaned in and kissed Taylor while she began to unclasp the garter belt and slowly pull the lace underwear down Taylor's legs. As Taylor kicked them to the floor, Brooke's eyes remained glued to the shoes still on Taylor's feet. "Are you going to keep your heels on?"

"Yes," Taylor said as she bucked her now bare hips towards Brooke. "It's part of the fantasy."

Brooke smiled as she ran her finger through Taylor's slick arousal. There was definitely not going to be any need for lube with how wet Taylor already was. Brooke teased Taylor's entrance with the toy before rocking it back and forth to coat it in her wetness. "What's the fantasy?"

"This," Taylor said as she grabbed Brooke's face to kiss her hard. "All of this with you."

Without removing her mouth from Taylor's, Brooke slowly inserted a finger into Taylor and felt her girlfriend grind on her hand. "Put it in," Taylor said amidst a moan. As instructed, Brooke replaced her fingers with the toy, slowly pushing it in and feeling Taylor tighten her grip around her back as she dug her dull nails into Brooke's shoulders. "Fuck," she groaned before she pulled back to push Brooke down on the bed.

She arched her back and bent the other side of the toy to visually align the perfect angle to please Brooke. "Are you ready?" she asked as she began to tease Brooke the same way Brooke had done to her moments before. Her fingers gently alternated stroking her clit and dipping inside of her, leaving Brooke longing for more. Payback was a bitch.

"Yes," Brooke sounded as she looked at Taylor staring back into her eyes. This was taking their intimacy to a new level and despite how internally wrecked she was, she was craving this; craving Taylor in ways she hadn't felt before.

When Taylor finally moved her hips to gently slide the hot pink toy inside Brooke, she wasn't met with any resistance. Brooke was ready for her.

"Does it feel okay?" Taylor asked sweetly as she seemed deep in concentration to not lose control of the piece inside of her. Two weeks ago, she joked that she started Kegel exercises to prepare her for this moment, and she probably actually did.

"Yes," Brooke whispered.

"Tell me to stop if it's not."

Brooke nodded as she felt Taylor slowly pick up her pace. There was no way she was ever going to tell Taylor to stop, not when it felt this good. Not when Taylor's breasts were bouncing in front of her, causing her to reach out to hold them in an attempt to feel more of her girlfriend.

"Tay," Brooke groaned as she felt her body already start to lose control. "You feel so good."

"Fuck," Taylor groaned as she gripped the headboard, trying to steady her balance as she focused her energy on her hips to pound into Brooke.

"Harder," Brooke moaned as she lifted both of her legs to wrap around Taylor's waist to hold her closer and provide an angle that felt even more satisfying than the one she was just in.

Taylor moaned deeply as she fell forward and clutched at Brooke's hands and intertwined their fingers in need of something to hold onto. Their bodies moved in sync, gyrating towards each other in desperation. When Brooke leaned up and brought her lips to latch around Taylor's nipple, everything that they were working towards was reaching the point of no return. This was the explosive sex that people fantasized about and it was real. And so fucking satisfying.

"Oh my God, Brooke," Taylor yelled out as she dipped her hand between their bodies to rub Brooke's clit as she still moved her body in a rhythm that only a woman who did yoga three times a week could manage. "Are you close?"

"Yes," Brooke said breathlessly. She was trying to do everything in her power to not find a release in this moment, not because she didn't want to, but because she was afraid it would be the last time they ever had sex. After tonight, things had to change, despite how good it all felt. These feelings were clouding her judgement and she needed to protect her heart more than her libido.

Every time they connected physically, she felt like it had topped the previous time but tonight was another level of ecstasy. Except this was all she was good for to the woman on top of her and technically inside of her. She never wanted this moment to stop but when Taylor started to tremble and scream out Brooke's name, she became undone. If this was the last orgasm she'd ever have with Taylor, it would be one she'd never forget.

After moments of silence other than their rigid breathing, Taylor leaned back to slowly pull out of Brooke and remove the contraption from herself. She tossed it onto the pile of her clothes on the floor before she pulled off her heels and dropped them beside the bed. She crawled back on the mattress and climbed her way back up Brooke's body.

"I love fucking you," Taylor whispered in Brooke's ear when she collapsed on her shoulder.

Brooke's body grew still. The tremors she was still experiencing suddenly disappeared to be replaced by the overwhelming slap of reality. Her heart had skipped a beat on those first two syllables only to then be shattered.

Everything became crystal clear in that moment.

Taylor loved fucking her. And she fucking loved Taylor.

A tear escaped Brooke's eye that she quickly wiped away as if it was a bead of sweat. It was believable considering what they just did and the slick sweat that was covering their tangled bodies. She tried to pull herself away from Taylor who only grabbed her tighter.

"Where are you going?"

"Bathroom," Brooke said as she found the discarded bathrobe and wrapped it around her body. She was vulnerable enough now; she didn't need to be naked on top of it.

"I'll miss you," Taylor said softly, yet echoing throughout the apartment and in Brooke's mind.

Brooke slowed her movements as she tied the belt around her waist. She wanted to believe it. She really did. But once the bathroom door was closed and she turned the faucet on, tears exploded from her eyes. She loved a woman who felt only love for her physically. She was just sex after all, and the events of tonight were proof of that. Despite how good Brooke felt and how much she loved having sex with Taylor, she felt used in this moment. And for that she cried even harder.

When she left the bathroom minutes later, she was prepared for Taylor to question what took her so long. Luckily, she was already fast asleep. Her chest lightly rising and falling against the mattress. Beautiful as always.

Brooke quietly got back into bed and rolled on her side to face her. She took one last look at the woman she loved before she wrapped her arm around her. If tonight was the last time they shared a bed, she wasn't going to spend it not holding her. She'd have a lonely lifetime of that.

Chapter Twenty-Two

What felt like minutes later, Brooke awoke looking at Taylor sleeping beside her with the same adoration she had before she closed her eyes. The same thoughts she had before she fell asleep now only sounded the alarm bells with greater intensity. The beautiful woman next to her could destroy her heart and likely would. Michelle made that pretty clear last night, and so did Taylor, which now left Brooke reeling as she felt all of her insecurities and fears pile up on her heart and mind. It was the reason she barely got any sleep, despite how tired she was, especially after the explosive sex that should have knocked her into a sweet slumber as it did her girlfriend. With one more glance at the woman next to her breathing softly, Brooke's heart told her to stay, but her mind was telling her to run before it was too late.

She quietly left the bed and tried not to disturb Taylor. Maybe she could discretely sneak out of the apartment and avoid having this conversation first thing in the morning. It would have been the first time Brooke ran out on her, which alone would have been telling. Despite Brooke hiding in the bathroom for a few minutes and not making a sound aside from the toilet flushing and the faucet barely turned on, she walked back towards Taylor's bed and saw her girlfriend was now wide awake.

So much for avoiding this now. "How's it feel to be thirty and two days old?" Brooke asked when Taylor smiled up at her as she sat down on the edge of the bed. She didn't know what else to say in this moment. A good morning kiss didn't feel right given what she was prepared to say and do, even if it was all she wanted.

"Good because I'm with you," Taylor said with that raspy morning voice that Brooke found irresistibly sexy.

Brooke stared at Taylor and felt herself start to spiral. Michelle's words last night slammed against her brain. Would someone who only cared about sex say this? Of course she would if she wanted to keep having sex.

Memories of their bodies moving in sync hours prior sent shivers down Brooke's spine. Taylor's messy light brown hair was a reflection of everything they did last night. Everything she wanted to do over and over again. Taylor never had any hesitance talking about sex with Brooke, but she never talked about her feelings or things she wanted in the future, besides a dog and moving to Europe. That much was becoming quite clear and started to echo in her ears. *I love fucking you.*

Brooke got up from the bed and started to find her discarded clothes from the night before. She couldn't spend the rest of the day lying in Taylor's bed pretending she was okay; that they were okay. "You know, I've been thinking you might be happier with someone your own age," Brooke blurted out, trying to rip the Band-Aid off and just let it out into the open to destroy her quickly.

Taylor laughed in response. "What?"

Brooke pulled her dress on over her head and fumbled with the side zipper. She wanted to blame it on the awkward position but it was because her hands were shaking from nerves. "Someone who will gladly stay out until two o'clock and eat Papaya Dog without having indigestion."

Taylor laughed again, clearly not understanding the serious conversation Brooke was trying to have with her. "Nothing good happens at two o'clock in the morning. At that time, I should be home in bed and Papaya Dog would give anyone indigestion." Taylor crawled across the bed and tried to grab Brooke to pull her down but she stepped further away.

"You say that now but things will change," Brooke said firmly without making any eye contact. If she looked at Taylor she would lose her resolve or open the floodgates of her eyes. "I don't want to wake up one day and you're not interested in me anymore because the sex isn't new and exciting and I'll be forty-five and doomed."

Taylor furrowed her brows and sat up in bed, not at all phased by the fact that she was completely naked. "Wow, way to be optimistic. That's five years from now."

"Exactly," Brooke said in frustration, trying to prove her point and not be distracted by the woman she loved staring at her. "I have to think about my future. I can't let my feelings cloud my judgment."

As a silence fell between them, Brooke felt all of those feelings she had for Taylor explode inside of her. This hurt too much. She didn't even know why she was doing this right now aside from the sheer panic of what someone she just met had to say to expose her greatest fear that had been percolating dangerously close to the surface for the past few weeks. That when she thought Taylor was going to tell her she loved her, she said she loved fucking her. It was too much. Too hurtful. Too terrifying.

"Are you saying you don't see a future with me?" Taylor softly asked as she pulled the sheet up to wrap around her body. She looked more vulnerable in that moment than she did when she was exposed and Brooke felt awful that she was the cause for it.

She did see a future with Taylor, but just because she saw it, didn't mean it was obtainable. And to not have that with Taylor who she already wanted it with and so much more made her absolutely gutted. "I'm saying I'm not sure you're thinking about *your* future."

Brooke could tell she was throwing Taylor into a tailspin. If she was on the receiving end of this conversation, she'd be equally as confused and adamant to disagree. Yet Brooke still found it hard to believe her even when she said, "I want to be with you, Brooke. Where is this all coming from?"

"Your friend has very strong opinions about your dating style. She must have heard it somewhere." Brooke finished putting her shoes on and tried to avoid looking at Taylor staring back at her. Bringing Michelle into the conversation wasn't what she planned to do, but she needed to get it off her chest.

"What-what are you talking about?" Taylor asked in confusion. "Did something happen last night?"

"I got a wake-up call is all and maybe you need it too."

Brooke grabbed her illuminated phone off the nightstand and stared at it in complete disbelief. This was not what she expected to see and deal with in the midst of ending something she wanted to have for the rest of her life. Her father's text stared back at her despite trying to blink it away. Her mother had a stroke and was in the ICU. They didn't expect her to make it past the day.

Brooke knew Taylor was still speaking to her, but all she could hear was a ringing in her ears until her mind re-focused and she could process Taylor's voice that now escalated into a yell. "This is a serious conversation you just dropped on me the moment I woke up and you're on your fucking phone?" Taylor yelled at her. "Are you working? Maybe you're the one not ready for a relationship. No wonder why your wife cheated on you."

Brooke looked up from her phone and finally met Taylor's eyes and couldn't control the tears that started streaming down her face. The words verbalized and the words on her phone screen had slammed into her like a pile-up on a highway and she wasn't making it out unscathed. "I'm gonna go."

As she started to leave the room, Taylor jumped up from the bed and followed Brooke towards the door. "Brooke, wait. I'm sorry, I didn't mean that."

Her mother was dying and she was here having a forced fight with the woman she loved because she was afraid of going too far and being hurt. And too afraid to be the bigger person and tell Taylor she loved her. "These past few months have been great and I care about you more than

I should but-"

"No buts," Taylor said as she tried to wrap her arms around Brooke. "Give us a chance. Tell me what's going on."

"I'm sorry, I have to go," Brooke repeated as her tears started to fall harder.

"Brooke, please talk to me," Taylor pleaded as she started to cry. "What happened last night? Did I do something?"

Brooke took one last look at Taylor and resisted the urge to collapse into her arms. "I have to go," she said again before she walked out of the door and let explosions of tears escape from her eyes.

Brooke kept re-reading her father's text message in disbelief that it was real. She missed his back-to-back phone calls because she was talking to Taylor and spontaneously deciding to end their relationship without so much as a proper explanation. She couldn't even formulate words after she read his text but the accusation that she was working hurt more than she expected. The Jaclyn comment was a massive low blow that sealed the deal. As tears fell down her face while she walked down the street, she wasn't even sure what they were for exactly. Her dying mother. Her failed marriage. The relationship she just self-destructed. Maybe all of the above and then some.

The moment Brooke left Taylor's apartment, the blindsided woman got back in bed and cried hysterical until she made herself nauseous. She couldn't understand what the hell happened this morning. Everything was fine. Until it wasn't. It was like Brooke woke up a different woman and decided she didn't want to be with her anymore. Taylor thought something seemed wrong at the bar last night, but she brushed it aside when they came home and had incredible sex that she could still feel pulsating her body hours later.

She sat up in bed and started to talk to herself in hopes it could bring some clarity to the situation, and process all of her racing emotions. She knew it seemed a bit crazy, but nothing was normal today so why not talk to herself and add to the abnormality? "Fuck, okay. I'll just give her space. I can fix this. I *have* to fix this. I've never met a woman like her and I don't care about a stupid ten-year age difference. Why does she? Jesus, it's not like she could be my mother or anything that would be weird. She's so sexy and fun I wouldn't even know we were different ages except she definitely has more life experience. Oh my God, maybe she thought I was a gold digger or something? No, it can't be that. Why would she think I don't want a future with her? What the fuck happened last night?"

Taylor spun around in the bed to find her phone, almost wishing that Brooke had already contacted her but there wasn't a single text or missed call on her phone. She decided to send out individual texts to all of her friends who came out last night to ask them what they thought of Brooke to figure out what happened and what Brooke meant about her friend having opinions. Every single one of them raved about her, just like they had previously. Everyone except for Michelle.

Michelle [12:34pm]
She's in a different place in life than you are

Taylor [12:35pm]
What does that mean??

Michelle [12:37pm]
You said yourself that you don't want to settle down. You don't want kids either

Taylor [12:38pm]
When did I say that?!

Taylor collapsed back on the bed as she started to put herself in Brooke's shoes to try to piece together what was going on. *Holy shit. Did Brooke want that with me?*

Taylor [12:39pm]
And what does that have to do with Brooke?

Michelle [12:42pm]
She's 40 and looks at you like you're the love of her life so obvi she's going to want a future with you... why would you get into that now??

Love of her life... no it couldn't be. Taylor couldn't be that lucky that Brooke loved her back and loved her with the same intensity she felt for her. If that was the case, then why did Brooke just run out of her apartment after seeming to abruptly break up with her without even a proper conversation? Brooke was too mature for whatever it was that just transpired. Something must have happened.

Taylor [12:44pm]
Did you say something to her last night?

Michelle [12:46pm]
We chatted for a bit

Taylor [12:47pm]
What did you say to her???

Michelle [12:48pm]
That you're not looking for anything serious and are just having fun

Michelle [12:48pm]
You're the one who told me that so I was only saying the truth

Fury coursed through Taylor's veins. Michelle was clearly the reason for Brooke's actions today. Whatever she said to Brooke hit below the belt and sent Brooke running. Michelle did this on purpose and Taylor knew exactly why. A drunken mistake coming back to haunt her for no reason other than pure jealousy.

Taylor [12:50pm]
I cannot fucking believe you!!!

Taylor [12:52pm]
I thought you accepted the fact that we would NEVER be anything more than friends... I'm truly sorry if our drunken makeout A YEAR AGO led you on but I was emotional and now I found someone I'm crazy about and you just had to go and sabotage it

Taylor [12:53pm]
What kind of friend are you??

Michelle [12:48pm]
If she's that into you she wouldn't end things over a conversation with me... it's clearly more than that. Wake up!

Taylor threw her phone on her bed before she pulled her pillow over her face and screamed into it. How did everything spiral out of control in the last twenty-four hours? She was on the precipice of telling Brooke that she loved her on Friday night and now she was apparently dumped on Sunday. This didn't make any sense and rather than try to plea for Brooke to talk to her, she decided to give her space. She needed some time to process her own feelings, and hopefully come to the realization that whatever Michelle said wasn't true and that she should just talk to Taylor about it directly.

In the meantime, she'd cry her eyes out. It was the only thing she could do.

Chapter Twenty-Three

Brooke grabbed another tissue from the now depleted box beside her. After she wiped her eyes and tossed the damp white cloth beside her on the floor, she closed her lids and tried to quiet the thoughts running through her mind. In the silence, she could hear her father crying in the room next door. Were these walls always so thin? How many late-night conversations did Brooke's parents hear over the years when she was growing up? Conversations her mother would never be privy to again.

By the time Brooke packed a suitcase and got on the next train to DC, her mother only had another hour left before she passed. It was almost as if she was just hanging on for Brooke to get there and that broke Brooke's heart even more. Right down to her final breath, Mary did everything possible for her daughter. Including stay alive for her. If only there was a flight that could have gotten Brooke to DC sooner, they could have had at least a little more time together.

As a deep sigh escaped Brooke's lips, she got up from the bed and walked out of her old bedroom to go downstairs to the kitchen. It was almost nine o'clock and the only thing she ate all day was a protein bar and a cup of coffee. She didn't have an appetite but she knew having something now would make the heartburn hurt less tomorrow. She opened the fridge and didn't bother to wipe away the tears that fell down her cheeks. The meals that Oscar prepared for him and Mary were still neatly lined on the shelves.

She pulled out two glass containers and popped them each into the microwave. She grabbed two forks, knives, and napkins before she carried everything upstairs and knocked on her father's door.

"Come in," he said softly.

Brooke walked into the room to find him sitting in the blue accent chair in the corner. He looked like a shell of a human curled up as he looked out the window onto a dark street. This was not the man that raised Brooke. The man who always was composed and vibrant. The man who never backed down from a challenge. The man who would constantly have a smile on his face anytime he was reading or sitting quietly by himself. "We need to eat," she said softly.

"I'm not hungry."

"Me either but we have to."

She settled the tray onto the side of the bed and cautiously sat down. This was her parent's bed that her mother would never sleep in again. Being in this house was unsettling. To know this was where her mother had her stoke just twelve hours ago but now would never return to. That the porch she collapsed on was one of her favorite places to sit and just relax yet it was the last place she'd ever be. The idea of eating in this house felt even more repulsive to Brooke now.

"Should we go to a hotel?" The words left her lips before she even had time to process them. She was trying to help her father any way she could, and the idea of him going to sleep in that bed alone tonight made her want to bawl her eyes out again. How do you go to sleep knowing you will never see the person you love again?

"No," he said softly before he finally turned his head back towards her. "Let's eat downstairs though."

Brooke nodded and carried the tray of food back downstairs where they sat at the dining room table mostly in silence. Brooke didn't know what else to say and her father seemed to feel just the same. After all their conversations with the doctors earlier, they were depleted. Tomorrow would be another horrible day of planning the funeral and having to tell people what happened to the woman they loved.

"Tell me something nice that's happened lately," Oscar finally said while clearing his throat as he pushed his mashed potatoes around in the glass container. "Anything."

Brooke thought back to her last week in New York and felt anything but nice memories. It was a terribly sad week that exploded right at the end. "Uh," she started as she tried to think of something, anything, to bring a smile to her dad's face. "Nina's daughter got in trouble at school for telling a boy that women rule the world and he'd be working for her one day."

It was a stretch, but it was nice to see the smallest smile appear on her father's face. "The future gives me hope," he said lightly.

"I mean, she's probably not wrong," Brooke said with a half-smile. "Nina is raising one fierce girl."

Oscar nodded along as he finally took a forkful of food to his mouth. Brooke couldn't help but feel relieved that he ate something, even if that would be the first and last morsel he digested. "How's Taylor?"

The question was normal, it was genuine, and yet it was the worst thing her father could have asked. Brooke couldn't tell him the truth. The last thing he needed was to worry about her and her broken heart. Brooke barely knew the truth herself and she was the one who lit the match and set everything ablaze. "She's good," Brooke said simply, knowing it was a lie. Taylor wasn't good judging by the tears in her eyes earlier in the day and their lack of communication since. That made two of them.

"Is she going to come down this week?"

The idea of Taylor wrapping her arms around Brooke in comfort sounded so wonderful but Brooke didn't deserve it. She abruptly exploded their relationship. She lied and hid the truth about her mother and her own feelings. She hid the love she had in her heart. She didn't deserve an ounce of affection from Taylor despite how much she wanted it. "I don't think so," she said softly, trying to find a way to not raise suspicion or paint Taylor in a bad light. "She has a work conference and

I'll be an emotional mess."

Oscar seemed to understand as he nodded along. Brooke knew that he was probably biting his tongue thinking that a girlfriend should attend their partner's mother's funeral, and he wouldn't be wrong. Brooke would be upset if Taylor hadn't attended if circumstances were different. But she had no idea – just another misstep that Brooke made. "I hope I can meet her one day. I know she's the only reason you've been smiling lately."

"She is," Brooke admitted sadly. Taylor was the joy in her life. The bright light in the darkness of everything. Three forkfuls into her dinner and Brooke decided she was done. She couldn't handle the grief over losing her mother and Taylor at the same time.

Fog. That's all Taylor saw and felt trapped by for the past two days. She couldn't focus at work. She couldn't shower without crying. She didn't want to talk to anyone unless they were Brooke. It was absolutely pathetic. When she got to the bar Sunday night after her disastrous morning, she contemplated quitting months earlier than she planned. She was exhausted in every possible way and it surpassed what just happened with Brooke. She had pushed herself to the limit the entire year in hopes that the payoff would be worth it.

Now that she was tired and in desperate need of rest and a reset of focus on herself, she knew it was time to leave bartending behind. She had gotten the money she wanted. She got promoted at her real job. She had a girlfriend she wanted to spend more time with. Well, maybe she lost that one now. But with or without Brooke, Taylor knew her worth and knew she could focus on herself the way she deserved. Even if she wanted Brooke to be a part of that.

"You're a hot mess today," David said to Taylor as she sighed at her screen for the fifth time in the last ten minutes. She couldn't focus on reporting when her mind was lost in other dimensions.

"I'm fine," she snarled back at him.

"Trouble in paradise?" he obnoxiously pressed on.

Taylor rolled her eyes because David was the last person on the face of the planet that she wanted to talk to about her relationship woes. "No," she said softly.

"Well, if it makes you feel any better, I'm telling Michael that I'm quitting today."

Taylor's ears perked up. Her day had quickly taken a turn for the better. "Oh!" she exclaimed louder than she anticipated. "You got a new job?"

"Yep," he said with a smug look on his face. "I realized that if you want something, you have to go for it. You can't expect it to just fall into your lap."

For a moment, Taylor contemplated jumping up from her chair to hug David. He might have been talking about himself and his career, but Taylor related it to her own life. If she wanted Brooke, she shouldn't be waiting for her to come around. She needed to go after her. "You're absolutely right," she said with a smile.

As David continued to ramble about the new job and the team he was going to lead, Taylor continued to smile and feel optimistic. Change was on the horizon. David was leaving. Taylor could fully enjoy her job once again. This good news is what gave her the motivation to pull her phone out and start to draft a text to Brooke. They deserved better than Sunday's unresolved conversation. Maybe something else positive could happen today. After she wrote and re-wrote the message countless times finding the right words to say.

Brooke sat in her parent's living room clutching a glass of red wine. It was her third of the night after her dad had one glass and went to sleep.

The alcohol wasn't lessening the chest pains either of them had over the death of the woman they loved. Would anything actually do that?

Brooke had been replaying the events of Sunday over and over again. From seeing her father's text message, to crying on Amtrak, to arriving at the hospital. By the time Brooke got to the ICU, the doctors already said that Mary would not be waking up. They gave Brooke and her father time to say their goodbyes before they began to increase the morphine dosage and begin the process of sending Mary into whatever afterlife there was, if anything. Brooke hated herself for not being there that weekend with her mother. She just saw her seven days prior and now she was dead. No matter how much she knew it was coming, it hurt like hell.

Oscar had barely left the bedroom since they got home from the hospital. He seemed to be in a complete state of shock and the weight of the planning fell on Brooke's shoulders. She was the one who spent the entire last two days informing most family and friends of her mother's passing. She was the one who organized the wake for tomorrow and the burial for the day after. Would it all feel even more real the moment that was done and nothing was left to plan for? She didn't want to find out.

She downed the remainder of her glass and went upstairs to get ready for bed. Tomorrow would be a horrific day that she'd give anything to avoid if possible. Anything to bring her mother home and back to their lives. She went into her old bedroom that was converted into her father's office and felt tears start to pour out of her eyes again. Her phone illuminated next to her and she picked it up expecting more words of sympathy or questions about the wake tomorrow. She wasn't expecting to see Taylor's name, despite how much she had also thought about her over the last forty-eight hours.

Taylor [8:42pm]
Hi. I've been trying to give you some space but I can't anymore. I'm really sorry about what I said Sunday. I

didn't mean it I was just blindsided that you wanted to end things which I know was immature and low. I also know Michelle said something to you and I'm beyond furious and pleading for you to know it's not true. I care about you so much Brooke. SO SO SO much. I want what you want. And I want YOU. Can we please meet up and talk? Please.

The words made her cry even harder. She screwed up pushing Taylor away on Sunday and now she was too distraught to fix it. She was so broken now that there was no way she could mend things properly with Taylor. Or even worse, Taylor wouldn't want to be with the shell version of herself she was quickly turning into. Or the liar that hid her mother's cancer like a coward.

Brooke [8:55pm]
My mom died

The phone immediately rang and Brooke closed her eyes looking for relief. She let it go to voicemail knowing she couldn't hear Taylor's voice right now, nor did she want to show just how broken she was.

Brooke [8:57pm]
I can't really talk now

Taylor [8:59pm]
Brooke omg. I am so sorry to hear that. I can't believe this. What happened?? How are you holding up?

Taylor [9:00pm]

What can I do to help?

Brooke [9:01pm]
I'm devastated

Brooke [9:01pm]
The wake is tomorrow so I'm just trying to get through that and the burial for my dad's sake

Taylor [9:02pm]
Where is the wake? I'll come

Brooke [9:04pm]
You don't have to do that. I meant what I said on Sunday that you should go live your life and enjoy your 30s. You deserve it and so much more than I can offer you. Especially now

Taylor [9:05pm]
Stop telling me what I want or what I should do. I want to be there with you. I want to be with you. Please let me be there for you

Brooke [9:07pm]
This is hard enough please don't make it harder. We can talk when I get back home

Taylor [9:09pm]
I'm sending you all the hugs from NY

Brooke didn't reply. She didn't know what to say back when all she wanted was to actually feel that embrace consume her right now.

Chapter Twenty-Four

The first time Brooke truly understood that people died was when she was eight and her grandfather died. Mary said that he had to go away up into the stars and would never come back. Brooke thought it was strange and continued to ask questions until her father told her that people cease to exist at some point. Sometimes because of old age. Sometimes from tragedies. Regardless the reason, it was part of the circle of life. Brooke had trouble sleeping for a full week after that, afraid that if she closed her eyes and went to sleep, she might not wake up.

All these years later, she still didn't have a grip on death. She'd definitely need to start seeing her therapist again now to cope with this and all of the feelings about life and loss that would certainly keep her awake for nights on end. Especially now that the previous reason for her angst was staring back at her.

Brooke didn't directly tell Jaclyn that her mother died. She hadn't directly spoken to her ex-wife in almost a year and Brooke would have preferred to keep it that way. Her father, unfortunately, was still close friends with Jaclyn's father and he told Victor that Mary died and the news trickled down.

"I'm so sorry," Jaclyn said as she held Brooke in her arms. "I know how close you were."

Brooke nodded and found herself confused at the sensation of being held by someone she shared an entire life with who now she felt like was a complete stranger. Who was this woman wrapping her arms around her? "I wish you told me she was sick. I would have been there for you."

Brooke stifled a laugh as she pulled out of the embrace. "I'm sure Charlie would have loved that." She didn't mean to have such a bite in her voice but she couldn't help herself. She was scorned and jilted after all.

"He knows that I'll always love you too, B. I was serious when I told you that."

Brooke shook her head in disbelief that even now at her mother's wake Jaclyn still had the audacity to pretend to love her. She had said the same lies after they broke up as if that was supposed to be comforting amidst a divorce caused by infidelity and pregnancy. Brooke could confirm with complete certainty that it wasn't. "You only love yourself."

Jaclyn reached for her hand to hold and Brooke didn't have the strength to tell her to stop. She was truly exhausted by the past week and if Jaclyn wanted to pretend and put on a show, she could be her guest. It meant nothing to Brooke. "I will always love you," Jaclyn repeated slowly. "Which is why you should have told me about Mary. How are you holding up?"

"Even though I knew it was coming it was still shocking," Brooke admitted, ignoring Jaclyn's love declaration.

"If only she stopped smoking years ago. Do you remember when you yelled at her for sneaking a cigarette when we took our wedding photos?"

Brooke smiled at the memory, even if Jaclyn was included. Her mother had disappeared right when the photographer wanted to take the family photos and Brooke was antsy to get it all over with so they could make it inside for cocktail hour. Her mother had decided to go for a smoke and talked a valet into bringing her a glass of champagne at the same time. Brooke wanted to be livid but Jaclyn had calmed her down with a kiss reminding her that they were finally married. It should have been all that she cared about. And for the next four years it was.

"She was relentless," Brooke said simply.

Jaclyn stroked her thumb across the top of Brooke's knuckles. It was such a foreign sensation. What used to give her butterflies now made her feel numb. "Like mother like daughter," she said softly. "Just in different ways."

Brooke always thought she was more like her father than her mother but maybe she had picked up her mother's determination, and stubbornness, over the years. "You didn't have to come today," Brooke said to end the trip down memory lane.

"Of course I did," Jaclyn stated as if there was no other alternative. "My parents still give me enough shit for our breakup. I'd never live this down if I didn't come with them."

Brooke sighed and glanced towards the back of the room where her former in-laws were seated when her eyes landed on Taylor two rows behind them. Her heart started to speed up at the sight and the realization of the situation she was currently in. The woman she loved and broke up with was staring at her holding hands with the woman she used to love who broke her heart. Maybe this was the karma she deserved.

Even though Brooke told Taylor not to come to the wake, nothing was going to stop her. Not even not knowing where it was. Taylor already knew all she needed. She was willing to call every single funeral home in the Washington DC area if she had to until she found out where Brooke was going to be. She wasn't going to let the woman she loved go through this alone. She might not be wanted romantically anymore, but she sure as hell wasn't going to not pay her respects to someone she wished she met to remind Brooke just how much she cared.

Luckily, a quick Internet search led her to Mary's obituary. No phone calls were needed giving her more time to pack a bag, book a hotel and a train ticket and less time to think about what was going to happen once she was there.

Now that Taylor arrived at the funeral home, she nervously looked around the crowded room at all the unknown people dressed in dark neutral colors. She never met any of Brooke's family and friends aside from Nina, but had seen photos in her apartment and on Instagram. That didn't help her in this moment as she looked for Brooke and tried to think of what would be an appropriate thing to say to the woman who just simultaneously lost her mother and dumped her.

As her eyes landed on Brooke at the front of the room, Taylor froze in her tracks. Even from afar, she could see how sad Brooke was. Her usually vibrant eyes were downcast and almost lackluster as she talked to a woman. Aside from the sullen expression on her face, she was still completely breathtaking. A woman shouldn't look that good while grieving.

"Brooke will be so happy you're here," a voice said from behind Taylor. She turned to see Nina, who was already leaning in to hug her. A hug that Taylor didn't even realize she needed.

"I'm not so sure about that," Taylor said nervously. She didn't want to overshare, especially in this environment, but she selfishly was hoping for words of encouragement.

Judging by the look on Nina's face and the way she squeezed Taylor's arm, she knew all about their current situation. "Ignore whatever she said. She's hurting and she wants you here, but maybe wait to go up and see her."

"Why?" Taylor asked as she glanced back at Brooke, still rooted in the same spot deep in conversation with the same woman who now was holding Brooke's hands in her own.

"You don't know?" Nina asked as she looked towards Brooke. "That's her ex-wife."

Taylor looked back towards Brooke and saw her now embracing the woman; the woman she used to be married to. From afar, Jaclyn was almost unrecognizable from the photos she had seen. Taylor knew now was not the time or place to be jealous, nor did she really have anything to be jealous over, yet she was. She was hurt that Brooke's ex-wife knew that her mother died and where the funeral was and Taylor, her girlfriend as of three days ago, was completely shut out and had to figure it all out on her own. What would have happened if Taylor hadn't texted Brooke last night? Would she have not told Taylor that her mother died?

As she continued an intense stare, Brooke looked towards the back of the room and noticed Taylor staring back at her, evident from the raised brow on her face. Without even thinking, Taylor stepped towards her, never breaking eye contact with each step. When she was a foot in front of her, all of her jealousy and emotions dissipated as she threw her arms around Brooke's shoulders and melted into her arms. "I'm so sorry."

It had only been three days since she saw Brooke last but it had felt like an eternity and everything seemed to change during that time. Now that she was holding Brooke in her arms, she didn't want to let go. Mainly for emotional support to let her know that she cared, but also because Jaclyn was staring right at them.

"I can't believe you're here," Brooke said softly in her ear as she rubbed the back of Taylor's neck to hold her closer.

"I had to be here," Taylor said as she clung to her.

Brooke tightened her grip around Taylor's body. "I'm glad you came."

When they pulled away, Taylor intertwined their hands together not wanting to break all contact. The fact that Brooke didn't pull away and let Taylor hold her hand gave Taylor a glimmer of hope that they could get through this together. Brooke finally removed her gaze from Taylor's eyes to look over at Jaclyn, who was glaring back at them.

"Jac, this is Taylor." Taylor knew a wake was not a place to judge but her eyes were like daggers on the woman who broke her girlfriend's heart. She never expected to cross paths with Brooke's ex-wife and the experience sent her mind into overdrive. She started looking for defects in this attractive woman's physical appearance but struggled to find any. Then she remembered just how hideous she was on the inside.

"Nice to meet you," Taylor said without releasing Brooke's hand to offer a shake, not that she thought Jaclyn was worth such nice pleasantries to begin with.

"I didn't realize you were seeing anyone," Jaclyn said to Brooke, barely giving Taylor any of her attention.

"I'm not just anyone," Taylor said defiantly. Brooke lightly squeezed her hand, which Taylor interpreted as her way of telling her to play nice. This was a wake after all.

"I didn't take you for the type to have a mid-life crisis," Jaclyn said with a smirk towards Brooke before she turned her attention back to Taylor. "Isn't it past your bedtime, sweetie?"

"I do my best work late at night. Right, babe?" Taylor countered back to the passive aggressive dig. Two could play this game and Taylor was not going to back down.

Brooke laughed before people turned to look at her and the inappropriate scene they were making. "Give me a few minutes, okay?" Brooke said to Taylor before pulling her hand away.

Taylor didn't want to leave. It felt like Jaclyn won and got to spend more time with Brooke. Time that she so desperately wanted. Reluctantly, she retreated to the back of the room and plopped down in a vacant chair as she began to question what exactly she was doing there. Were they even girlfriends at this point? Did Brooke really not want to be with her anymore? If that was the case, why did she bother to introduce her to Jaclyn and hold her hand? Unless it was just a ploy to make her ex jealous that she had also moved on. Maybe that's all she was to Brooke. A relationship rebound.

Nina sat down beside her and looked at her sympathetically. "I'm way out of line here, but you should know she didn't tell you her mom had stage three cancer because she thought it'd scare you away."

"Are you serious?" Taylor questioned sharply. Her mother was sick while they were together and she never mentioned it? All those trips to DC she pretended were nothing important? All those days she was exhausted and never shared what was really bothering her? Taylor felt betrayed that Brooke hid an entire portion of her life from her. Maybe she didn't care about her that much after all.

"And I quote: 'what thirty-year-old who can have whoever she wants would want to settle with a divorced forty-year-old with chronic migraines and a dying parent?'"

Taylor casted her eyes up to the front of room, watching as Brooke was still talking to Jaclyn. Despite how hurt she was, nothing compared to the wounds the other woman had. "I'm that thirty-year old," she said softly.

"I hoped you'd be," Nina said with a smile. "But she's absolutely terrified of you hurting her and not wanting the same type of future she does. You've got a lot of walls to knock down. Jaclyn did a number on her and now losing her mom was the final blow."

"What do I have to do?" Taylor asked in desperation as she turned her body towards Nina. "Please help me. I'm crazy about her."

Nina glanced up at her friend and sighed. Maybe this was too big for even her best friend to assist with. "Give her time. This loss isn't going to help anything."

"How much time are we talking here? Weeks? Months? Years? I can't sit back and watch her find someone else without giving me a real chance."

Nina looked between Taylor and Brooke before she opened her purse. "Give me your phone number. I'll try to help play Cupid if I have to."

Taylor happily read off her phone number before she started to question why Nina was so adamant about helping. Was there something that she knew? Did Brooke feel just as strongly about her as she did? "Why are you doing this?"

"Because I love her like a sister. She deserves to be happy and my intuition says you're it," Nina said with a smirk. "Don't prove me wrong."

"I won't," Taylor replied with a matching smile.

When she saw Nina's eyes travel upwards, Taylor followed her gaze and saw Brooke approaching them. She was finally free from Jaclyn and giving Taylor a moment of her attention. "Come with me," she motioned to Taylor before she started walking towards the front of the room again. Taylor smiled at Nina before she followed Brooke as she approached her father, which Taylor only knew from photos. This was not a circumstance Taylor ever imagined could be how she'd meet Brooke's father for the first time. "Dad, this is Taylor."

A wide smile crept across his tired face. "Taylor, it's so lovely to meet you," he said as he extended his hand to shake Taylor's. Without any context of who she was in Brooke's life, Taylor wondered if he knew. *What* he knew.

"I'm so sorry for your loss," Taylor said softly as she held onto his hand. "I can't imagine what you're going through."

His smiled softened as he squeezed her hand before releasing it. "I don't think I'll ever accept it but I'm just glad she's not suffering anymore."

Taylor wished she knew more to fill the silent void but Brooke kept her in the dark about what happened. "She'll always be with you," she opted for before she looked at Brooke and felt herself fight back a wave of her own emotions and feelings. Looking at Brooke reminded her of everything she could lose.

"Thank you for making the trip here," he continued as he placed his hand on his daughter's arm. "She could really use a reason to smile."

Brooke diverted her eyes away to look towards the floor. Was it guilt? Admission of feelings? General confusion? It didn't matter to Taylor; she just wanted to see those gorgeous hazel eyes again.

"I'd do anything to see her smile," Taylor said simply as Brooke raised her watery eyes to meet Taylor's gaze. A smile wasn't on her face but her eyes told Taylor everything. She was barely keeping herself from falling apart. And yet, despite the pain, she was still radiant.

"Me too," Oscar said before he cleared his throat. "You ladies go talk before I start crying."

Oscar turned to step away and return to the group he was talking to before Brooke introduced Taylor. Brooke motioned to the empty seats behind Taylor and they sat down in silence. "You really didn't have to come," Brooke finally stated.

"I did. And I'd do it again just to see that look on Jaclyn's face."

Brooke smiled and for the first time in days, Taylor felt herself relax slightly. "That was quite priceless."

"How come you told her your mom died but not me?" Taylor immediately asked, finding herself unable to rationally process what was going on and what this all meant.

Brooke looked down at the floor and avoided Taylor's questioning gaze. "I didn't. My dad told her dad – I had no idea they were coming."

That seemed like a situation Taylor could understand to be true, but it still tugged at her heartstrings. Jaclyn had a way to find out Mary died. Taylor was completely in the dark about a huge portion of Brooke's life. And while she wanted nothing more than to console Brooke during this time, she couldn't help but think about the reason *why* she didn't know about Mary's cancer and just how bad everything was. Why Brooke lied to her. Why she was in the dark. "Why did you hide this all from me?" she asked softly.

A puff of air left Brooke's lips before she looked back at the younger woman with tears in her eyes. Those hazel bloodshot eyes that silently screamed heartbreak. "Can we not have this conversation here?"

"Okay, but can we talk later?" Taylor asked as she nervously spun her rose gold ring around her finger. "I'm sure you'll be busy with your family but can I see you for a little today or tomorrow? Get dinner or a drink? I just want to talk and know you're okay."

Brooke seemed to be processing Taylor's request as she held Taylor's gaze, only momentarily breaking it to blink. What was going on in that brilliant mind of hers? Was she weighing her options, including whether Taylor was the right woman for her? Was she too devastated to think about anything other than her grief? Taylor could accept the latter, but the former gave her pause. She needed them to put Sunday behind them so they could move on, together.

"Let me take my dad home first then I'll stop by your hotel. Text me the address." Taylor didn't know why she was disappointed that Brooke didn't invite her over but she knew these were abnormal circumstances. She just hoped that what was to come wasn't going to be just as abnormal. All she wanted was some normalcy and her girlfriend back. Otherwise, she'd never get her heart back.

Chapter Twenty-Five

Brooke sat in her father's sedan parked down the block from Taylor's hotel. She wasn't emotionally or mentally prepared for this conversation. Physically, she yearned for Taylor's arms around her to make her feel whole again, just like it had a couple of hours ago at the wake. Losing her mother was devastating, yet the idea of losing Taylor also hurt so much, just in different ways. How much pain could one person handle? She opened the car door vowing to endure the pain now rather than down the line when she was more invested, when she'd be older and even less likely to get the happy ending she longed for. Time was slowly running out.

As soon as Taylor opened her hotel room door after Brooke gently knocked, Brooke felt herself immediately start to crumble. Could she really leave this woman behind? Taylor was already in her baby blue satin pajamas and looked completely adorable as she grabbed Brooke to pull her in for a tight embrace. The scent of her coconut shampoo filled her nostrils as she nestled herself into Taylor's neck. She could stay here forever.

Taylor dragged her towards the bed and sat them down, not removing her eyes from Brooke's as she broke the looming silence. "Are you okay?"

For such a simple question, it was the most complicated to answer. She wasn't okay, but admitting that to anyone, even herself, was always difficult because she never wanted to be weak. Even if it would be completely understandable in this situation. Brooke decided to shake her head from side to side rather than try to find words.

"Why didn't you tell me your mom had cancer?"

A shaky breath left Brooke's lips. She knew in her quest to make things easier, she wound up disappointing Taylor, which wasn't her intention to begin with. "I didn't want to cloud what we were starting with something so serious."

Taylor reached for Brooke's hand in her lap and laced their fingers together. A perfect fit. "I'm your girlfriend, I should know these things. I would have been there for you and helped you however I could."

Nothing Taylor did could have helped the situation or saved her mother from her inevitable death. "I didn't want you to pity me and stay with me only out of guilt."

Taylor scoffed in response. "That's ridiculous. I would have only cared for you even more, Brooke."

Tears swelled Brooke's eyes as she processed those words; too afraid to admit that could have been an option. Maybe Taylor would have cared initially but over time that would waver. She would have gotten just as stressed out as Brooke had and decided that Brooke wasn't worth it. If it wasn't her mother's illness, it would surely be something else to send Taylor running. Brooke wasn't strong enough to wait and find out what it would be that would destroy them. "This has all shown me how not ready I am for love again," Brooke shamefully admitted. "I've been so scared you're going to hurt me and now I just lost another person I love. I can't lose you too so I have to be the one to let you go."

Brooke knew she basically just confirmed that she loved Taylor without actually saying it and as much as she hoped Taylor didn't pick up on it, she hoped she did. Maybe Taylor could reciprocate the feelings and save Brooke from her despair.

"To do what?" Taylor sharply asked, not acknowledging love at all. "Be single forever? To find someone else who will actually hurt you? I'm not going to do that. I'm not Jaclyn."

She wasn't, but that didn't mean she still didn't have the capacity to hurt her. When Brooke got divorced, she was convinced she'd never fall in love again, either because of slim chances of meeting someone decent, or because of walls she'd put up to protect herself. Now as she stared back at Taylor, she realized the complete opposite had happened. She did fall in love with someone incredible and she was putting the walls up after the fact to not find out if they felt the same. How disappointing would it be to know that Taylor didn't share the same feelings? That Taylor didn't want a future that included marriage and kids. That Taylor was too young to even think about these things. At thirty, she probably did only still care about having sex and Brooke was just a reliable means to an end. Brooke decided to just not give Taylor a chance to prove her fears wrong. "We want different things in life."

Taylor jumped up from the bed to walk back and forth around the hotel room. "Says who?" she almost shrieked in frustration. "You? Jealous Michelle? Not me. When have I ever said I want different things from you?" Taylor's voice had escalated and it was jarring for Brooke to see and hear what she was doing to the person she cared about. "When have you ever asked me what I want, Brooke? You never asked. You just assumed."

Brooke grabbed her arm to stop her from pacing and a way to avoid answering that question. "You are the most incredible woman I've ever met. You have no idea what I feel about you but I can't go down this road. I have to protect myself now. I'm sorry."

Taylor stepped between Brooke's legs and wrapped her arms around her neck as she started to cry. Tears poured out of Taylor's eyes onto the top of Brooke's head and Brooke's heart ached in a resounding dull pain. "Don't do this to us. I know you're so devastated right now but don't throw us away. I can't lose you."

Brooke pulled Taylor down towards her and wiped tears off her cheeks. She wished that Taylor wasn't upset like this, knowing that *she* was the reason for the pain. Maybe Taylor truly cared about her as well, but that didn't erase the risk of how painful it would be to lose her and the life she so desperately wanted to have. "I will cherish these last few months more than you will ever know," she whispered as she started to cry as well, unable to control her emotional tidal wave.

Against her better judgment, she leaned up and brought their lips together for the last time. Brooke expressed everything she wanted to say in a kiss. She let her lips and tongue tell Taylor how much she loved her. How much she wanted her, not just now, but forever. But she learned the hard way forever didn't exist and she wouldn't take that chance with someone who had a higher likelihood of not wanting the same future as her. She didn't want to ask knowing priorities could easily change and vows could be broken. Jaclyn proved that tenfold. Taylor couldn't be her second mistake, even if she'd be the greatest gift in the process.

Taylor's tears blended in with Brooke's as they cried and kissed, their lips moving in harmony to the sound of Brooke's breaking heart. "You're making a mistake," Taylor said when she finally pulled away. "I'm all in."

"For now," Brooke countered.

"For always."

Brooke became still in Taylor's arms and wanted to confess everything but she opted for silence and a kiss on Taylor's forehead before she slipped out of her arms. She needed to pull herself together, not only for herself, but for her father who needed her to be a rock tomorrow at the burial.

"I have to get back to my dad," Brooke said as she wiped her tears and looked at the wall, trying to hang on to the microscopic thread of composure she had left. "Thank you for coming today. You have no idea how much that meant to me." She avoided looking at Taylor knowing she was still crying by the sounds of her whimpers. If she turned around and looked at her, she would fall apart. She needed to leave. "Goodnight."

She walked to the door and when Taylor didn't try to stop her, she decided she made the right choice. At least for the initial moment she walked down the hall. By the time she got in the elevator and released another wave of tears, she knew there was a reason she only said goodnight. She knew she could never actually say goodbye to Taylor Thompson.

Eleven minutes. That's how long Brooke stayed in the hotel room. She managed to shatter Taylor's heart in eleven minutes and walk out the door like she didn't feel an ounce of the same pain. Taylor wanted to be mad at her, furious even, but she couldn't. Brooke just lost her mother, and that was a lot more important than what was going on between them. Brooke probably wasn't even thinking clearly. Or maybe she was. That thought hurt even more.

Taylor got under the white bedsheets and cried as she wondered where she went wrong. Just like Sunday morning, Brooke left her reeling with her mind spinning in a million directions. The latest direction was what she did to cause this. Taylor thought she must have done something to give Brooke the impression things wouldn't work between them long term. As she replayed back their entire relationship she wondered if it was because she never talked about what her future aspirations were. Because she never said she was secretly a hopeless romantic who did believe in marriage and that she did want a family with the right woman. A woman she thought was Brooke. Did that allow Michelle's words to have extra weight and impact? If Brooke really cared about her, wouldn't she have looked past that and trusted her actual girlfriend rather than someone she met once?

Taylor let out another onslaught of tears realizing she never stood a chance. Jaclyn told Brooke fake promises too and then blindsided her with a pregnancy. She was getting married to him now too, clearly getting what she wanted after all while Brooke got nothing but heartbreak. Taylor knew Brooke was the woman for her, the one she never wanted to let go of and that's why she decided amidst her tears that she wouldn't give up yet. She *couldn't*. She convinced herself that time would be on her side here despite how shitty she felt in the moment. There was too much left that was unspoken.

How do you let the woman you love go without even telling her? Knowing she can't receive it properly? Knowing you might not hear it back? You just do and remember that your soulmate will always come back to you, if there's even such a thing. If it's meant to be, it'll be. At least that's what Taylor told herself as she drifted to sleep.

In the morning, Taylor went to the church where the mass was being said for Mary. She contemplated whether or not she should even attend given the events of the night prior, but she felt like this was the right thing to do. This had nothing to do with Brooke – she was simply going to pay her respects to a woman who deserved more time to live. Taylor listened to the priest give Mary a final sendoff while she sat in the last pew. A closing prayer for peace that Taylor hoped would help heal Brooke and Oscar's hearts.

When Brooke walked down the aisle of the church towards the doors, her eyes met Taylor's as she slowed her pace, processing the fact that she was there. For a moment, Taylor thought that Brooke was going to approach her or extend her hand for Taylor to join her. Instead, the faintest heartbroken smile appeared on Brooke's face before she walked out the door with her father. Taylor interpreted it as Brooke being happy she was there. It was the hope she'd hold onto for weeks to come.

By the time Taylor made it outside, Brooke and Oscar were nowhere in sight. Taylor had no idea if Mary was being buried or cremated, but maybe they were already enroute to that. Or heading back to their house for a family gathering that Taylor would never know about. Could today really have been the last time Taylor saw Brooke? She'd remember that devastating sad smile for the rest of her life if that was the case.

"Glutton for punishment?" Nina asked as she walked up to Taylor on the sidewalk. Taylor raised a brow in confusion. "You still came after what happened last night."

"I guess you heard she dumped me. Again," Taylor admitted, embarrassed and ashamed.

"I didn't hear that," Nina clarified. "I heard she walked away because she's a pussy."

Taylor stifled a laugh, realizing that outside of a church where a funeral was just held wasn't an appropriate place to appear to be having fun. "That's not quite how I would describe it."

Nina looked around at the remaining people on the street hugging goodbye before walking to their cars. When Nina's eyes became fixated in one place, Taylor turned to see Jaclyn talking to an older couple, probably relatives of Brooke's. Her former family. Maybe they were all going to Brooke's house together. "Are you hungry?" Nina asked as she finally looked back towards Taylor. "There's a diner not too far from here and I could really go for some cheap coffee and pancakes."

"You want to go with me?" Taylor asked in confusion. If there was a gathering, Nina surely would have been invited. She seemed more like family to Brooke than Jaclyn was now.

Nina smiled as she dug in her purse for her car keys. "There's no one else here now is there?"

Having a meal with Nina felt comforting, yet dangerous. Brooke would probably see it as a betrayal; her best friend talking to the enemy. Yet in this moment, Taylor didn't care what Brooke would think because she was too fixated on this possibly having a chance of reuniting them. Nina seemed like the one and only person who could get through to Brooke and Taylor wouldn't miss that opportunity. "You drive, I'll buy."

"In that case, I'll get some bacon and eggs too," Nina said with a smile as she walked off to the parking lot with Taylor trailing behind her.

Despite how nervous Taylor thought she would be having this one-on-one time and conversation with Nina, she was oddly relaxed. Nina was nice, and funny, which Taylor already knew from the Billy Joel concert. It was no wonder Brooke cared about her as much as she did, and the feeling seemed to be mutual. All Nina did was rave about Brooke, until the moment she called her an idiot for running away from Taylor. The jilted woman had to admit that felt good to hear.

"I'm going to tell you two things because I think it's important for you to hear," Nina said as she wiped the sides of her mouth to clean remnants of maple syrup. As promised, she did order pancakes with a side order of extra crispy bacon. "One, Brooke was absolutely blindsided and completely devastated by Jaclyn. I'm talking non-stop crying and self-loathing thinking she did something wrong when Jaclyn was just a fucking bitch."

"Did you not like her?" Taylor interrupted; her curiosity getting the best of her.

"I did for a while. They seemed happy together. But a year before she got knocked up, I walked in on her and Charlie practically pressed up on one another at her and Brooke's Halloween party. I told Brooke and she brushed it off because Jaclyn naturally brushed it off and she turned up the charm, taking Brooke to Turks and Caicos like two weeks later as a surprise but it was all a coverup. Fucking bitch."

Taylor tried to picture Brooke in that moment, feeling so secure in her relationship that she didn't see the signs. Now she was nothing but insecure. "Fucking bitch," Taylor echoed.

"Number two," Nina started again. "Your friend Michelle said something to her at your birthday. She hasn't told me the exact details yet but it's what triggered this whole thing. She panicked and then she got the text her mom had a stroke while you were arguing and it spiraled out of control."

Taylor froze as she looked at Nina across the booth. "Wait, she found out her mom had a stroke while at my apartment?"

"Yeah, she said her dad called and texted and that's when she left."

"Fuck," Taylor sounded as she dropped her face into her hands. Waves of regret washed over her as she thought about Sunday and the words that were said that she wished never left her mouth. If she didn't say those words, would everything be different now? "I accused her of working and said maybe that's why Jaclyn cheated on her."

Nina was silent. Stunned into silence possibly because when Taylor raised her head and looked at her, she was wearing an expression that was on the border between disgust and rage. "I didn't mean it and I told her I was sorry but I was hurt and she was just sitting there on her phone ignoring me after she dropped a bomb saying we shouldn't be together."

Nina finally looked away as she picked up her coffee mug. "The fact that you willingly told me that shows you're honest but fuck, you couldn't have said anything else?"

"I'm sorry, it was terrible and I regret it so much," Taylor said exasperated. "I had no idea that's when she found out. Jesus Christ, why didn't she tell me?"

If she had a time machine, Taylor would go back a month and tell Brooke she loved her the first time she wanted to confess her feelings. Everything could be so different now.

Nina sighed heavily as she leaned back against the blue pleather booth. "I told her to tell you about her mom but she was worried it would scare you away. Then she got scared you might never want a real future with her. Then whatever your friend said to her scared her to the point of no return. And here we are."

"What do I do?" Taylor asked, finding herself only caring about the solution. She'd apologize for the rest of her life if she had to, as long as it meant she had a chance to save her relationship.

"You give her time," Nina repeated her suggestion from the wake the day before. "She needs time. Time to process her mom. Time to accept what's happened. And time to wake the hell up and realize she misses you."

"What if she doesn't?" It was certainly a possibility, even if Taylor didn't want that to be the outcome.

"She will and soon enough she'll admit it to me," Nina said with a smile. "And I'll tell her 'I told you so' and we'll probably argue. She'll cry and be super dramatic before she admits she made a mistake."

"You say that like you've been here before," Taylor said with a sad smile.

Nina bit off a chunk of bacon. "I can say that I've never seen her happier than I have with you. So, this might be unchartered territory."

"Thank you," Taylor said softly. "You've given me hope."

"And thank you," Nina said with a smile. "You've given me bacon. And a lot of jealousy over your sex life."

A blush took over Taylor's face. She couldn't miss out on that sex for the rest of her life. She might just need to purchase more bacon breakfasts in the future to help her get there.

Chapter Twenty-Six

Brooke sat at her office desk staring at her computer screen in a daze. She had so much work to catch up on after her bereavement leave but she couldn't focus. How could she? Her mother just died two weeks ago. She broke up with her girlfriend. The idea of getting through another day of work and meetings about people's public images and press appearances made Brooke want to just turn around and go home. None of this mattered. Life was short and she was going to waste it working on making other people's lives better when it was her own life that needed reviving.

Right now, all she could think about was that she needed something positive to look forward to and she hoped that Nina could deliver it. She was her last hope.

Brooke [11:23am]
Can we meet for dinner tonight? I really need a shoulder to cry on

Nina [11:37am]
Come over after work. Bring wine

Brooke [11:39am]
Might need tequila

Nina [11:40am]

I'll make tacos

Brooke smiled and placed her head down on her desk. She should have taken more time off – she should have pushed herself to fall apart completely before she could pick up the pieces and move on. Instead, here she was, in the middle of a busy office where everyone could see her through the glass windows barely keeping herself together. Would she even care if people saw her have a complete meltdown right now? She didn't think so. Everything else mattered so much more.

Later that night, Brooke arrived at her best friend's apartment with a tequila bottle in hand. She hoped that she was making the right decision. Nursing her pain with alcohol was a terrible idea any day, but especially on a Thursday night with tequila. The Friday recovery would be rough.

"How's your dad?" Nina asked while she diced tomatoes and Brooke prepared margaritas in the blender.

"He's thinking about going to spend a few weeks with my uncle in Miami to give himself a breather for a bit."

"That's a good idea, it could be helpful for him. Maybe you should do the same."

Going away wasn't something in the cards for Brooke now. "I'm so busy at work, I can't take a vacation right now."

"Work remote. You're going to burn yourself out."

Despite knowing it was true, Brooke didn't want to admit it. As much as she hated having to work now, and spent the better part of the morning contemplating if she could just quit and retire earlier to work part-time somewhere else, it was the only thing giving her a distraction from her personal life. "That might not be the worst outcome."

She turned the blender on and watched the machine roar to life, swirling the much-needed ingredients around. "Are we making slushies?" Andrew asked as he ran into the room and yelled over the blender. "I want one!"

"These are adult slushies," Nina yelled back to her son. "Only for me, daddy, and Aunt Brooke."

"Not fair!" he complained before storming out of the room.

Brooke poured them each a glass and glanced at the white icy concoction looking for answers. She learned her lesson almost twenty years ago that tequila was only good for one thing: forgetting the present.

"Have you talked to Taylor?" Nina asked as soon as they took their first sip.

Brooke knew the question was coming. There was no way Nina wasn't going to bring up Taylor, or that Brooke wouldn't bring her up herself. This was partially why she wanted to see her best friend today – to have someone to talk to about what was eating her alive. Yet, the idea of actually talking about Taylor now made her want to walk out the door and go back to hiding in her lonely apartment. "I'm going to need more than one sip if we're going to talk about that."

Nina lowered her eyes onto her best friend. "We're going to talk about it now before you have one drink and start crying."

Clearly Nina was still holding on to old memories and the effect tequila had on Brooke during college. In Brooke's defense, it had the same effect on Nina but she didn't bother to bring that up knowing Nina would just accuse her of deflecting from the topic at hand. "She texted me a couple times but I haven't responded."

"What is wrong with you?" Nina barked back as she slammed her glass on the kitchen counter. Brooke was not prepared for this strong of a reaction so early into the conversation. "You love her. She's done nothing wrong and you just broke up with her in a panic."

Brooke took three long gulps of her margarita to help prepare her for the onslaught of what else was going to be thrown her way. She knew Nina would scold her, and deep down she knew she needed it and deserved it, but it was still jarring. "I'm saving myself from future heartbreak."

"You are making a huge mistake," Nina declared with enough force to make Brooke actually listen to what she was suggesting. "I've never seen you happier. *She* makes you happy. She wants to be with *you*. You're putting words in her mouth and making fictious decisions for her."

Hazel eyes drifted towards the marble countertop. Nina was right. Brooke knew that despite how much she didn't want to admit it. With a heavy sigh, Brooke decided to finally tell Nina about the hay that broke the camel's back and sent her spiraling down into quicksand.

"Her friend Michelle told me that I was just sex to Taylor and that she'd never want something serious with me," Brooke admitted when she sat down on a bar stool. She had briefly told Nina that something happened that night at the bar but it was very much overshadowed by the events that transpired the morning after. "I literally wanted the floor to open up and swallow me whole. It was like my worst fear was being confirmed and I could only see Taylor as this young girl who wanted to have fun who isn't even thinking about her future. Isn't thinking about *me* in her future." She sighed deeply and ran her fingers through her hair. "And then we got home and had mind-blowing sex. I'm talking Taylor in lingerie and double-sided strap-on sex."

Brooke paused to look up and saw Nina with her mouth slightly ajar. "That's hot."

"And then Taylor said she loved fucking me," Brooke continued, feeling her heart break all over again. "I thought she was going to tell me she loved me and she said the one thing that confirmed Michelle's statement. I love her and she loves fucking me."

Nina sat down beside Brooke and placed her hand on her arm. "Okay. I can see how you might spiral from that but did you talk to Taylor about it?"

"A little," Brooke started before she shook her head. "I mean, no, I didn't flat out ask if it was true, but she told me that she found out about it and it was all lies. It's just scary to believe that Michelle might be telling the truth. What if Taylor only does enjoy having sex with me? What if that's all I am to her?"

"You'll never know by running away."

Brooke was never a runner. She always accepted every challenge head-on. Hell, sometimes she thought she loved a challenge too much. At least at work. Yet, now she was fleeing the second it got hard. And it wasn't even hard, it was just unknown. "I don't want to waste time with someone who doesn't want to ever get married or anything. And obviously, I don't mean now or anytime soon. I'm not crazy," Brooke said before she picked up her drink and took a long sip. "Or maybe I am crazy. Crazy enough to leave her."

"Mommy! I'm hungry!" Andrew yelled out from the other room.

"Dinner will be ready soon!" Nina yelled back and sighed in frustration. "Are you sure you want little demons in your life?"

"I do," Brooke said almost under her breath. What she wanted felt so far away from her in this moment that she started to give up hope that it could even be obtained.

Nina got up and returned to preparing the dinner that her children were antsy to devour. "I have a feeling Taylor would want the same with you."

Brooke stared at Nina's back and questioned what she knew. "What makes you so sure?"

"She's clearly in love with you," Nina said as she continued to chop onions. "And not just in love with fucking you. If she wasn't, she wouldn't have found out where the wake was after you told her not to come. She wouldn't have stayed for the mass after you pushed her away. She wouldn't have texted you. She's committed to you."

Brooke drained the contents of her glass in one final gulp. She was so terrified about the negative what ifs, she had overlooked the positive what ifs. "What do I do?"

Nina turned around and looked at her friend with a lopsided smile. "First, you make us another round of drinks. Second, you eat with us and be the good aunt my kids love and wish I was. Third, you text Taylor."

"I can do that," Brooke said with more optimism than before. "But I might need more than just one more round to make it to number three."

"I'd expect no less," Nina said with a smile.

Maybe Brooke could pull herself together and make this right. Maybe. If she didn't wind up throwing up all night instead.

Chapter Twenty-Seven

I'm going to need a new apartment. Taylor blasted music and tried to drown out the thoughts in her head. Nina's advice of giving Brooke time wasn't working – it was driving Taylor mad. And now her own apartment that used to be her safe haven was the equivalent of the lower level of Hades. Every inch of the studio reminded her of Brooke. The kitchen where Brooke made her breakfast. The couch where they made out like teenagers. The bed where Taylor could still feel Brooke surround her. Consume her. And then ultimately destroy her. There was no escaping Brooke in a four-hundred-fifty square foot box.

Moments like this made Taylor angry, maybe even a tad spiteful, because she hoped that Brooke would suffer just as much. That she wouldn't be able to look at her apartment without thinking of Taylor. That she couldn't cook in the kitchen without thinking of the night after the work gala and the things they did on the kitchen island. Or seeing her face on the silly photo Taylor left the last time she was there. Although maybe she already threw that out just like she tossed Taylor.

Taylor rolled over in her bed and grunted in frustration. Despite how mad and hurt she was, she still couldn't actually wish harm on Brooke. She loved her too much. She cared too much and knew Brooke was grieving the loss of her mother. That was so much more serious than what was transpiring with them, but that knowledge didn't make this waiting game any easier.

When "Lisztomania" by Phoenix came on her playlist, she sat upright in bed with an idea. There was one way she could help clear her mind and it wouldn't be in this apartment. She needed a change of scenery. She needed something that Brooke was never associated with.

"So, what do I owe the pleasure of my baby sister showing up unannounced?" Harper asked when she let Taylor into her house after hugging her tightly on the porch. Her white Shih Tzu dog, Minnie, finally stopped barking the second Harper broke their embrace and finally looked down at her ignored pet. "Mom said you dropped in unannounced a couple of months ago. Don't you know how to use a phone?"

"Can't I come spontaneously visit my childhood hometown for no reason?" Taylor questioned as she looked around the house almost expecting two excited children to be smashing into her legs upon hearing her voice.

"You could," Harper said before glancing over at her sister, "except you always say how much you hate it here when it's hot and you also look like complete shit."

"Thanks for the compliment," Taylor said as she dramatically threw herself on the couch, making herself at home. She hadn't been in her sister's house in almost two years and right now it felt a lot homier than her own apartment did. Being here was what she knew she needed; a break from reality that was long overdue.

"What's going on?" Harper asked as she sat down on the couch and looked at her sister with curious and worried eyes.

Taylor wanted to talk. It was the reason she flew here on a whim knowing her sister was the only one who could logically understand the situation she was in, but all she could do was burst into tears. All the pent-up emotion from the last two weeks exploded out of her and onto the black throw pillow nestled into the corner of the couch.

"Tay," Harper sounded as she jumped to wrap her arms around her sister. "What's wrong?"

When the younger woman finally found the strength to stop crying, she told her sister about everything that happened the past two weeks. From her birthday and Michelle's apparent conversation through the wake and the ignored text messages from days prior. She confessed how hurt and devastated she was that she didn't seem to have a girlfriend anymore. Not just any girlfriend. *Brooke*. She lost Brooke and didn't even understand how when everything seemed to be going so well right up until the last night they had sex. She got chills thinking about that night, and every other one with Brooke. About how she cried kissing Brooke in the hotel room after the wake. About how she could still close her eyes and see Brooke clearly before her.

"Sounds like you really love her," Harper said softly, bringing Taylor back into the conversation.

"Yes!" Taylor yelled out. "I am madly in love with her and she just shut me out and now I'll never be able to tell her."

Harper sighed and rubbed her sister's back trying to offer support. Yet, despite how nice it felt, it wasn't healing any of her wounds. "Let me make you a cup of tea. Tea always helps me calm down."

"It's a hundred and one degrees out I don't want tea," Taylor complained. "Make me a cocktail."

Harper obliged as she went to the bar in the corner of the dining room. Taylor watched her mix a gin and tonic in anticipation of having the alcohol calm some of her anxieties. If that was even possible.

"I want to know how you got over Michael and were able to remarry," Taylor said after she took two long sips of her drink. It might have been one in the afternoon, but she really needed that reprieve.

Harper furrowed her brow in confusion. "Why?"

"Because maybe I can learn what to do so she'll trust me and want to be with me."

"You can't force people to be with you, Tay," Harper reminded her.

Taylor sunk further into the couch, wishing it could just swallow her whole. She felt like she was a pathetic woman desperate for someone to love her back. "But to be honest she might just be scared."

"Why would she be scared of me?" the younger woman questioned with hostility. "I've given her nothing but affection and my complete attention. I'm not a bad person. We were so perfect together."

Harper reached over and held her sister's hand. "But you have the power to break her heart."

"I won't!"

"Says everyone who's ever dated someone before," Harper said while rolling her eyes.

"I'm serious I won't!" Taylor yelled back. She was aware that her raised voice could imply she was being defensive, but in her heart, all she knew was the truth about her feelings. "I've stupidly spent entire nights thinking about a real future with her one day. Getting married. Having kids. God, it's all so picture perfect."

Those visions felt so real to her she could almost feel them. She could feel Brooke in her arms at family holidays. Waking up in bed together every day. Going grocery shopping and planning their weeks. Going on lavish vacations and taking touristy photos around the world. She knew these were all long-term goals and visions but she'd never get there if Brooke didn't let her be her girlfriend now in the present.

"When Michael and I got divorced, I was terrified of dating again," Harper shared as she leaned back on the couch. "I didn't want to feel like a failure again. I went out with some really decent guys and some I thought maybe could be real but it fizzled out and it hurt more than I thought it would. When I finally met Bryan, I had lowered my expectations and he was patient with me. Maybe you just need to be patient with her. If she truly cares about you, she'll appreciate knowing you're still there willing to give her time to accept she's worthy of a real relationship again."

Taylor processed her sister's words, and she completely understood what she was saying but she still felt hopeless. "I'd happily be patient if she gave me a chance but she just dumped me and acted like she didn't care."

"From the sounds of it she cared a lot and her tears and words were proof of that," Harper pointed out. "But her mom just died, Tay. I can't even imagine having that weight on top of trying to accept someone wasn't going to hurt me. I would have called it off with Bryan too if I was in her shoes."

Brooke losing her mom was what bothered Taylor the most because she wanted to be there to comfort her. To hold her. To tell her she loved her and that Mary would always be with her. To not be able to do that felt almost like a cold betrayal of her own identity and the role she wanted to fill.

Harper continued to give her sister advice. "Give her some space. Try to remind her that you care about her and hopefully when she's not so hurt, she'll come back to you and you can talk all of this out. If not, it's her loss."

Brooke not coming back was something Taylor knew was now a possibility but not something she wanted to be a reality. "Thanks for the pep talk," Taylor finally spoke. "Can we go do something fun tonight now that I just showed up on your doorstep?"

"Yes, but you owe me," Harper said with a smile. "One day I'm going to show up at your place to escape my kids."

Taylor smiled and thought about how nice it'd be to have Harper in New York for a weekend without Bryan or her two kids. She just hoped Brooke would be around to meet her. "Deal."

"And I need you to do one more thing," Harper said as she waited for Taylor to meet her gaze. "Stop being friends with Michelle."

"Tell me something I don't already know," Taylor said with a sigh. As much as she wanted to blame Michelle for everything, there was a part of her that was also responsible for this happening because she never told Brooke how she really felt. If she only told her she loved her on her birthday, would this have all been avoided? Or was this how it was destined to be so she could fully understand her feelings and what she wanted?

She'd never know.

Chapter Twenty-Eight

Brooke found herself staring at her ceiling feeling more heartbroken than she ever had in her life. She still couldn't believe her mother had died and she wasn't there in time to say goodbye with her knowing she was there. All of the preparation for what was to come didn't lessen the blow of this loss and the ache in her chest that she'd never have phone calls or dinners with the woman that raised her.

And then there was the incredible sadness of pushing Taylor away. She thought she was doing herself a favor by ending things before she got hurt down the line but now, she questioned her actions entirely. Maybe she acted too hastily. Maybe her judgment was clouded because of her mother. Maybe she should have given Taylor a chance to explain Michelle's comments. Asked her what she really wanted for the future. Asked her if she thought they had a real chance. Maybe it was the tequila still in her system a full twenty-four hours after she was at Nina's. The hangover she endured today was enough to make her work from home and hide in the dark all day.

"God damnit," Brooke said aloud to herself as she rolled over in her empty bed. She looked at the side where Taylor would sleep. She closed her eyes and imagined what it would be like to have her there now to comfort her. To tell her everything would be okay.

She grabbed her phone and started to type, *"I'm so sorry"* before she deleted it. *"I fucked up and I hope you can forgive me."* That didn't work either. *"I made a huge mistake pushing you away when I needed you the most. I hope you can forgive me."* Too dramatic. *"I love you."* She had no right to say that now. Especially via text. So instead, she deleted it all and closed her phone before she picked it up again and decided to not overthink it.

Brooke [2:04am]
I'm sorry

It was a good thing she wasn't expecting a response because it never came.

"Aunt Taylor! Throw my ball!" Eli yelled at his aunt.

Taylor had just sat down after helping Ella push her bowling ball down the lane. She helped her niece get a strike which sent the young girl into a fit of hysterics, and now her brother, into a fit of competition.

"Okay, but next time you're going to push it yourself, okay?" Eli nodded furiously as Taylor picked up the green ball and placed Eli's small hands on it before she released the ball down the lane with extra strength. Her luck of getting a strike had run out when only five pins fell down. That was enough to get Eli to say he would do it himself.

Taylor sat back down and picked up her beer as she watched her nephew manage to place the ball in the one spot where no pins were standing. She turned her head and saw her sister staring at her with an intense gaze. "What?"

"I think you'd make a pretty awesome mom," Harper said with a smile.

Taylor rolled her eyes. "That's just because you want a babysitter."

"Does Brooke want kids?"

It had been twenty-four hours since Taylor heard the other woman's name verbalized. That's not to say she wasn't thinking about her, because she honestly couldn't stop, but to hear it reminded Taylor that Brooke was real. She wasn't just a figment of Taylor's imagination. She was real enough to text Taylor in the middle of the night. Not that Taylor had any plans of responding while on this trip. She didn't intend to play games, and she desperately wanted to talk to Brooke, but she needed this time away to clear her own mind. "I think she does," Taylor said softly as she thought about how sad Brooke always looked whenever she mentioned Jaclyn's child. "I think that's why she's so worried about age and the future. And what her ex did to her."

Harper nodded and looked at Ella inching closer to the wax part of the bowling lane. "Stop there, Ella!"

Taylor could just picture the catastrophe that would ensue the moment Ella slipped on the lane and then Harper have to struggle to pick her up. It might have been the comical relief she needed.

"What does her ex have to do with it?" Harper questioned.

Jaclyn seemed to have played a large role in their relationship, unknowingly and certainly unwanted. "She cheated on Brooke with a guy and got pregnant. They're getting married next month."

"Fuck," Harper sounded.

"Bad word, mommy!" Ella scolded her mother.

Harper patted Ella on the head. "You're completely right." As Ella jumped up to plot how to push the ball with Eli, Harper looked back at her sister. "You failed to mention that very important detail."

It was a detail that Taylor didn't mention because it shouldn't have mattered. She was not Jaclyn.

"You do realize why she's so scared then, right?" Harper continued. "You don't just forget about something like that."

Taylor knew that but all she could do was shrug in response. She knew she'd never do that to Brooke. She wished Brooke trusted her. She wished Brooke talked to her about any insecurities she had. Once Taylor had that thought, she also felt guilt rise to the surface. She should have asked more. She should have given Brooke more reasons to believe in her. She should have reminded Brooke that she was serious about everything and that she was nothing but loyal.

"So hypothetically speaking," Harper started, stopping Taylor's running thoughts as she looked up at her sister. "Would you carry the baby?"

Harper's question was a legitimate one, and one Taylor had already spent some time pondering herself. If she and Brooke were to ever cross that bridge, Taylor would most likely have to carry otherwise they would need to adopt. She would have been fine with either option but these were all grandiose thoughts that didn't warrant any additional mental energy in the present. There is no baby without the two moms being together. "I guess so," she answered quickly. "But can we not talk about her for the rest of the weekend? I kind of need a mental cleanse."

"Fine," Harper agreed as she took a sip of her beer. Just because her sister didn't talk about Brooke, didn't mean Taylor stopped thinking about her. She wouldn't know how even if she tried.

Brooke didn't know exactly what she was doing but she was most definitely mindlessly pacing the hallway of Taylor's apartment building. After she stopped by the bar and didn't see her there, she made the impromptu decision to show up here in an attempt to mend her heart. Except Taylor wasn't home. Brooke sat outside the apartment building for an hour and fifteen minutes, and was contemplating just how long she'd be this pathetic waiting for Taylor to either answer the doorbell or come home. She was on the verge of leaving when Mr. Jefferson, Taylor's next-door neighbor, arrived at the building carrying groceries. Groceries that Brooke was quick to help grab and help him inside to bring her a few steps closer to the woman she loved.

Another forty-seven minutes of waiting and pacing left Brooke feeling hopeless. Of course, Taylor wouldn't be home. It was a Saturday night and for all intents and purposes, Taylor was single. Once that thought entered Brooke's mind, she felt herself crumble even more. Maybe Taylor was out with Michelle and other friends laughing over their entire relationship. Maybe she was already looking for someone else to be with. Someone to sleep with. Someone to make her get over Brooke and all the hurt she had caused her beautiful soul.

Forcing herself to the apartment was a massive step and Brooke knew if she didn't get these feelings off of her chest now, she'd lose her nerve. She was terrified of the rejection but she was going to take a chance anyway. What's the worst that could happen? They were already broken up.

Chapter Twenty-Nine

When Taylor got home from her sister's house late Sunday night, she was surprised to see an envelope on the floor when she opened the door.

"Great, a rent increase is all I need right now," she said aloud as she bent down to pick up the blank envelope. When she pulled out the paper inside, she was shocked to see a handwritten letter rather than a cold typed-up statement informing her that her rent would be increasing or the elevators would be out of service. Again.

The white paper started to tremble in Taylor's hands as her eyes scanned the words and she understood who it was that slipped this inside her apartment when she was in Phoenix.

"Dear Taylor,

I know this might seem old fashioned, but I still find written letters romantic. Although, I wish this letter was being dropped off in better circumstances. Or have better things written in it, even though this might be the most important declaration of my life.

I'm sitting in the hallway outside of your apartment and you're not home. I know that sounds creepy but I came here to get a few overdue things off my chest. I don't want to miss the chance to say this tonight so I'm writing it instead before I chicken out.

I want to tell you that I'm sorry. I'm so incredibly sorry for pushing you away when I needed you most. I'm sorry for not telling you about my mom to begin with. I'm sorry for not meeting your parents in Santa Barbara.

I'm sorry for not introducing you to my parents when they were in town. I'm sorry for hurting you. I'm just truly so deeply sorry and wish I could take it all back.

If it's any consolation, I hurt myself just as much. If not even more because I'm absolutely crazy about you. My feelings have terrified me for a while now, maybe since we met if I was being honest. It's not that I actually care about our age difference, it's that I deeply care about YOU. I've been consumed with worry that we're in different places in our lives and you'll grow to find that you want different things than I do. That you don't want to get married and have kids one day – not saying with me, but just in general. Although I'd be lying if I said I didn't want that. Hearing Michelle verbalize my fears and tell me I was nothing but sex to you felt like a confirmation based on the assumptions I had already made from things you said, or didn't say. I simply panicked.

And then my mom died. I was hiding her diagnosis and struggles from you because I was scared of that too. Scared I'd lose you in the process and be even more heartbroken. Scared you might only stay with me out of pity and break up with me down the line, blinding me the way Jaclyn did. It's taken me a while to recover from her destruction and it's obvious I'm still a bit broken and I wish I wasn't. I'm trying not to be but I'm just terrified.

I know how much I screwed up and that these are just words but I'm truly so sorry, Taylor. If I could do it all over again, I'd tell you everything sooner before I destroyed it. I'd take the chance on you because you are worth it all. Even if we never lasted, at least I would have tried and had you for as long as I'd be lucky to be granted.

If you can ever forgive me and want to talk, you know how to reach me.

Yours,
Brooke

P.s- Mr. Jefferson told me that I owe him a slice of cheesecake (his choice) for letting me borrow a pen and paper. If you could get him one for me, I'd appreciate that. I don't like not delivering on promises."

Tears were streaming down Taylor's face by the time she put the letter down on the kitchen table in front of her. Why didn't Brooke just call her and ask to see her? Then again, Taylor was the one who decided not to reply to the "I'm sorry" text at two o'clock in the morning thinking it warranted more of a conversation, especially after Taylor had sent her long messages asking for another chance and an opportunity talk. She interpreted the "I'm sorry" as Brooke's inability to give her what she needed.

Taylor firmly believed that relationships should never be difficult. Of course, there would be difficult moments and challenging times to navigate, such as a sick parent, but the feelings and desire to be together should never be complicated. Now that she knew how Brooke felt and what she wanted herself, it was time to make a change.

Taylor spent the next three days deep in thought. More accurately, she was like a hamster on a wheel going in circles and getting nowhere. She didn't know *how* she wanted to see Brooke because each option included talking to her and the outcome was unknown. Brooke asking for forgiveness in the letter didn't mean that she wanted to get back together and Taylor needed to keep reminding herself of that as she processed how they should reunite to talk.

If they went to a restaurant, they would have a very public outing and she didn't want that. There could be tears, likely Taylor's. Did she really want to be publicly humiliated at a restaurant? Of course not. She could just picture herself showing up there and crying while their waiter would interrupt asking if they were doing okay and she'd be far from okay.

But did she really want to prolong this stress and the words that so desperately needed to be spoken? Telling Brooke she loved her at a restaurant didn't feel right either. If she was going to have done that, it should have been on her birthday before it all went to shit.

Taylor sighed and rolled over to grab her phone to turn off the pop song that was blaring through her speaker. She was in the mood for something more soothing when her brain had enough blaring beats. Music was always Taylor's source of comfort. Rather than shrivel up and eat pints of ice cream or drown herself in a bottle, she lost herself to lyrics and let that motivate her to process her feelings and take action. It was clearly what prompted her spontaneous trip to Phoenix as well.

When Nina Simone's sultry voice came on, Taylor felt a lightbulb go off in her brain. This was it. *Nina*. She could ask for a favor and surprise Brooke. It was a bit blindsiding but it was the only option that could guarantee that Brooke would be taken completely by surprise. Taylor knew she could have just contacted Brooke directly and avoided playing any games but part of her wanted to catch Brooke completely by surprise. She wanted her to not be in her head and worried about their meeting in an attempt to, hopefully, let all her walls down when they were reunited.

At least that's what Taylor hoped would happen. She truly had no idea how things would go especially when Brooke was expecting dinner with a friend and instead would be met with the woman that had apparently thrown her life for a curve.

Taylor [3:39pm]
Hey! I don't want to put you in an awkward position or anything but can you call me when you have a chance? It's about getting Brooke back

Nina [3:52pm]
FINALLY!!!! Call you in 10

Ten minutes later, Nina called as promised. She said she was breaking all types of friend code cooperating but she wanted this to work out. She wanted Taylor and Brooke back together. It was that commitment to Brooke that got Nina to ask Brooke if she could come over on Saturday night for a girl's night. She promised wine and charcuterie and Brooke agreed. Because of course she would. Brooke would never turn down cheese.

Chapter Thirty

An hour before Nina was set to arrive at her apartment on Saturday night, Brooke contemplated cancelling. She knew Nina meant well but she wasn't in the mood for company. She wanted to just lay on the couch in her feelings and thoughts in the same leggings and hoodie she had been wearing all day. Nina might not let her relish in self-loathing alone but she surely wouldn't care if Brooke didn't dress up to see her. At least she didn't need to put pants with buttons on.

When the doorman buzzed Brooke's apartment stating her guest was there, she unlocked the door and got back on the couch. After a knock on the door, Brooke yelled out, "It's open!"

Brooke waited for Nina to burst through the door with the same boisterous announcement she usually made declaring she had arrived. Instead, she was met with a soft angelic voice she thought she was imagining penetrating her ears. "Hi."

Brooke spun around on the couch, her neck almost breaking to join her heart in body parts that needed repair. "Taylor," she said softly, frozen in place on the couch.

Taylor walked into the apartment and placed the two bags she was holding onto the floor. Brooke immediately questioned what was inside. Was it the spare clothes she left in her apartment? Any item she purchased to erase her from Taylor's life? "Can I come in?"

"Of course," Brooke said as she finally stood up and wiped the sweat that was suddenly swarming her palms onto her black leggings. "Nina is on her way over though."

"I'm Nina," Taylor declared. "I did bring you charcuterie as promised if you want to put it in the fridge."

Baffled, Brooke stared at Taylor unsure how to even form words. She was set up. Did Taylor think Brooke wouldn't want to see her if she asked? Was this Nina's brilliant idea?

"Oh, ok, sure," Brooke fumbled over her words as she cautiously stepped towards Taylor and grabbed the bags. Keeping her hands busy was the only way she'd avoid doing something embarrassing like awkwardly go to hug Taylor potentially against her will. She placed the bags in the kitchen and started to pull out carefully wrapped cheeses and meats from Murray's Cheese – her favorite cheese shop. And also where Taylor had gotten supplies for their picnic back when things were simpler. Happier.

At the bottom of the second bag was a bottle of champagne and a bottle of red wine. "Um, did you want to drink this?" She asked as she held the bottles up and saw Taylor standing in the living room with her hands clasped in front of her. She looked as uncomfortable as Brooke felt.

"No," Taylor said as she looked up to meet Brooke's gaze. "Can we talk?"

Brooke nodded before placing the red wine on the counter and the champagne in the fridge. Her anxiety intensified with every step she took towards Taylor and this unexpected conversation. She quickly sat on the couch to stop her legs from shaking and giving out underneath her. She wasn't nervous, no. She was *terrified*. When she motioned for Taylor to do the same, the younger woman took the furthest possible seat on the other end of the couch and looked at the wood coffee table instead of Brooke.

"How are you?" Taylor finally asked.

"I've been better," Brooke said honestly.

Taylor nodded. "Ditto."

Brooke ran her teeth over her bottom lip waiting to find out what exactly Taylor wanted to talk about. It surely wasn't just a curiosity into how she was doing.

"I got your letter," Taylor said while keeping her eyes laser focused on the coffee table. "You know that was a cop out to just write that and not say it to my face. I deserved better."

Judging by the bite in Taylor's voice, the letter wasn't well received. Just another thing that Brooke fucked up lately. "You're right," Brooke admitted, knowing that much was true. "You did. You still do. After waiting outside your apartment for two hours like a crazy person, I didn't want to lose my courage and not get it off my chest that night."

"You could have waited longer," Taylor argued.

She could have. She would have waited forever if she thought she had a chance to fix the mess she created. "I started to think maybe you'd come home with someone else and I didn't want to be there for that."

Taylor finally moved her gaze off of the table and onto Brooke. Her eyes were watery and filled with pain and sadness. "I was at my sister's house in Phoenix."

"I guess I'm selfishly glad you weren't on a date," Brooke forced a smile. Now that those green eyes were staring back at her, she felt like she was sitting there naked, completely vulnerable and embarrassed, to have hurt this heavenly creature.

"Taylor," Brooke sounded as she closed her eyes; the image of Taylor seared into her eyelids. "I'm so sorry for everything," she finally said softly. "I got scared and then losing my mom hurt so much and I didn't want to give you ammunition to leave so I did it myself. I know it's not an acceptable excuse but I'm sorry and I wish I could take it all back."

"It's not acceptable," Taylor said firmly. If Brooke's heart wasn't already broken, it would have shattered. "You threw away everything without even talking to me like a human being. Like your girlfriend. I expected better from you."

"I'm sorry," Brooke said as she felt tears swell her eyes. She was a complete disappointment.

"I'm not a child either, Brooke," Taylor said while throwing her hands in the air. "I'm thirty years old and I have my shit together. Who are you to tell me what I want?"

She was right again. The only one who did anything wrong here was Brooke and she had nothing left to lose. She already lost herself, her mom, and the woman she loved. "You have every right to be mad at me and I know I don't deserve the chance to even talk to you right now but I need you to at least know I'm sorry."

As silence piled up between them, Brooke could hear her heart beating in her chest. If she listened close enough, she thought she could hear Taylor's, but that was her own wishful thinking that Taylor was just as scared as she was.

"I know you are," Taylor finally said softly as she looked up towards the ceiling, a heavy sigh escaping her lips. "You really hurt me though. I felt blindsided and betrayed. And so fucking sad."

"I'm sorry," Brooke repeated like a broken record. "Words will never convey how sorry I am. I'm sorry for not being able to undo that. I never wanted to hurt you and I hate that I did."

"Stop saying you're sorry," Taylor said coldly. "I believe you, I really do," she added as she looked into Brooke's eyes. "But I need you to accept something now. I need you to know that I'm not Jaclyn. I'm not going to hurt you."

"Thank God you're not her," Brooke said with a nervous laugh. When the smallest smile appeared on Taylor's face, Brooke started to feel some of the tension release from her body. The discomfort she had was now disappearing to only leave room for one emotion: love.

"I have to tell you something else I didn't put in the letter," Brooke started, finally giving in to her true self. Finally accepting that whether or not it was well received, it would be out there. At least she was finally being honest, even if it was far too late. "The truth is," Brooke started again before she felt her throat go dry. She really could have used that champagne or wine to loosen the grip around her heart. When Taylor finally looked back into her eyes, she felt herself fall. "The truth is that I love you. I love you so much and it's terrifying because I didn't want to lose you and I wound up doing just that."

She didn't even realize that she was crying, but the damp sensation on her leggings filled her in that while she was professing her love, her eyes were releasing their pain and sadness. Taylor stared at her with a blank expression on her face – it was clearly too late. It was the wrong time to say something so right. Rather than pretend it didn't happen, Brooke dug herself in even deeper. "You are the most perfect person I have ever met, Taylor. So beautiful inside and out. So caring. So funny. So exhilarating. You make me feel things I didn't even know were humanly possible. God, I'm so in love with you that I could actually envision us being together forever and having that pug you wanted and everything was just so perfect. I didn't want you to break that vision in my mind by you not wanting the same, by not ever being ready, or just not wanting it with me. I panicked and I should have told you sooner. I know you deserve better than me but I needed to finally tell you how I feel."

When Brooke closed her eyes to avoid looking at Taylor's stoic face staring back at her, a hand crept into her lap. Fingers were laced together before squeezing tightly. "Can I tell you something now?" Taylor asked. Brooke nodded with her eyes still closed, preparing herself for the worst. "There is no one better than you," Taylor said softly. Brooke's eyes slowly opened as her body transported to another world where there was hope for them to make it through this rough patch. "Panicked or not, it didn't change the fact that I love you, too. I'm so in love with you that besides the pug, which I still want by the way, I could picture us getting married and having kids. I *do* want a family one day, but only if you're part of it. That's just how wrong you were about everything."

Brooke didn't expect to hear those words said back to her tonight, or ever, but it seemed only fitting. She didn't expect to meet Taylor at the bar. She didn't expect to kiss her at Stonewall. She didn't expect any of this to happen and maybe that's why they were meant to be. They found each other when they least expected it.

Tears started to stream down Brooke's face again. "Do you really mean that?"

"I don't say things I don't mean," Taylor stated firmly. "I didn't tell you sooner because I didn't want to scare you away. I knew you had been hurt before and I can't promise to be perfect all the time but I can promise to be loyal and love you and want the same things you do when we cross that bridge."

A gasp of air left Brooke's lips before she closed her eyes and winced. "I fucked up so badly. I'm so sorry."

"I'm sorry, too," Taylor admitted as she inched closer on the couch. "For giving you any impression that I didn't want a real relationship and a future with you. That I wasn't head over heels in love with you. You were never just sex to me. You've been everything to me all along."

Brooke couldn't stand the distance anymore. She leaned over and wrapped her hand on the back of Taylor's neck to pull her in for a scorching kiss. A kiss felt so much different now with love on the table. This was a kiss full of honesty; no fears, no secrets, just pure love.

"Wait," Taylor said as she pulled away and held Brooke's face in her hands. "I want to do this right."

"Me too," Brooke said softly, even though she didn't really know what could be more right than what they had both just declared.

Taylor jumped up from the couch and ran over to the fridge. She grabbed the bottle of champagne and two glasses and sprinted back towards Brooke before jumping in her lap. "I want to celebrate us. The way we should have been doing all this time. No tears, just love."

"Just love," Brooke repeated as she wiped the remaining tears off her face. "So much love."

Taylor dramatically popped the cork off the bottle and poured it into the glasses in Brooke's hands. "I love you so much, Brooke," Taylor said as she looked into Brooke's eyes. "I want to toast to us and make a promise to each other. Let's always be honest and tell each other exactly how we feel. Let's always be there for each other no matter what. And most importantly, let's promise to keep having the best kisses and sex of my entire life."

Brooke laughed and felt herself start to come alive again. "I promise. To us."

Taylor leaned in and kissed Brooke softly before pulling back. "And to Nina. You owe her a text message."

Brooke smiled as she rested her head on Taylor's shoulder. "I have so many questions."

"We have forever to discuss it," Taylor said sweetly before she glanced towards Brooke's phone on the table. "But seriously, text her before she melts in anticipation."

Brooke leaned over and grabbed her phone, wanting to quickly return to the woman smiling back at her.

Brooke [7:02pm]
She loves me

Nina [7:03pm]
Omg are you serious?!

Nina [7:03pm]
I didn't see that coming

Nina [7:04pm]
I mean NO SHIT SHERLOCK!!!

Brooke [7:04pm]
Thank you. For everything

Nina [7:05pm]
Thank me later. Have all the makeup sex in the world now

Nina [7:05pm]
I bet it'll be even better with FEELINGS

Nina [7:05pm]
Just don't get pregnant before the wedding

"Tay," Brooke sounded when she locked her phone, suppressing the smile on her face. She'd let Nina get away with these comments tonight. After all, she owed her immensely. "What do you say we have a repeat picnic now?"

Taylor leaned down and placed her lips upon Brooke's. "That was my plan. Hopefully this night will end just the same as well."

Brooke laughed and wrapped her arms around Taylor to hold her tightly. Just like that night five months ago, she didn't want to let her go. "I wouldn't have it any other way."

Epilogue

Three Years Later...

"Come here, baby! Come here!" Oscar's voice yelled through the phone. "That's right, sweetie! You can do it!"

Brooke stared at the screen in complete adoration. She couldn't remember the last time her father smiled that hard. He wasn't even smiling that widely on her wedding day last year because he had been alternating crying and drinking tequila with Bryan. Whoever thought it was a good idea for him and Taylor's brother-in-law to discover their love of the Mexican alcohol in the middle of a wedding was surely someone who wanted to see the epic mess it turned into of poorly executed dance moves. It was Nina, because of course it was.

"My good girl!" he yelled out again in glee. "Say hi to mommy."

"Hi baby!" Brooke yelled back into the phone. Staring back at her in complete confusion over the fanfare of simply walking from her fuzzy bed to the couch was Sprinkles. The two-year-old black pug, who judging by the looks of it, had been getting more snacks than she should have in grandpa's company. "Mommy misses you. Are you being a good girl for grandpa?"

Sprinkles tilted her head to the side at the sound of Brooke's voice. "How many snackies has he been giving you?"

Snackies was a trigger word because Sprinkles took off in a mad dash towards the kitchen; her little curled tail sprinting into the distance. "Not enough snackies is the correct answer," Oscar replied as he held the phone back towards his face. "Where's Taylor?"

"I'm right here," Taylor sounded from beside Brooke in bed. "Judging you crazy dog people."

Brooke playfully slapped her leg as she looked at her wife. "Coming from the woman who told me to FaceTime dad so we can see her."

Sprinkles barked in the distance, sending Oscar into a panic that he was not being a good fur grandparent and that he needed to hang up and not be distracted.

"I miss her so much," Brooke said as she laid back down next to Taylor.

Taylor smiled and reached for Brooke's hand to hold. "Me too, babe. But I'm so glad we're here."

So was Brooke. This was a vacation that was purely about Taylor. All week they did exactly what Taylor wanted. When she wanted to go to the pool, they went to the pool. When she wanted to nap, they napped. When she wanted to eat six tacos and guacamole, they did just that. When she wanted to rip Brooke's clothes off, Brooke gladly allowed her. This vacation surely surpassed their honeymoon in Bali. This week in Cabo was everything because of the reason why they were there.

"How do you think Sprinkles will adjust to not being the baby anymore?" Brooke asked as she gently caressed Taylor's expanding stomach. Underneath that soft skin was their five-month-old baby girl, getting bigger every day and bringing them closer to the family they so desperately wanted.

Taylor laughed and pulled Brooke closer to her. "Kind of like you when you realized you weren't *my* only baby anymore," she teased, referencing how Brooke once said Taylor was more excited to see Sprinkles than her. She'd never live that down. "Overly emotional but easily swayed back by food and kisses."

Brooke rolled her eyes as she leaned her head on Taylor's shoulder. "I was not that emotional."

"Sweetie, you're a complete mush."

Okay, so maybe Brooke *was* a complete mush. Ever since she finally caved in and declared her love for Taylor, everything changed. She felt freer. Happier. Constantly in a daze over how much she loved Taylor. Luckily, the feelings were one thousand percent mutual. So much so that Taylor made sure she was the one to propose to ensure Brooke knew just how much she loved her. Those nights working at the bar quickly shifted to saving for a massive engagement ring once her loans were paid off.

Brooke encouraged her to quit bartending soon after and Taylor happily agreed, especially when she got an engagement ring on her own hand that she never wanted to take off or damage. Those rings were now accompanied by the wedding bands that expressed so much more than just a declaration of love. It was a symbol of what they had been through and how they were always going to move on together, stronger, and always be fully honest.

"Did I ever tell you how much I love you?" Brooke playfully asked.

Taylor pretended to be deep in thought as she looked up at the ceiling. "You know, I recall you saying it over and over again on our honeymoon but I was a bit busy between your legs at the moment."

Brooke laughed and tried to roll away from her wife. "Stop that, our baby will hear."

"I didn't hear you complaining last night," Taylor teased as she wrapped her hands around her wife's waist to pull her closer and bring their lips together. "But I love you, too."

It still hadn't gotten old. It never would.

About The Author

Rachel Murphy has spent her whole life daydreaming about being a writer. After taking years off to focus on her non-writing career, she's diving back in to return to her passion of Sapphic love stories. She's a Native New Yorker who refuses to move out of the Big Apple, except in the world of fiction. Follow her on Instagram @rachelmurphybooks

instagram.com/rachelmurphybooks

Also By

The 1,308 Days

After years out of the spotlight, actress Isabella Cruz finds herself back in the center of attention in anger management of all places. She doesn't have much hope for this rehabilitating her image tarnished in the tabloids.

Until her eyes land on the alluring Katelyn Hughes. Then she has hope for everything, including love.

As the women's friendship quickly blossoms into something much more serious, they have to find a way to balance their passionate feelings, all while Isabella experiences increased notoriety from her comeback TV series. Despite whatever curveball gets thrown their way, the one constant is their desire to build a future together, and the desire they have for each other.

Available on Amazon

Made in the USA
Middletown, DE
29 August 2023

37556463R00175